Published by Influx Press
49 Green Lanes, London, N16 9BU
www.influxpress.com / @InfluxPress

All rights reserved. © Wayne Holloway, 2019

Copyright of the text rests with the author.

The right of Wayne Holloway to be identified as the author of this work has been asserted in accordance with section 77 of the Copyright, Designs and Patents Act 1988.

This book is in copyright. Subject to statutory exception and to provisions of relevant collective licensing agreements, no reproduction of any part may take place without the written permission of Influx Press.

Printed and bound in Great Britain by Clays Ltd, Elcograf S.p.A.

Paperback ISBN: 978-1-910312-29-2
Ebook ISBN: 978-1-910312-30-8

Editor: Kit Caless, Assistant Editor: Sanya Semakula
Proofreader: Momus Editorial, Cover art and design: Jamie Keenan

This book is sold subject to the condition that it shall not, by way of trade or otherwise, be lent, re-sold, hired out, or otherwise circulated without the publisher's prior consent in any form of binding or cover other than that in which it is published and without a similar condition including this condition being imposed on the subsequent purchaser.

This is a work of fiction. Names, characters, businesses, places, events, locales, and incidents are either the products of the author's imagination or used in a fictitious manner. Any resemblance to actual persons, living or dead, or actual events is purely coincidental.

*For my Nan, Winnie Pallen, 101, for the gift of her life and memories, as a grandson and a writer I couldn't ask for more.*

# INCITING INSTANCES

**EXT. SEGUNDO BEACH CALIFORNIA - DAY 2036**

MUSIC MIXES BACK UP: WE PICK UP THE END OF 'THE EARTH IS BROKEN' BY TIM BUCKLEY.

Slow motion: Through a shimmer of heat haze we watch two mangy, skeletal dogs scuffle on the sidewalk. It's hot, they pant, sweat and drool, but still they go at each other pointlessly.

Close-up of an old army boot fills the frame: The boot is crumpled, the heel worn down, and the sole has a hole in it. Sun pours through it as it is held up for inspection.

                **FRANK V/O**
  Shit.

A DIRTY FINGER POKES THROUGH, FEELING THE
HOLE OUT.

**CUT TO:**

SHOTS OF A HAND RUMMAGING IN A BACKPACK. THE
HAND FINDS WHAT IT'S LOOKING FOR: A KNIFE, A
PIECE OF RUBBER AND A TUBE OF GLUE.

The hands mend the boot, expertly paring back the
worn edges of the hole, cutting the piece of rubber
to size and gluing it over the hole from the inside.

The hand holds the boot back up to the sun;
it blocks it out, there are no gaps.

FRANK'S voice grunts in approval. He places it
on the ground to dry in the sun. This is FRANK,
mid-forties, a hard life written on his face
and in the way it pains him to move.

The two dogs now lie side by side in the
shade of a rusting truck, their chests
heaving up and down with exhaustion, anger
spent, flies buzzing around their muzzles.

**FADE TO BLACK**

### LAVISH DIAMOND REYNOLDS, FACEBOOK LIVE FEED OF THE MURDER OF HER BOYFRIEND PHILANDRO CASTILE, 7 JULY 2016

'Please don't tell me my boyfriend's gone! He don't deserve this! Please, he's a good man. He works for St. Paul Public Schools. He doesn't have a record of anything. He's never been in jail, anything. He's not a gang member, anything.'

*She prays aloud.*

'Allow him to be still here with us, with me... Please Lord, wrap your arms around him... Please make sure that he's

OK, he's breathing... Just spare him, please. You know we are innocent people, Lord... We are innocent. My four-year-old can tell you about it.'

**CUT TO:**

'I need a ride I'm on Larpenteur and Fry. . . My boyfriend, I don't know what condition he's in, I don't know if he's OK or if he's not OK, I'm in the back seat of the police van car, in the back seat of the police car, handcuffed, I need a ride, I'm on Larpenteur and Fry, they got machine guns pointed.

(Aside to four-year-old daughter Dae'Anna) 'Don't be scared.'

'My daughter just witnessed this, the police just shot him for no apparent reason, no reason at all. I can't really do shit 'cos they got me handcuffed...'

Dae'Anna: 'It's OK. Mummy.'

'I can't believe they just did this. I'm fucking, what the fuck is that?'

*Crying, keening noises...*

Dae'Anna: 'It's OK. I'm here with you.'

*More sobs, feral pain...*

'Y'all pray for us, Jesus please I ask everybody on Facebook, everybody that's watching, please pray for us.'

**FADE TO BLACK**

# PROLOGUE

*God's Heaven,*

*New Orleans, Louisiana, 2024*

Survivors zigzag across Crescent City Bridge, trying to get out of the city with whatever possessions they can carry. A man staggers, struggling to carry a 60-inch TV, the mains and HDMI cables trailing behind him, tripping him as he lurches forward, constantly changing grip, swapping out sweaty hands, wiping them dry on increasingly damp jeans, swapping hands again, an absurd dance/performance, his heroic attempts to gain purchase and move forward with the television set intact, screen unbroken and cables still attached.

Abandoned cars, some on fire, litter the bridge, mirages billowing thick oily black smoke across the road, obscuring the exit in an impenetrable flux of heat haze and particle suspension. Frank hugs a baby close to his chest, under his shirt, protecting it from the hard sunlight and all else. Sweat pours from him, baptising his child into the world. The baby's hand tangles in a set of dog tags hanging from his neck. At the far end of the bridge, a line of cops hastily forms in front of their patrol cars.

Gretna Parish cops armed with shotguns, glimpsed through the smoke, warped by the heat which kneads the light. These wobbly cops now conjure as infantrymen looming out of smoke cover from fired cannon, Confederates in this new civil war.

A song, a classic old-time tune, earworms its way into Frank's conscious mind, as if it didn't have enough to consider, something that had been playing on 98.5 WYLD right before the last hurricane made land. Now it plays as his personal soundtrack for what happens next.

*'I got shoes, you got shoes, all God's children got shoes.'*

The crowd approaches the line of cops. A loudhailer click, click, clicks into life. Inertia keeps them stumbling forward, desperate, almost lifeless automatons. A scene familiar from the zombie show craze, to those on both sides of this particular line. Nervous gallows humour prompts mimed head-shots from a few of the younger cops, straight out of the *Walking Dead* playbook.

'Keep back, this is a final warning, no City residents to be allowed off the bridge, return to your homes and await further instructions. I repeat, return to your homes…'

Those that can hear shout back they have no homes, their homes are under water, but it's no good, the scene is set and it's only going one way, and that's off the bridge.

*'When I get to Heaven gonna put on my shoes, I'm gonna walk all over God's Heaven.'*

The river roils below with detritus borne upon the surge, deep currents and oily foams pushing up as well as along, startling those on the bridge who care to look down. This water is not an escape option, as horizontally impassable as were the vertical walls of water held back by the God magic of Moses.

The white cops raise their shotguns for real and the mainly black crowd freezes, re-calibrates itself. The opening chords to a familiar, bone-deep dance. The guy lugging the huge TV now crouches behind it like a 16:9 ratio aspect Roman shield. Frank finds his anger, which brings him round like a dose of salts. He shouts, moves towards the line, shames them with his son held tight to his chest. A few step back, step back, but they all keep their weapons raised, they all keep their weapons raised.

*'Everybody talking about heaven, ain't going there Heaven, Heaven, Gonna walk all over God's Heaven.'*

Frank carefully prises the dog tags from his son's hand, a gentle out of place gesture, a tender untangling of soft little fingers from a mesh of chain metal links. He rips them from his neck, holding them up, dangling them in the cops' faces, as if some charmed amulet or ancient Kamea.

The singing voice is familiar, but the name escapes him.

*'I got wings, you got wings, all God's children got wings.'*

A red weal glistens with sweat across his muscle-corded neck, red on black.

*'When I get to heaven gonna put on my wings, I'm gonna fly fly all over God's heaven.'*

The boy let's out a cry, and the cop nearest Frank wavers, his gun droops, his face questions. But by now other survivors have broken through, have managed to get behind the line of cops, a moment of hesitation passes before all hell breaks loose.

Batons swing, and the front line of cops charge forward into the crowd, others still staying back, preparing to fire rubber bullet, or tear gas rounds over the heads of their fellow officers.

The crowd breaks, some drop, the rest run back towards the drowned city. A shotgun offloads, a low resonant note, followed closely by the rest, deep thuds in battle order, provoking return pistol fire from the crowd, a defiant high-noted *crack*, summoning others like a string of Mardi Gras firecrackers; *crack, crack, crack*, in response to their *boom, boom*.

Frank turns his back to the cops, his son's last defence, the muscles, ribs and spine of his father. Frank is dropped to his knees by a round of some kind, a rubber bullet or tear gas canister. Not mortally wounded, but bleeding freely from a head wound, blood stinging his eyes, running down his face and onto, flowing over his child, a second baptism, Frank's arm miraculously still cradling him, the other raised, dog tags glinting in the harsh sun, talisman bright.

The earworm finally surrenders its name. *Johnny Cash*, Frank can't help but think, *Johnny Cash*, blinded now by blood in his eyes and no spare hand to rub it away. Tears chase the blood from his face, yet his son is strangely silent, safe inside the crooked arm of his father as the deep thuds are replaced by live round explosions in the soundtrack of what happens next.

*'Everybody talkin' 'bout Heaven. Ain't going there Heaven, Heaven, Going to fly all over, going to shout all over, Going play all over, gonna walk all over God's Heaven.'*

# THE BLACK CHARLIE CHAPLIN

*Hollywood Hills, Los Angeles, 2016*

A black man, a handsome black man in his mid-thirties, an actor, a celebrity, sits at the breakfast bar of a large open-plan kitchen. Opposite him, a white man, a chubby faced Jewish man, hands the black man, his client, a movie script. The kitchen opens onto a terrace latticed by animated ropes of light bouncing out off the swimming pool. The filter system hisses and hums pleasantly. Cloistered in a humid microclimate, the borders of the garden are planted with banana trees, brightly coloured Hawaiian Hibiscus in tastefully made, hand-aged terracotta pots and beds of chubby Echeveria cacti. Trailing the back wall on trellises, the purples, reds and yellows of Fuchsia and Mimosa. This the work of a contract gardener with a taste for fancy cocktails.

Reflected inside, the black and orange of juice and coffee on the counter. The agent drinks coffee, his client OJ. The black man wears a white cotton gown, his agent a creased, expensive, light blue linen suit. A huge flat-screen TV plays 4k UHD sports mutely on the wall behind him.

The actor reads the cover page of the script: 'If it's broke fix it. Bindlestiff, the story of a black Charlie Chaplin.'

A pause as he thinks about what he's just read, he doesn't look impressed.

'Who wrote this shit, man, "A black Charlie Chaplin"? What the fuck does that even mean?'

His agent shrugs.

'Who cares? It's the best film script you've been sent in five years. I never heard of this guy, a commercials director is what I was told, a Brit. His lawyer sent it, Lichter, she's connected, so he must be kosher.' The handsome black man smiles at the word *kosher*, chases it with a sneer.

'A Brit. Shoulda known it, a Brit looking down his nose at us poor Americans.'

The agent raises his eyebrows. 'Just read it Forest.'

'Bindlestiff?'

'I googled it. From the Depression, what they called tramps, hobos. The main character is an ex-marine, a hobo, it's kinda set post-apocalyptically…'

'I ain't playing no broke-ass black space tramp. Stereotype bullshit. Who else they send it to?'

'It's not set in space. He says he wrote it for you.'

'He a fag too?'

The agent, Morris, raises his eyebrows, finishing his coffee in silence.

Silence.

Forest paces a little, eyes the terrace.

'OK, OK, I'll read it. You wanna swim? I wanna swim.'

'"Broke-ass black space tramp?" Did I miss something?'

'Yeah, you did. How about Prometheus? They had one in that.'

'I know, you were up for it.'

'Touché, Morris, I'll read it.'

They both smile. The handsome black actor Forest Speaks,

famous for action movies and perfume commercials, takes off his towelling robe and goes outside. Morris Vogel finishes his coffee, fat fingers pumping his phone, desperately communicating how excited his client is to read the script...

Splash.

# BEVERLY HILLS ADJACENT

*Los Angeles, 2016*

In the argot of Californian realty, (a standalone word and not a slurred take on 'reality', although it is also most definitely that), properties not in Beverly Hills but close by are designated *Beverly Hills adjacent*, spoken with as little pause between each word as possible. There is also *Beverly Wood* and *Beverly Wood adjacent*, but you get the picture. Like side pitching a B-level director off the back of an unavailable A-list one, in the argot of film and advertising. In both cases you get the frisson but with a smaller overhead. Just how far this adjacency extends depends on the bare-faced cheek of the sales rep concerned. In L.A. bare-faced cheek sells a lot of real estate.

Meet Tommy X, denizen of Beverly Hills Adjacent. Onetime TV actor in a big network show, cancelled after three series, turned producer, nicknamed Tommy Adjacent due to his Industry aspirations and personal proximity to people way more successful and famous than he is. Tommy is one of many fish in the sea, who, like the rest, swim adjacent to their dreams, which always lie tantalisingly just out of reach. He lives in

South Cathay, Beverly Hills Adjacent to the max, with his wife Monica and their four, count them, children. Back east he had been a roommate of David Schwimmer and now his eldest son plays soccer with Tom Cruise's kid. They had two kids, a boy and a girl, were happy with that, but then fell pregnant with the twins. He took on some commercials, (he has a great head of hair), they paid the bills and then he took more to pay some more bills and the movie world receded into the black blue of the distance, yet never fully out of sight. He went to Scout camp once with his youngest daughter and woke up in a tent next to a groaning seventy-odd-year-old Warren Beatty and his twelve-year-old boy.

'What the hell did I do to deserve this?' Warren laughed with Tommy over the 7 a.m. campfire coffee.

It pays to have children, right? Just get them into the right school, playing the right sports, and hey presto!

Everywhere this guy turns there's proximity. He is (unconfirmed, but possibly) actual friends with Laura Linney. Anyway, define what 'friend' 'actually' means, right? If Tommy puts a call in to Schwimmer, it's probably 70/30 he'll call him back, although he no longer has his current 'cell' number. Old friends for sure. . .

Monica is a landscape gardener. Vibrant cocktails of colour are her signature and through Laura and her adjacency, their circle expands. To mix metaphors, they keep their heads above water. Tommy drives a leased Audi A8. Parked it once next to Forest Speaks and neither of them could recognise their own car. Same colour, (white), same lease, same inability to remember the license plate. They shared a joke, exchanged cards, well, Tommy gave Forest his. At a meeting later that week Tommy could say, if it comes up, and you can always make anything come up in these meetings, 'Forest Speaks? Yeah, I know Forest, a great guy, you wanna get to him?'

Hollywood is a casino which operates like an enigmatic

Blockchain in which adjacency is one of many currencies which you can spend in the game. Exchange rates are in constant flux, so it is advisable to play with several. The thing is, here's the thing, most of the floor players are several paychecks away from sucking dicks to pay the bills. Sitting on top of the pile, remote players shall we call them, are the elite who have amassed so many future cheques, leveraged so much projected real estate income from flipping their way to the top, backed by so much offshore investment, with such a diverse portfolio of assets, that the possibility of sucking dick against one's will, involuntarily, recedes beyond your death and hopefully that of your children, and God willing their children too. That's the dream. To rise from the gambling floor. No need for comped drinks or rooms, they own it. For the working adjacent, the trick is to know when to put the money in the slot, when to play your hand, and when to cash in your (bit) coins.

For the rest of us the single figure ceiling still pertains. The true adjacency of this business is credit scored; translucent figures shimmering above each person's head – like the glowing credit poles in Gary Shteyngart's novel *Super Sad True Love Story* – our rating glowing a healthy green for high numbers, amber through the middle numbers and a flat red for single figures and a flashing, beeping blood red for the final countdown like Tommy's leased Audi A8 parking assist 5,4,3,2, the last paycheck representing as a solid flat-lining red; a synaesthesiastically transposed dead phone line tone your ever-present companion through the last week, day by day, minute by minute.

So, you get the picture. A town with a lot of flashing red lights floating above heads. That's show business. Dead phone lines and a lot of blow jobs.

Tommy has company for his troubles, some of it good. What I'm trying to say, maybe not hard enough because he's an easy target in a town full of big fat easy targets, but what I want to say for the record is that he's not a bad guy, not a bad apple, probably not a bad husband or father in a place where it is difficult to be either. But the erosion, the constant knock-backs, the wearing down of your sense of self-worth, the mirror that lurks, lies in wait in the bathroom every morning and the way in which Tommy finds himself constantly parlayed by others, all of this and then some, adds up to more than a cautionary tale, it's fucking 'Ivans XTC' on methamphetamine.

Tommy's mother was a Holocaust survivor, from Hungary. Now she deals antiques in Westwood Village ('Neighborhood Charm, City Style'). As a rich kid in Budapest she rang a silver hand bell whenever she wanted something to eat or a drink. Her nursery was at the top of the house, servants brought it up four flights of stairs. She was six in 1944 and lost a tooth to the whip hand of Josef Mengele as she darted behind him to be with her mother on the railway sidings at Auschwitz. Now her gold front tooth glitters in the West Coast sunshine. Or so the story goes. If you lose a tooth at six, don't you get a second chance toothwise? Wouldn't that have been a milk tooth? Maybe the root got ripped out by the lash of the whip, making the gap permanent, so that a tooth could never grow there again. Or the lack of nutrition, the starvation she endured, deprived her of her dental maturity? I don't know, I'm not a dentist. Anyway, who would make shit like that up?

Then again, there's no business like Shoah business, right? How many times I gotta say that?

Now the thing is, Tommy's problems began and ended with his mother. He hated her, she him.

'Would have been better for the brownshirts to kill me than to live to have a son like you.'

I'm no shrink but this has got to fuck you up, especially in the self-worth department. Is that why Tommy became an actor? To crave affirmation outside of the family? Love beyond the limelight? Can you become somebody else in order to survive being born you?

Either way, Tommy's mother's experiences of World War Two twisted her into the piece of work she became, or was it that spoilt six-year-old, high up in her bedroom ringing the shit out of that silver bell, was that the problem? I don't know. Never met the lady. In these stories there is rarely, if ever, any before-the-Holocaust story that isn't coloured by it. 'The Holocaust', a rare historical moment that rewrites the past and rewires the future. Perhaps that's why Primo Levi threw himself down the stairs forty years after surviving the death camps. Now that's a desperate way to kill yourself, a stark unravelling of civilisation reclaimed, the horror of what must have driven him to do that, the seizure that must have taken over his body.

That's what the Holocaust does, it reaches forward and takes you back. Whatever car you drive, however fast you drive it, the repo man will always be ahead of you, waiting with his engine running.

I know Tommy like a face in the mirror. Lies, self-hatred, paranoia, ambition, greed, self-delusion, laziness and a non-rational Arab-hating ultra-Zionism, all tucked away behind a veneer of normality and general good guy persona. And as I already mentioned, great head of hair, a really great head of hair.

It's a heady mix. Not to say a volatile one. A personality that would veer, flip, turn itself inside out from one day to the next, over lunch, between toilet breaks, beats of the heart even. 'Check please', who picks up the tab? Somebody has to pay, and this is what you get. The mask slips at every bill time, every check is an axe that falls, and the rest of the time is only the run-up to the next bill. Each one an execution. This is his interior life, his emotional life, how he's wired, the way this town has wired him.

This is a man, crucified.

You put this Rat King of a fuck-up into the movie business. Good luck. A guy in his early fifties, good looking in a very Semitic way, dark, tanned, looks great in a suit, has great hair, I can't mention that enough, voluminous even, but whose haunted eyes, freighted with such black bags, tell of a hunt that has always been on, the sunken coal black pits reflect the real Twentieth Century Fox, snarling and feral snapping at his heels and stinking in heat, for it is a vixen and his nose twitches with her cunt stench as he scrambles from one unproductive meeting to the next, from one valet parking to another, ten bucks to ten bucks, that's twenty bucks for two meetings, and lunches, minimum a hundred bucks sans booze, constantly weaving a way forward, pressing hard towards his goals, from one dodged tab to the ones you can't dodge, it's fucking life as pinball with the flippers snapping at your heels, as you, Tommy, are the last ball on the table, bouncing who knows where, triggering who knows what consequences, if any. And the smell of fear, of the hunted, the vixen close and getting closer, that smell, lodged in your sinuses for all time, always a disrupter, wrenching you back, back in time, tossing you forward, forward in time.

This is the guy who landed up with the *Bindlestiff* script in his lap. This guy.

His boy plays soccer with Tom Cruise's son. They stand together on the touchline. They talk soccer. It's a big thing with L.A. people, soccer. A beautiful world sport, everybody wants it except the American TV advertisers who can't find a way to throttle it, two 45-minute halves with no commercial breaks what the fuck is that about? The boys are on the same team, the dads on the same touchline. So far, so far.

At the office (a generic pay-by-the-week rental space), a pile of books appeared on Tommy's desk. Books about Scientology. His wife gave them to him. She popped into the office with them poking out of her wicker tote bag. He was getting shepherded towards Tom. A chunk of their weekly food budget on these books, tuna steaks from Santa Monica seafood skipped without comment that Thursday, a week's worth of valet parking, two dry lunches even. This guy who loves being a Jew, thinks they're the best, this 'Go IDF go!' type of Jew, boning up on L. Ron Hubbard in the office.

The apex of this story is a movie script stuffed into his back jeans pocket that Saturday morning at kids soccer. It is around this script that the story turns. The script he knows he shouldn't get out, never having told Tom what he does for a living, as if Tom Cruise can't smell a producer like shit on his shoe, but as long as it's just kids and soccer, it's OK, they can 'shoot the breeze'. Don't do it Tommy, don't go there, don't speak of what you do, don't ask him to read anything. I think the script in question is some returning home from war dreck set in the bayou written by and/or starring his buddy from the *Star Trek* franchise.

Whatever it is, you don't go there.

'Hey Tommy,' Cruise didn't even open a door with a question like, 'Had a good week?' Just 'Hey Tommy' leaving him hanging with the only place to go the safety of the touchline and sports small talk.

Cruise wants to be a regular guy, a regular dad *for a few hours each week*. But that involves you playing ball too, in fact it involves you acting. Without being asked, that's the unspoken plea of 'Hey Tommy'. Shit, celebrities pay escorts to piss on them for similar reasons, to be brought down to earth, to feel reviled for a change, like judges in diapers, to be degraded, to feel the boot on the other foot, or however the saying goes. Tom just wants to be treated like a regular guy, or his version of what that means. Hell, he may even know vaguely who you are, but don't go there. And you know what? Tommy didn't. 'Who we playing today?' is the line he delivered, as scripted, and Tom played it from there.

After a week the Scientology books disappeared unread from his desk.

His son still plays football with Tom Cruise's, they continue to be football dad buddies. The script in the back pocket stays invisible and tuna steak is back on the menu.

Because Tommy, despite and maybe because of all I have

written about him, is a good guy. Or more precisely, has the capacity, to be better than some of the rest. That's who he is. That's a tight spot in which to turn. He has the balls to yank himself off the fucking cross, nail by nail, but still endure another crucifixion when Saturday comes.

Fucking soccer, every Saturday morning, an anticipation of more humiliation. For Christmas he thinks about buying his son a basketball, a hockey stick, an anything.

And, by the way, fuck Tom Cruise for creating that bad energy whirlpool, for sitting in the eye of his own storm whilst everyone else drowns. Fuck him, Tommy. For you.

Another story is infinitely sadder and has no negotiable ending. When Tommy finally got to produce a TV show, a pilot that gets picked up, you know what? He was rude and nasty and treated those below him like shit, aping those he imagines were above him, beyond his adjacent ceiling, in a psycho fantasy cliché of how a studio guy should behave, and nobody liked him, or trusted him. They laughed behind his back, at times in front of his face and I saw him turn, get nasty to the little people, runners, interns, caterers, crew, throw his weight about humiliating them and it never has to be like that, but somehow it always is, his beloved Israel surely the shining example of that shit truth, the smell of fear once again defining him, owning him in the American idiom, and send me to hell for writing it.

This guy.

This guy is looking to set up *Bindlestiff* in this town. Now who would ask him to do that, what writer would allow this to be so? A case of desperation, of cluelessness, above all a Writer/Director with no other option, would be my guess. A guy who was about to run out of dimes, every call he makes put on hold, or stonewalled with 'Can I take a message?', like a career flat-lining in a soon to be cancelled hospital soap opera. A guy just like @waynex.

This guy.

# THE MONEY CHUCKLES

*Rodeo Drive, Los Angeles, 2016*

A bustling eatery off Rodeo Drive in Beverly Hills, in the style of a mid-twentieth-century French/European dining room; abuzz with the tinkling of glass, clinking of silverware and the snap of crisp white tablecloths dressing solid looking cherry wood tables. Bustling waiters and discrete sommeliers vie with the clientele for aisle space to and from the tables, the kitchen, the toilets and the hatcheck. As in all good restaurants the world over this dance works, looks pleasantly choreographed – the trained staff, performers elegantly dodging the untrained clientele.

One of the odd things that keeps you off kilter in this town is the mismatch between the soulless sanitised streets and boulevards and the seeming authenticity and elegance of the food and service and the architectural appointments of the interiors. As soon as you look closely, these interiors are as fake as the streets are real, all chipboard and varnish. But if you don't look too closely and don't literally knock on wood, then they project a studied realism. The trick is never to look too closely at anything.

'So, great news, just spoke to his agent and Forest Speaks loves the script, wants a meeting.'

'Huh. What about Jim Hawks?'

'To play a black Charlie Chaplin?'

'Black Charlie Chaplin? Gimme a break. Means nothing, some writer's hocus pocus, who cares.'

Tommy Adjacent watches incredulously, as his lunch partner expertly mixes wasabi paste and low sodium soy sauce with the tips of his chopsticks, and the focus of a modern alchemist. In Hollywood the obsession amongst certain classes with sushi is acknowledged by the menus of even mid-century French/European restaurants; here too you will find sashimi, nigiri, assorted 'hand rolls' and the vintage sakes to go with them.

'What do you think about the script changes? We lost the back story, opening scenes really fizz now.' Tommy attempts a diversion, fails.

'Hard to cast a black lead in such an indie project, in terms of finance. Forest is a mid-budget action hero, he ain't gonna do shit playing a tramp. Look what happened to Wesley Snipes.'

Tommy flashes on the Snipes story. Wesley holed up in the presidential suite of the Hojo in downtown Bucharest, hookers, coke on call, a Benihana one floor below, staffed with exiled Japanese dope-smoking sushi chefs from the Paris franchise on punishment rotation.

The Howard Johnson hotel in Bucharest. Snipes banished to this eastern frontier, dodging bullets with fading stars and cheap home-grown gangsters. Health and safety deficient pyrotechnics, injured crew, lawsuits, tight budgets being pushed to the max in the wild East until inflation closed the gap on the noughties and they flushed clear out of there, further east, accountant navigators blazing a trail, Mason-Dixons of the next best margins, profit panzers aiming for the production friendly service cities of Almaty, Tbilisi, Ulan Bator.

'Even if we make it for under ten, say for five, six mill?'

An apologetic, quietly desperate rearguard action to protect promises and integrity, not to say a friendship, albeit a Hollywood one.

The Money shrugs. Eats his sashimi with relish. Ebi, tuna, yellowtail with ponzu sauce sprinkled with juniper berries. So many great flavours, clean and intense.

'Under ten? Then why we eating here? That's salt beef and bagel money.'

Tommy nurses a Diet Coke, his plate empty of the sushi that sits between them.

'Well, maybe with a little rewrite. Hawkes looks like a fucking tramp, right?

'You been to that Sushi Nazi place by the 405? Fucking chef grows rice on the roof, there's no menu, he looks at you and gives you what he thinks you will enjoy, place has got like five tables. 300 bucks a head. What a gag. Organic rice. Gimme a break, on that roof? Spitting distance from gridlock. You not eating?'

Tommy shakes his head, gulps his drink, thinking over other black options.

'How about Don Cheadle? Or the slave guy, what's his name, Chewy. . ?'

The Money shrugs again, incredulous, Chewy Who Cares.

'Chewy, urgh, what's his damn name, anyway, well, what about Ice Cube? Will Smith? Drake?'

The Money raises an eyebrow.

Too late. Chiwitel Ejiofor.

'Black leads are tricky in this type of movie. Look at Danny Glover. You know he wants to make a movie about fucking Haiti and some fucking slave uprising?'

'Toussaint L'Overture. Liberated Haiti during the French revolution.'

The eyebrow arches a little 'you shittin' me?' higher. After a beat he recovers from any intuited slight…

'Never gonna happen, never heard of the guy. Maybe if the shvoog put in some of his own money. . .'

Tommy has nowhere to go, doesn't have the data to hand, figures to back up the viability of black leads in mid to low budget movies to overcome this prejudice, he's just not that buttoned up. Now this is a good guy, but a desperate one, and without the stats at his fingertips? In this town? Being good ain't good enough, in fact it's bad, it's a wasted opportunity. Besides, Tommy is two payments away from being on the street sucking dicks, so we must forgive him for being constantly distracted, juggling projects, bills due, solving day-to-day issues before they escalate into bigger problems, operating under pressure from the triumvirate of home, work and self. Beyond distracted, it's almost like a cosmic persecution he's suffering from, the torture of being him. He is an installation of all these things: *The Crucifixion Of Tommy Adjacent* now showing at LACMA; the invitation to the private view written all over his face, dark lights flickering behind his already inky eyes, the storm of who he is constantly threatening.

Integrity doesn't come on an instalment plan.

'French blacks? You gotta be kidding me, right?' The Money straight up taunting him, bullying his lunch companion to agree with the racist absurdity of French black people.

Tommy flashes on the chopsticks sticking out of this fucker's eyes, blood squirting out and ruining his $500 shirt. There was never any wriggle room, and what wriggle room there never was he's now run out of. He says nothing.

The Money stabs the last piece of tuna, swallows it. The Money is always hungry, and Tommy has no appetite, his stomach full of acid. It's a boxing mismatch, almost a con if you're the audience, having paid good money. Tommy could never make weight with this guy.

He palms a Pepto Bismol in the toilet, tamping down his sour bile. He has run out of moves. He splashes water on his face, psychs himself back up in the mirror, shaking his head left to right.

'So, let's talk about Jim Hawks.'

Back at the table and he's got a second wind. He segues, something he's good at, a necessary skill in this town, especially if you can't run the numbers, you move on, which is what you have to do above all else: keep in the game, keep the ball rolling, and never let the money leave the table.

Tommy buys time on the ropes.

'I loved Hawkes in *Martha May Mary Marlene*, a very strong performance. You wanna make the movie, right? Or what are we doing?'

The Money stabs his chopstick towards Tommy's eye. A gob of soy-drenched wasabi flicks God only knows where. Tommy flinches, eyeballs his shirt, it's clean. If he had been eating this, his roll would have got stuck in his throat, stuck in his craw, sideswiped by this shark's persistent and focused intelligence.

Tommy has to fight back, offer resistance. 'It was *Martha Marcy May Marlene*.'

Custer's last stand in this room, now.

The Money pours another glass of wine, a delicate Pinot from the Alsace, doesn't miss a beat. The only response to this outré correction is to pretend he never heard it, that it never left Tommy's mouth, so he covers the transgression, smothers Tommy's resistance with a smile, a dazzling seal on the last stand that never was.

The shark smells blood, circles his prey.

'Are you 100% attached to this project as the producer?'

'Yeah, for sure, the writer is a good friend, let me talk to him.'

'And he can't direct it, you know that right? He's a fucking nobody.'

Swims in close for the kill.

'I'll talk to him. He's coming in Wednesday to work on the script.'

'It's a great story is what I'm trying to say Tommy, it'll make your career, pay a few bills right?'

He finishes the last of the ebi, hesitant chopsticks and raised eyebrows do a so-so impression of asking permission, his first irony.

Blood swirls in the water.

'Delicious.' Patting his thin lips with a napkin.

'Yes, it's a fucking great story.'

'Stupid title. Who gets it? *Bindlestiff*? I was thinking how about we call it *Land of Hunger*, suggests a bigger canvass right? A bigger movie. What d'you think?'

What bigger canvass?

'I'll suggest it,' Tommy mumbles.

Unconditional surrender. He prays the victor will pick up the tab, his only consolation.

The Money surveys the table, the empty plate of sushi.

'Tommy, you didn't eat a thing!'

'Nah, I hate sushi.'

The Money chuckles. They clink glasses. Warm Diet Coke, room temperature Pinot.

Check.

# MAN'S BEST FRIEND

*Hollywood Hills, Los Angeles, 2016*

Forest Speaks studies the *Bindlestiff* script sitting by the pool. His dog, a Schnauzer called Bullseye, snoozes at his feet.

The pool hums, Forest reads aloud, in a flat voice.

*'Now girl, you know how much we both like that dim sum. Well, here's where it's at, every day. Don't look at me like that damn dog.'*

He runs the sentences together to get a feel for them, repeating them two or three times searching for the voice of the character speaking, getting a steer from reading the script direction.

```
FRANK buries his face in the dog's ear,
whispers, hides his tears.
```

Forest clears his throat, ruffles the fur of his sleeping dog, tries it again. This time he stands, adds moves to the words, and this time he inserts a pause before the line.

*'Don't look at me like that damn dog.'*

He likes that delivery, nods his head and continues reading. Forest hunkers low to his dog, the words now coming in a hushed voice, as he doesn't want to be overheard.

*'You know I love you, and I be back, you and me come a long way together already, and this ain't the end of the journey, this isn't goodbye, no sir, it's just a vacation, something I gotta do.'*

FRANK stands up, hands the lead to Mr. KIM. Digs around in his bag and hands him a tattered camouflage dog coat.

Forest stands.

*'She gets cold nights.'*

A tin bowl hangs from his backpack, he unties it, hands it to him.

*'And this here her bowl.'*

'Shit, this Brit thinks he can write Black, Asian, anything he damn likes. Not perfect, but not bad.' Forest scribbles in the margins.

Forest continues the scene, reading Mr Kim's lines in a flat neutral voice, but inhabiting Frank's as his own.

*'She'll be fine with me, but you come back Frank.'*

*'She'll eat anything, ain't no trouble, just sit her in the sun out front. Hates the damp, loves the sun. That's my dog. Now stay girl, stay.'*

WE TRACK IN ON DOG'S FACE AS FRANK SHUFFLES OUT THE DOOR.

The Schnauzer looks up, breaking the actor's concentration. 'Not you Bullseye, I'm talking to... hell, I'm just talking.'

He puts the script down. It looks well-thumbed and has pencil revisions all over it. He has edited some dialogue, tweaking the idiom and the resulting cadence of the spoken words.

'We never met, but he says he wrote the script for me.' He shakes his head, rubs his hand across his mouth. In order to not just stand there, to move things on, Forest Speaks dives into the pool.

Splash.

# THE CARD PLAYERS

*Transatlantic, 2016*

> *'The hand that signed the paper felled a city;*
> *Five sovereign fingers taxed the breath,*
> *Doubled the globe of dead and halved a country;*
> *These five kings did a king to death.'*

— Dylan Thomas
  'The hand that signed the paper.'

'What's next?' is what @waynex felt as much as thought as he waited to board the plane. He was full of expectation, a not wholly unpleasant anxiety and an existential lightness of being he hadn't felt since college, albeit leavened with the dread and foreboding that colours, drop shadows, the same.

'The 11.30 flight to LAX is now boarding, will Upper Class and Gold members please proceed…'

Virgin Premium Economy, upgraded with points to first class. Prepare to experience an upper-class moral makeover. There will be blood.

'Boarding all the winners at gate 24, will the losers please make way. . .' An old joke but not far off describing the entitlement on show at the priority boarding gate and the weakness we others display when offered temporary membership of the international jet set.

The Virgin departure lounge is bright enough to wear sunglasses, so you wear them. A blank thousand-yard stare as you get up and walk past the rest. Slow-motion smugness, attitude lifted from their TV commercials.

At the end of the tunnel, you reach the aircraft door. Which way do you turn, left or right? Your life now reduced to these two options. Left or right. Us and them. The Masters of the Universe turn left and for today, for one day only, you can too. With a quick glance at your ticket the gatekeepers usher you forward. The trick is to pretend that this is how you always fly. You don't turn left in awe, but rather as you would go upstairs on a bus. To trudge left is the trick. Where else would you go? And besides, it's all a chore. Seated, you pass up the champagne as being a little too in your face for 11 on a Tuesday morning, this communicated by a casually dismissive minor shake of the head, left right, left right, accompanied by a momentary frown above disappointed eyes.

A soft crackle of nylon and one of the flight attendants lowers herself down to you, pen and clipboard in hand ready to tick you off.

'Can I offer you one of our in-flight massage services, sir?'

'No thanks, it's fine,' mumbles @waynex, friendly but with a frisson of 'It's not for me'.

Upper-class travel is an extended exercise in exquisite self-denial, because the ultimate pleasure is in being better than all the other fuckers. Better than either the turn left or God forbid turn right subsets of humanity. And never make eye contact with either. This best pleasure is transglobal, sustained authenticity is the prize. Better how? Morally? What moral code do you subscribe to? Socially, what class do you claim membership of? Intellectually, what justifies this sense of superiority? How can you travel authentically? Flying prompts these useless thoughts, perhaps as a diversion from worrying about the act of flying itself, the stark hubris of flying. The approximate 1 million people plus in the sky at any moment, sitting in 10,000 planes, 10,000 spinning plates in the air.

Focus on the mundane, home in on familiar details: menus, complimentary toiletries, the hot towel that cools rapidly on your face and is removed surreptitiously with tongs, your first drinks order, what films to watch and asking when does the in-flight service begin. Remember, it's just you, the crew and your safety and comfort.

Makeover complete, last prods on the phone screen, then swipe up for flight mode as you taxi to the runway and accelerate down it. In this critical moment of screaming engines and liftoff, you cannot but wonder at the miraculousness of all that weight, all those people, all that luggage, kilos of overhead duty free, hauling itself off the ground at what untold engineering cost; critical stress points red-lining, popped and sheared rivets up and down the fuselage; it is in this split second between heaven and earth that your true identity floods back, your fragile flesh and blood and crushable bone returns as reflux in the back of your throat threatening to flood your mouth. As the anonymous and unheralded aircraft hauls itself once again into the breach of the sky, the details of who you are, your identity, your 'soul on board' – to use the technical term that designates us when we are airborne – a single line item, one of many, inconsequential in the face of all the others, hand-written on lists, printed on manifests alongside and given equal weight with (manifestly) present or missing cargo and carved into innumerable memorials, this infinitesimal facticity of 'you' overcompensates, punches above its weight, seduces you back, to the memories of others who bore your name, who came before, who thicken your bloodline, beating a path to your door with their genes. Showing you the tail of the comet that is you as projected by your ego, that will always rage against the dying of the light, or any hint of it. Therefore, in this moment of technological marvel @waynex flashes on his family and their stories, the source in so many ways of his.

The Neckinger river lies buried under the streets of Southwark, a two-mile loop under the neck of the mother Thames. The threads of one end, three millstreams dug to feed the river itself, just by Shakespeare's Globe and the OXO Tower, and the other end where it rejoins the Thames at St Saviour dock where they hung pirates in the 1600s. The hangman's noose, the Devil's neckcloth, the Devil's Neckinger, at the site of the Dead Tree public house. When you bury rivers, islands disappear. Bermond's Ey for one, Jacob's Island another. Buried or not they still mark boundaries between places, landmarks which divvy up the land between Man and God and where between them they made things happen.

Neckinger Road. 1919, 1920 or 1921, the Star Music Hall in Bermondsey. Winnie, @waynex's nan remembers going to see Charlie Chaplin with her mum. She was four years old. Her birthday present was a bag of pink and white icing, an orange and a King William pear. She dropped the orange trying to peel it. Her mum Daisy's hands were red raw from scrubbing, (she was a skivvy, a cleaner), so she always, even on her birthday, got her daughter to peel the fruit. She also bit her nails down to the quick but that was out of habit. Winnie fumbled the orange, and it rolled down the aisle towards the limelight. She ran down to retrieve it and Chaplin beamed down at her. In 1920 The Star was both a music hall and a cinema, and Charlie Chaplin was either on stage or on the screen. A moment of historical overlap when the tide was turning but had yet to turn and the two arts lived side by side in temporary cohabitation before one superceded the other. His nan couldn't remember which it was, a real in-the-flesh Charlie Chaplin or a projected one, but she remembered how damp it was in there, always had been.

The truth of the story lies in the memory of the rolling orange and of a smiling Charlie Chaplin, that she had seen Charlie Chaplin, but now aged ninety-seven, is unable to remember whether he had been on the stage or on the screen. Her memory encompassed both possibilities, and that's how @waynex approached writing. Truth always lies between things; facts, memories, delicately balanced between them. Memory is a multiverse, or to be exact, it generates multiverses, its function to bridge gaps between things, to allow them to have meaning and tell stories. Memory is the art of connecting the now of the thinking moment and the then of what it is you thought about and writing is the act of crossing those bridges, constantly recrossing them also, taking and bringing back, but also creating physical proof of the journey, signposts for those that follow such things, however temporary footsteps in the snow they may be.

Bill Sykes' house was on Jacob's Island, Southwark Council considered putting up a plaque there in 1855. The stone and wood, wattle and brick of the city itself rubbed themselves into the pages of Dickens' stories, along with the people – the soft machines that inhabited it. Sykes drowned in Folly's Ditch, the fictional stretch of the Necking before its confluence with the Thames, a river as yet unburied.

King Cnut flooded a ditch for his boats to attack London avoiding heavily defended London Bridge, forging his way from the south-east into the heart of enemy territory. Cnut's trench became the Neckinger where it crossed the Kent road, a crossing site which became locally known as the 'wateryng of Saint Thomas' famously re-penned 'St Thomas a Watering', a meeting point for the players of the *Canterbury Tales* on their way to the shrine of St Thomas a Becket, followed later by a site for public execution, perhaps in honour of the namesake;

the mid spot of a river already with a noose at either end. Shakespeare's Globe at one end, executions almost nightly and the Devil's neckerchief where it ends at St. Saviour dock, executions by appointment.

*Bing.*

The plane levels, the seat belt signs go off and the next passage of time and travel gets under way. In the past this was the cue to light up a cigarette and enjoy the high life. Now a mundane anxiety fills the void.

@waynex shakes off the shackles of his imagination and stretches his legs, checking out the lay of the land. Business types and once-in-a-lifetime retired couples sipping champagne or bucks fizz, the latter already gagging to be standing at the bar exchanging pleasantries with the staff and rubbernecking any celebrities.

The high life.

Once @waynex had been in the Virgin lounge in L.A. and then on the plane with Keira Knightley and her boyfriend, who were both absurdly thin and gamine. Her boyfriend was reading the collected works of Samuel Beckett and wore a beany hat. He was 'scruffy', it was a well-thumbed copy of the book, but thumbed by whom?

Can you pay to have somebody thumb books for you? Like you can do with online multi-player games like *Warcraft* when you are away on holiday? Somebody, probably in a South East Asian internet cafe with huge broadband keeps your mage or warrior levels up. Protects your hoard, increases it. The game doesn't stop, it's global, when millions of players sleep, other millions are playing, passing the baton of the game forward, bridging past into the future through a hyper ever-presence. Rich sleepers can play the game on a global 24/7 timescale, true masters of the games universe.

Back to Keira Knightley's boyfriend and @waynex had imagined Chinese or Taiwanese sweatshops full of thumbers, maybe being read to, like in Cuban cigar factories where an overseer reads aloud the news, the sport, the celebrity gossip. Being read to from the books they are thumbing through, the spare prose of Beckett in translated monotone from behind the lectern. Possibly inscribing themselves into the very books they were breaking in...

Knightley may have married this guy. Or not.

Another time at the Chateau Marmont, @waynex had seen Kiera K and her mum climb into a huge gold Hummer that the studio had sent them to drive. This is the same driveway on which Helmut Newton had a heart attack and died crashing his car into a wall. They must have been shooting pick-ups for one of the *Pirates* movies because other cast members were staying there as well. The pleasant Australian actor and the skinny hapless British one, who kept losing his eyeball. This was before the Chateau became Lindsay Lohan's front room – or was it Britney Spears – or one of the numerous 'new vodka' brands that tricked out the hotel as a product launch/event venue?

Back when the Chateau was private by nature of its discretion and Jerry Stiller swam morning lengths in the pool unremarked.

The sight of Keira Knightley's mum, as tiny as her daughter was tall, with long salt and pepper hair, worthy of her status as a playwright, hauling herself up into the driving seat of this beast and ferrying her daughter to the studio just about said it all. All of this normalised for her by its sheer everyday facticity.

Drinks.

'A virgin Mary please.'

He didn't say 'A Virgin Mary, please'.

@waynex's mind spinning all those thoughts, brought back to the present by the slight annoyance at having to use the brand name of the airline to order his drink, when he meant to use it as a normal, unowned phrase. Better just to ask for a bloody Mary without vodka, only to elicit the face of crew member lighting up as they got to use the word Virgin in a different context than the drills they all underwent in training.

'A Virgin Mary sir? With ice and a slice is that? Spicy?' extracts a staccato sequence of minimal nods. She repeated his order but with a capital V for virgin. Try ordering a coke at a KFC and it plays out like this; 'Is Pepsi OK?' Or worse, 'It's Pepsi, is that OK?' which is a little more dangerous, as there's a little more wriggle space for inserting a 'No' which really fucks things up. We pity the low wage staff the world over who have to make this brand correction to common usage. Up in the air and things are different, there is a relish in the correction.

'Bloody Mary without vodka please?'

'Is a Virgin Mary OK. sir?'

*Or would that be...*

'A Virgin Mary Please.'

'Is bloody Mary without vodka OK?

*or ultimately*

'A virgin Mary please.'

'Is a Virgin Mary OK?'

Which leaves it all down to the delivery...

@waynex walks up and down the aisle. No Keira Knightley or her mum this time. Today it's just Mr. and Mrs. North-East cement factory owner and some curled up deshabille fashion PR's working it with their points. The midweek flight, nothing special. The cement factory owner looked like the guy who invented the Segway and rode his over a cliff. He had made his fortune from putting rocks in cages and selling them to the military as sand bags on steroids. His next idea killed him.

The mind unravels on planes, as you chase thought turds up and down the aisles, turds like the ones in the only good Franzen novel.

Back in his seat @waynex fires up his laptop, but immediately spills some of his V(v)irgin Mary on the keyboard. It always happens when you take out the swizzler, its job done, darkening the blood red of the tomato juice with swirls of Worcester sauce, but where to put it? How to get it back on the little napkin? It's in this little journey across the table that it, without fail, drips onto the laptop.

He wipes it down, stressed, some juice has got under the keyboard, and inside the machine. He stares at the screen, distracted by pre-cognition of the smell of rotting tomato to come.

*Bindlestiff.*

He stares at the title page. Changes to the script would be inevitable. He was pragmatic; it wasn't his money. Not for him the airless precincts of high art. They had paid well for a spec script; he was lucky to get the rewrites. He had everything to lose. He was a commercials director where compromise and collaboration was the norm. You're just selling something, right? Rewrites were king. Make it better, or at least get it made. It was made up mostly anyway, or googled, or adapted from hearsay. Frank, a black Charlie Chaplin? Had a great ring to it, 'if it's broke fix it' a 'clever' twist on a commonplace, a classic Adland inversion. But really, what exactly about Charlie Chaplin did his main character have in common, other than being transient?

On another level @waynex knew he was retrofitting his rationalisation to accommodate present circumstance. A black Charlie Chaplin was a good marketing gag but also reflected a genuine desire to see more black characters and actors in films as leads. If others didn't want that what could he do? All he could do was write it. He knew the chances of Frank staying black were close to zero even if somebody like Forest

Speaks wanted to do it. A black action hero in an indie drama. Some chance. Like in a Percival Everett novel where nobody notices or says anything, where you can be kidnapped, erased or mistaken for a famous celebrity. No one says anything, the swap out is invisible. @waynex wrote Frank as he came to him. If they wanted a white lead, then as long as they say it, and don't pass it back unsaid onto him, fair enough and on their head be it. It was no different in advertising where euphemisms smuggled racism onto our screens year in, year out. The casting needs to be more upscale (White). It's just too Urban (Black) for our audience. We love it, it's brave (diverse) but it's not right for this campaign (Our Brand full stop).

The game is rigged, the odds are against change, just take the money. @waynex, one voice among many competing for control of the story. Is there another level of consciousness, one of impotent rage and disappointment, of crushed idealism, and yet another where it screams that everything else is the fake noise of deceit? That only down at some kind of base level, or up on some higher plane, does 'truth' reside, albeit a ganglion of self-love and self-preservation. The super Ego running on the fumes of a recently disabled Ego. Can, in fact, you be 'value' without substance, can the super Ego stand in for, replace, the Ego after it has been beaten down and denied, can it in fact do the Ego's job, become in fact a new, improved (super, even), Ego?

At Sapien level, the Original you, where creative or moral concerns don't fit into any meaningful category. The brain grows from left to right, adding bits as we develop, but not changing what's already there; the core, the bit at the back is still the most important, the most functional. You can fuck around with the front, all of our complexities, but damage the cortex and you're dead.

We are soldered together.

Base and superstructure.

Onion and chive pretzels.

The bag rips open and they spill all over the floor. @waynex bends forward to scrabble around to retrieve them from under the seat in front and his blood pressure soars, roars in the ears.

'Here sir, have another packet.'

'Thanks.' Craning neck up, twisting it to make eye contact, as he slumps back and the pressure eases.

Was it possible he wrote Frank as a black character because that is who he is? However stupid that sounds, however unsophisticated. Because that's the story as it came to him, out of his mind, his imagination, but also out of history, out of the world, as it presented itself to the mind of the writer. Mind as filter, mind as originator, as subconscious re-teller in the relay race of human ecstasy and suffering? Mind as the organising mystery. Sorry to be pedantic here, as @waynex hurtles above the Atlantic, flying to his doom (chuckle, chuckle), but this is important shit. 'Story' is held in delicate balance. His grandmother's memories were just one fragment of what made him think about Charlie Chaplin; the comic pathos of this character in a broken-down future America, a post-federal, post-industrial depression too good to pass up as it flickered through his mind's eyes, both conscious and savvy and subconscious and savvier. The possibility of innocence, a rugged wonder in the face of who we become. Frank is of this world. He lives, albeit inconveniently so.

@waynex closes his laptop after shaking it for pretzel dust. *Bindlestiff*. A black Charlie Chaplin. Kind of. Either way, it's a good attention-grabber, a gag with which to sell it in. Enough of the introspection, you always cry at movies on planes, anyway. Come to now, back to the hustle.

'If it's broke, fix it.' Snappy.

Back and forth, these layers mutter to themselves, minds within mind. @waynex was no neophyte to the world of film production, that's not the story. He is not innocent of the process and practice of making moving images. The truth was an open secret. An old director friend once told him a story of meeting with a studio exec whose punchline was:

'You bring me the best script you can write, gimme your best shot. It's my job to turn it into mincemeat.'

This guy, who told @waynex this story, now runs successful vintage and rare clothes stalls at street markets in London and Paris, hunting online and off for rare pieces of salvage jean, early and one-off Bape and Supreme T's and bespoke designer collaborations. But he was once a successful music video director and wannabe screenwriter, who earnestly took Polaroids of everyone he had a meeting with for his own personal career collage. As soon as he heard this punchline he gave up the ghost.

Taxi, LAX and out.

The process of making a movie means that a script gets processed. Hollywood is a factory; how else would it operate?

Lunch is served. An Irish organic beef stew, some red wine, a Grenache-Carignan blend from the Languedoc, earthy and tannic. An honest red. He eats. In Upper class they were trusted with metal knives and forks.

Zeitgeist. If something's broke *we* don't fix it anymore but buy a new one. The poor mend things or borrow money on credit to buy new ones. Strange that you can mend or fix your credit rating, that's the language they use, to mend, to fix credit ratings, to mend your score? Odd to use that metaphorical topology. Flash on the title of a book once read, a college classic, *All That's Solid Melts Into Air*. Maybe it's the inverse of this? We use metaphor to make sense of thin air, we talk of what's not there with what is.

In an award-winning short film about the women who recycle western garments back into their constitutive parts, threads, buttons and zips, at a depot in northern India, the workers assumed we had a water shortage in the West, which was why we threw away good clothes, we had money to buy new ones but not the water to wash the old ones. The poor mend, the poor sew, the poor make do. The image of a tramp wriggling his finger through a hole in the sole of his shoe is timeless. It's Chaplin. It's a visual lesson. How to mend a shoe. This shit should be up in space showing aliens or whoever wants to know, who we are, at least who we were. That's how @waynex wrote the opening scene of the film. Folding the past into the future. An ex-marine hobo who can turn his hand to anything: car engines, refrigerators, air-con units, microwaves. All that stuff that nobody bothers to learn. #ThisHobo learnt it in the army.

Will work for food. Digging holes and picking fruit. That was what writing *Bindlestiff* was about. The humour of life on the road, the episodic nature of taking the road that leads to the world and the contingent fortunes of those that take it. A retort, a rejoinder to the pompous gloom of films like *The Road*. Too white, too tragic, too doomed.

We will go out with many whimpers rather than a single bang, and in amongst all the whimpering there will be bursts of laughter, exchanges of stories, characters of strength and hope and many small redemptions and remissions. That's what @waynex really wrote.

And now he was on the plane. *Bindlestiff* renamed *Land of Hunger* and most of the back story deleted.

And @waynex had agreed to it all. For money. And it wasn't over yet as there would always be more money and with it more revisions.

At that textile depot in India the first job was to slash the clothes to make them worthless, so nobody would steal them. After this they ripped out the zips and cut off the buttons, to be re-purposed, revalued and thrown back into the supply chain. All this, all these steps flashed through his mind as the drive of his laptop spun up for the second time during the flight.

@waynex's characters:

Frank, ex-marine, latter-day hobo, broken down drunk, hurricane Katrina survivor, gambler, father, husband, widow, learning to catch trains across a broken, yet still beautiful America. The mystic Larry, his nemesis the hobo killer, the marines Kenny, Sinclair, and Madero, Lap Dances with Wolves, the half-Cherokee meth addict saviour of the story, all of them swim before his eyes from the original draft.

They stare up at him from the page in inert sentences just like these. @waynex clicks open the current draft, the third draft, replaying the telephone conversation he had with his producer Tommy less than a week previously.

'We open with Frank leaving his dog with the Chinese guy, right?' (@waynex muttered, 'He's Vietnamese, Mr Kim, he's not Chinese. . .')

'Why does he have to leave his only friend, his dog, where's he going, what's driving him to leave a place of safety, right? Hook the audience with these questions.' ('What about him mending his shoe, then catching out, riding the rails, the mystery of this, isn't that hook enough?')

'Bear with me pal, follow the logic here, so he has to go, to leave safety, to leave the coast, head inland into the horror right, you wrote that, the horror of America, this fascist dystopia, right?' ('I never used the words horror or fascist, Tommy.')

'Then the audience discovers why, when we are already on the journey! The dog is the hook, believe me, the dog hooks us into Frank's story without us having to tell it. Now they're on the road with him and we're golden. To find himself and the family he betrayed by his drinking and gambling, separated physically by a bankrupt America in free-fall. There's the jeopardy right there. That's the heart of the story and we are not changing that, just clearing out all the deadwood, weeding it all out, giving the audience a reason to care, right? You can see that, hell you're the writer. Jettison the back story and we're good to go.' ('. . .')

'Great man, I knew you'd get it, the rest will fall into place when you get out here, and don't sweat it about Frank…' (Breathes. A few deep breaths, in and out, before putting the phone down.)

@waynex presses the service button. The air hostess rustles down to him from two seats up.

'Another bloody Mary please.'

'Tabasco in that? Ice and a slice?' Questions parsed once again by curt nods. 'Celery?'

@waynex needs a drink, some Dutch courage.

'Yes, the works.' He mutters the commonplace.

He reads.

What about the card players? Inciting moment or just weeds? (His updating of the Decameron had fallen on deaf ears, blind eyes or barren soil.)

The cursor blinks. 'The card players.' His other nan, Rachel, had this ornament on her polished walnut sideboard. A fine, delicate ornament, made from Capodimonte porcelain, all thin fingers and playing cards, all four suits rendered immaculately in miniature. The players sporting cocked crushed hats and red rimmed eyes. Brimming with Neapolitan sentimentality, quintessentially Italian in its woe, its pathos. The intricate detail of cross-hatched sewn coloured patches on baggy trousers, the bindle, the tramp's bag made up with a piece of cloth, his dirty feet protruding from the peeled back uppers of his shoes, a skinny hand held high, almost triumphant but always and forever on the point of triumph, a Pyrrhic moment this, *about to lay down the winning hand*; wrist bone visible under parchment thin skin, painted hearts and clubs grasped up above his head forever, or until broken whilst being dusted or brushed past.

A whole series of these porcelain figures went by the name of 'Giuseppe', the everyman tramp of Southern Europe, a memory of the medieval ever-presence of hunger and landless labour, but also of a carefree rural idyll that the people with mantlepieces to put these figures on, have lost. Hobos, tramps, Bindlestiffs.

His fingers hover over the track pad.

His drink arrives, he takes a gulp; the spices burning his top lip, the vodka sharp on his tongue and in his throat. He takes another; the celery banging against his nose. He squeezed his eyes shut wishing the bloody Mary would give him the courage of one of Fox's Martyrs, to take his hand out of the fire. Instead, his finger presses the track pad, moves on it highlighting his what appear to be, surprisingly even, so late in the day, precious words.

His Bermondsey nan had a ceramic music box, two tramps drunk as skunks under a streetlight, one swinging from it, the other slumped below it, an empty green bottle hanging at his side, they both serenade the moon and stars in a much cheaper and more indelicate statuette than their Italian counterparts. The song it played he could never remember, but it was something sentimental, something music hall, something very British. It sat on her mini bar, a small MDF semi-circle with a faux leather studded front, pride of place in her small tidy front room. Baby Cham, Cinzano, Advocat at Christmas, snowballs, sherry, lemonade, tramps and hobos.

@waynex deletes 'the card players' as the plane begins its descent. The song finally comes back to him.

'*How dry I am*
*How dry I am*
*Nobody knows*
*How dry I am*
*How dry I am*'

They don't make them like that anymore.

@waynex shuts down his laptop, his splayed hand resting on it as if in benediction.

Touchdown.

'Ladies and gentlemen, welcome to LAX.'

# IRASSHAIMASE!

*Santa Monica, Los Angeles, 2016*

> *'As I was a walking one morning in Spring,*
> *To hear the larks whistle and the gully-birds sing,*
> *I heard a sweet maiden a making a moan,*
> *But alas, I'm a stranger a long way from home.*
> *I came from Sweet England with my mother and dad,*
> *And I thought in America all could be had,*
> *Of Gold and of silver and acres galore,*
> *And I'll never meet hunger and poverty more.'*
>
> — Shirley Collins, Sweet England

Tippins picks me up from the airport in his new ride, a discrete looking but powerful Mercedes AMC Sedan with cigarette burns all over the trim. The last owner was Robert Downey Junior 1.0. That figures, they both chain smoke white tip Marlboro Lights.

'Here, I got you some fags.' I pull out two cartons of Marlboro Gold, the brand name for Marlboro Lights in the U.K.

'Thanks mate. Good flight?'
'Yeah fine.'
'How's the family?'
'Great, you?'
'Yeah, all good man.'
'Let's get loaded.'
Tippins leans across and pops open the glovebox.
'Perfect.'
These are the conversations of men.

Inside the glovebox there's an eight-ball, the surefire solution for beating jetlag. That and a night at our favourite Izakaya 'Musha' on Fourth and Wilshire, chasing Asahi beer with cold Hananomai Sake and snacking on the signature spicy tuna dip, and their crack-like MFC, Musha fried chicken.

Tonight I was staying with the legend that is Sean, 'tip-top' Tippins, DGA Assistant Director in good standing. Surf his couch, catch up and decompress from the invincible feeling of being in a movie you get after a long flight, where each step of the journey is something you've seen in films or read in stories, and now you have been through it, processed through each station of this crossing, a cosy familiar rhythm takes over. Ringing ears from the air pressure changes further enhance this out of body feeling, this discombobulation, so a line of coke off the dashboard in the car park feels as natural as not doing a line of coke off the dashboard in the car park.

Tommorow I was moving to the Chateau Marmont for a week to work on the script, then down the street to the Standard when the family arrive. From a thousand bucks a night to three hundred. Someone else's coin but fair enough, the Marmont wasn't what it used to be, anyway.

Later in a back booth in Musha, six beers in, chased by three bottles of sake tamping down the jet lag, my mind whirls, detached once again from the here and now.

Rushing a long piss to get back to the table, shaking drips

over my shoes and jeans, back to the yellowtail sashimi with juniper berries, the booze, Tippins smoking out front, I check my phone: two missed calls from Tommy. I'll call him tommorow, tonight is ours.

I'm back at the table pouring sake, spilling it also, which in fact is lucky, a sign of prosperity, spilling it into the Masu bamboo box, drinking it from there, spilling yet more down my shirt. Tippins returns, eyeing the table swimming in sake and my shirt the same. 'Fucking mucky bastard', he laughs with a slight hiss through false front teeth.

'When you gonna stop smoking, Tips!'

I had seen cigarettes kill Sean's step-dad less than a year before, walking at his dad's snail pace across the car park, to get to the Coach and Horses for a Sunday roast, a journey that took forever to a soundtrack of cancer wheezing.

The stories of our lives took over. Catching up you can't do on the phone or by email and besides we were shit at both. Life was to be lived face to face. Now a river of sake and beer rushed over the stones of our lives, abrading our bones, sifting through the gravel that made us.

'I need a piss.' Sean lurches up, finishing his glass on the way to standing.

I come up for air (against my will, my desire being to stay deep in the moment, but an almost cosmic force of buoyancy pushes me upwards) and gasp snatches of Frank, passages of dialogue, arcs of narrative, the reason I was here in L.A. Frank drinking, the cliche of drinking away your troubles, of responding to trauma with drink, a classic trope of fiction, of men in stories, the sentimental drunk imagination of men, of 'Harvey' the invisible white rabbit, and I ask myself, what crap is this I've written? Frank in a bar on a military base, screaming at the war on the TV, triggering memories of his wars at home and abroad. The déjà vu of these broken-down old vets, their bitterness and thinking, is it even the timeline right for this, wouldn't the future look different, couldn't I have imagined it any differently? Another few drinks in and it should go, I'll cut it all out.

Talking to myself silently waiting for Sean to rescue me.

But there's an attachment to something already written down, a lingering nostalgia for cliches, a fear that without them all we have is a blank page.

'Wanna go to the Lost and Found?' Sean returns, in the nick of time, writing the next chapter of our evening, usually the last.

'Great fucking idea.'

'Left you a line in the toilet under the bog roll.'

'Great.'

'I'll be outside having a smoke.'

An easy guy to assassinate Sean Tippins, just wait across the road from any bar and wait till he comes outside for a fag. That or buy him some duty-free cigarettes.

# HOWLING AT THE MOON

*Hollywood Hills, Los Angeles, 2016*

It's nighttime up on Wonderland Avenue, the susurration of cicadas soundtracks the scene. As soon as there is pause in dialogue it washes over any silence, owning the night, becoming louder somehow the more it is heard, parsing out the spaces between spoken words, adding to their meaning. Behind both, intermittently, distant traffic and other random city sounds are brought on the wind, or by their proximity.

Listen.

Underwater lights spill from the pool, Forest and his agent Morris are playing cards on a table in the garden's candlelit gazebo. For the sake of further clarity, they are not 'playing cards'. They are scene reading from the *Bindlestiff* movie script.

Morris reads the other characters, so Forest can concentrate on Frank's lines. He's bringing it to life as much as he can, to the surprise of Forest who is both impressed and amused by his agent's acting bones. The moment takes on its own valency. They are enjoying themselves, the script neutral territory between who they are and what they do (for each other). It's probably the second read through, so they are deep in it, not to say also deep into the bottles of Pinot and one of Courvoisier that litter the table beside them.

So, in the spirit of now, we are:

EXTERIOR HOLLYWOOD HILLS - NIGHT.

The card playing characters are:

EXTERIOR BOARDWALK - DAY - 2036

The boardwalk in question is in the post-federal US marine veteran enclave of El Segundo, with its derelict power station looming over them in the background. America has become a patchwork quilt of federal remnants, corporate, military and ethnic minority powers all living in uneasy alliance in a world still dominated by other nation state 'Superpowers'.

Morris turns the fourth card, revealing the Ace of Spades.

*'Face the turn, face the turn. What you got?'*

Forest, *'You know I ain't got any real money.'*

Morris, *'What else you got?'*

Forest reads the scene directions.

'FRANK stares at his two hole cards. He places a set of rusty car keys on the table. One of the onlookers, SHAKES, picks out a chord on his guitar.'

Forest places the keys to his leased Audi A8 on the table. Morris sniggers, *'You all in.'* He pours them both refills from the bottle of cognac.

Forest savours the liquor in his mouth, reluctantly swallows, stares Morris in the eye.

*'Don't sell me short man, this is my one big hand.'*

Morris places his wallet on the table, full of bills. Forest mimes another blues chord from an invisible guitar.

*'Where you get all that damn money, Charlie?'*

Forest has settled on a soft southern accent, different from before, slower, a voice that's seen life, been hurt by it but not necessarily made any wiser.

An owl hoots, a rare addition to the soundtrack of the Hollywood Hills and they both start.

'Shit's that?'

'Just an owl man, an owl.'

We gift agency to noises in the dark, our imagination priming us to defend ourselves from any threat. We are hard-wired to assume intent out there beyond the circle of light where there may only be a benign darkness.

Forest winks at Morris. 'Concentrate'

He continues, *'Where you get all that damn money Charlie?'*

Morris winks back, *'Playing cards Frankie, playing cards.'*

Forest, *'Fuck you, man.'*

Morris, *'Now we see what comes down the river.'*

Morris reading out loud.

```
'The dealer, JOE, hesitates not wanting to
continue the game. SHAKES fingers glide up the
fret.'
```

Forest, *'Will you stop fiddling with that damn guitar Shakes?'*

Morris again.

```
'His fingers freeze on the strings. His hand
shakes.'
```

Morris, *'What you waiting for Joe?'*

Morris is now 'Joe' with a different voice. *'This ain't no high rolling Indian casino boys, come on let's call it off.'*

Forest, deadpan.

```
'He looks at each of them, they keep staring at
the cards and each other. Their blood is up.'
```

Morris switches back to Charlie, *'You want Joe to turn that card?*

*Turn the card, turn the page, could be a new beginning, a whole new life...'*

Morris continues the scene directions.

```
'FRANK looks at the cards on the table, dabs
his brow. Joe looks anxious, drinks deep
from his shorty. Frank rubs his dog's neck
meditatively.'
```

Forest, now at the heart of the scene, deep in it, leans forward in his chair over the table and up into Morris's grille, his voice tamped down, quiet, a hard and flat compression of the physical tension of the scene, hard enough you can hear time ticking between the words, let alone the cicadas, on a track that nobody needs to lay down, because it is us, *we* are time ticking; we own it.

*'I don't want a new life Charlie, just looking to fix the one I got.'*

Morris switches back to Joe, *'No, no Frank, oh man, cards don't fix shit, you know that. We don't have to turn the damn card. Tell him Charlie.'*

And back, *'Joe's right...'*

Forest fills in.

```
'FRANK takes another slug, retrieves the
unopened letter from his top pocket, turns
it over in his hand like a fetish and finally
replaces it.'
```

Morris, *'We can call it off right now, no one's gonna blame you Frank, call you chicken.'*

Forest, *'You always have to turn the card Joe.'*

His finger jabs towards the deck.

Forest, *'Card's made to be turned, just like a wheel.'*

Zooming out. 'That's a cheesy line, a little too OTT, right?' says Morris as Morris, pulling out a cigar from his sports jacket pocket. He cuts it, but can't find his lighter. Forest leans in again and lights him, ignoring his out of character remark.

*'Joe, turn the card, turn it.'*

Reluctantly JOE turns the last card, a seven of Spades.

Morris, *'You ain't got shit.'*

Forest, *'Fool never had shit before, why his luck change now?' Is that what you're thinking Charlie? But every dog has his day, isn't that what the Bible say? Every dog has his day.'*

Zooming out. Morris chuckles *'Every dog has its day? What Bible is that in?'*

*'Sure gotta be in the dog bible Morris'* Forest makes a Forest joke which could also be a FRANK one.

Forest stands up. Sways a little, throws his two hole cards down onto the makeshift table. SHAKES picks up the refrain as the chorus of Seasick Steve 'Doghouse Boogie' mixes up.

Forest's got three sevens. More than a little drunk, he bays like a dog at the sky. Disturbed, his dog joins in.

Morris: *'When's a man gonna learn, that river card only ever gonna bring him trouble. This is all too much a Robert Johnson deal with the Devil rip-off, like we're in a fucking theme park of life, fate and cards.'*

Forest ignores him, stares at the cards in Morris's hand.

Morris shrugs, lays his hand face up on the table. Full house. He snatches up Forest's keys in his hand. They both bay to the moon, this odd slightly drunk couple, laughing at themselves and the melodrama of it all.

In the movie about making the movie we would crane up and out over this scene to take in the house, the hills, the location, both physical and psychical of where this actor lives. Forest Speaks, probably the only black man on Wonderland avenue.

It's enough to say in this reading scene that 'the Hobo/Black Film Star/Jewish Agent dissonance amplifies itself into glorious cinematic metaphor.'

To quote a future critic, not my words at all.

# LOST AND FOUND

*Mar Vista, Los Angeles, 2016*

In a strip mall next to a Chase bank on National lies a mecca for old-school booze hounds. Entering the Lost and Found through its padded western style cherry red swing doors is to step back forty years. This place exists at the other end of a wormhole. 'Cocktails and dancing' reads the sign outside, although inside you will find a lot of one but not the space to swing a cat in for the other. It's in Mar Vista for fuck's sake, the land that time forgot circa 1975.

The Lost and Found, somewhere yet to be fucked with. Two bucks a vodka and tonic, don't ask what brand or the barman will punch you. A wide heavy wood-clad L-shaped bar puts distance between you and him although his reach probably renders this depth irrelevant. You sit on a stool and there's a lot of space for drinks, the bar a launchpad for the soon to be loaded. No bar snacks, the bar was uni-purpose. Behind it was a birthday peg board with the irregularly spaced names of regulars and their dates laid out across the year's calendar. Names spelt/misspelt/deleted as the regulars came and went or died. Above this a wonky 'U.S.A.' titled the board – patriotism of a kind, even in these far western parts. All the letters ran across higgledy-piggledy horizontals, wagon rail ruts if you will, heralding days of celebration to come. Local heroes, pioneers of booze. This was a community spot, not unlike Cheers albeit to a certain extent, a community of the damned.

There was a free popcorn machine and celery salt cellars on the tables. There was a pool table where the ambulatory under thirties would play pool. Out back you could smoke in the yard. One buck per play on a jukebox spinning Pat Benatar, Rick James, Hall and Oates and oddly enough, Shaggy. Cash only, cards put in their place, strictly for chopping lines in the shitty toilet.

One night a few years before, (it was a buy 4 get 1 free Saturday), we had settled in after wrapping a headache powders shoot, throwing back one after another of the cheap V&T's. Two blasted looking blondes came in and sidled up to us. Regulars, no doubt with names up on the board. Soused up already, primed, like skint kids do, pre-load on cheap drinks at home before hitting the bars, although this bar was probably cheaper than most homes. Swedish coke and booze hounds probably fifteen years younger than they looked. Fresh off a boat that had sailed a long time ago, every drink, cigarette, blow job and general life disappointment, was posted on their face(book). Within twenty minutes one of them offered to suck me off if I gave her some coke. I had none, never did and didn't really want a blow job, but no story writes itself so I said 'Yeah come on then, in the toilet, let's go.'

The Lost and Found generates its own bad choices amongst its clientele, has its own transgressive grammar, with which to write your sentences, a sociopathy you pick up on pretty quickly.

So we went back through the bar and into the stinky urinal and just as she was about to kneel, I said 'I'm joking, I don't have any coke and I don't want a blow job thanks.'

She shrugged, was all 'whatever' about it and so we went back to the bar where her sister (I assume) was draped all over Tippins and we all did some coke anyway, which Sean always had on him. A wrap here, a wrap there, one in his shoe, one behind his ear, you get the picture. We sat there and hit a few bumps off our thumb webs, shaken out of little vials, another one of Sean's magic tricks. The barman didn't say shit. It was like Christmas come early for the Swedes, faces all lit up. Booze would kill them before the coke, it eat them up as they drank it, like the dissolution of the Mummy. Shit, they seemed happy enough, free coke and some drinks and they didn't even have to suck anybody off.

I couldn't shrug off this memory lurching back from the bogs, legs heavy with jet lag, head muzzy with booze. What happened to those two Swedish women? Were they still around, still regulars? Were they dead? Or had they saved up the fare for the trip home. Had somebody in their family, their parents maybe, wired them the money, or flown out to take matters in hand, to bring them home? Why would I even think that? They must have been in their late thirties. When was home ever a solution to anything? Why would it be an option, a solution to a situation I literally knew nothing about? All conjecture, bad imagination playing tricks on me. How do any of us end up as we are, happy, sad or any point in between? Which decisions are irreversible, which less so?

Life in real time rarely serves up a back story. Tippins was on a barstool at the corner of the bar. We always sat there if we could. Best seats in the house; on point in the Lost and Found, waiting to be entertained.

'Come to now,' as Charlie Manson once sang.

As if on cue, a has-been actor came in with his bodyguard. Only in L.A do has-beens and fading stars still have bodyguards. Usually related to them as it works out cheaper. Dumb 'what the fuck do we do with him' nephews are always a good bet, or brothers, older or younger; the Fredos' of this world stop gap the need to pay professionals.

Once famous, always famous somewhere. They were there to prop themselves up, to console each other on the lives they once led, hookers they had once procured, the meals, the comped seats, the freebies of all kinds they had enjoyed, the gravy they had swam in. Now the tide was low, (or was it high?) this ticket to ride had expired. Like next stage cancer they had moved on, drinking out on threadbare tales of shows and flicks now forgotten or at very best dredged up on quiz shows and vestigial trivia pages on the web preserved in digital aspic by the browsers, way-back machine.

As he zigzagged to the bar, we couldn't quite place him although he did look like he had been somebody. His buddy was as forgettable as he had always been, which in this context gave him a stronger presence, a continuity of being rather than the sadness of former celebrity that haunted his employer. What is that look? How do you inhabit a body as if it had once been somebody? Broad shouldered, he had a remnant presence, which he was carrying on those shoulders, a burden, a ghost presence, that gave off an odd familiarity, like the smell of ozone. We got talking to the guy, he was already loaded, but funny as fuck and his bodyguard was too; foil to, as well as protector of, his faded celebrity. This was their half life and they shared what remained of it generously.

'Hey Tony, you remember we ate so much fucking crab you said we had to exit the fucking restaurant sideways? You ever eaten so much crab, so much fucking crab?'

I bobbed my head at this priceless anecdote, wanting more. Fabulous meals are all that stand out from the humdrum routine of more lives than you would imagine. Gargantuan, fantastical celebratory feasts in the face of it all; these culinary victories valued above all else, when everything else falls away, what remains to be recounted from our singular Odyssey, steaks yay big.

Tippins grinned, chuckled, 'Hey, Richard Tyson right?' Funny how celebrities eat this shit up. Tyson's eyes lit up, a round of drinks on him soon followed. I give Sean a 'how the fuck did you know who he is?' look. Tippins shrugs, smarter than the average bear that's how, he slides off his stool and goes for a smoke.

Tyson was like Dennis Wilson, a big, brawling fella, fuelled by booze and an idea that somebody owed him something. A guy who would throw sloppy but effective punches, ones you would feel in the morning. Tyson had starred in an unfinished version of *Ghengis Khan* alongside Charlton Heston back in the nineties. That's the kind of guy you meet in the Lost and Found and what makes it the place it is. Remnants, leftovers, self-haunted half-lings, crab eaters.

Us.

'You know who Richard is, right?', whispers Tony the bodyguard to me as Richard stumbles to the head.

Toilets/the bogs to Brits like me, but I love this word 'head'. Tyson must have been in a WW2 navy drama, the word suits him, he conjures it. 'Where's the head at?' For guys like Richard Tyson the head originated in the services, the navy, the era of 'Uncle Sam needs you' and a tour of duty somewhere you got to by boat; an echo of maritime order from the wars of the 20th century and beyond.

The war in the Pacific. The Pacific ocean echoes of that war are surprisingly close to the surface, in bars like this, bars like the Captain's Table on Main Street in Santa Monica, despite the gentrification, the blandness of wealth spread up and down the coast, the Captain's Table or Sean Penn's favourite bar back in the day, 'Chez Jay', boy you bet Sean soaked up those vibes; of the night before shipping out, the drink, the dames, the last sweetheart kiss, then embarkation, trips to the head, the sea, and the fate of war. Echoes almost European in their intensity of connotation, puncturing the shallowness of time present.

'You know who he is?' Tony tries again.

'Sure.' I snigger like Muttley into my N'th vodka and tonic.

*Pacific Ocean Blue*, Dennis Wilson's solo album that also channels this proximity to such a vast volume of time and water, one in which he would eventually drown, all boozed out like his face-sake Richard Tyson, back from his trip to the head, holding down the bar from floating off with one huge ham fist.

I had first heard this album in the sitting room of Lewis Taylor, his favourite album, this Jewish Prince. Like his Purple highness, he played all his own instruments, did his own production and arrangements, but his sweet yet powerful falsetto modulated more like Marvin's. Audiences thought he was black, but no, he was this short hairy Jewish guy from Willesden Green. But what a voice, what a guitarist, me doing coke, him heroin, both digging this album, as far away from the sea, from the Pacific Ocean Dennis Wilson drowned in as you could get, maybe it was his blues we shared, or some small part of it.

The Lost and Found is one of the few authentic bars left in the City of Angels. It was ever-present, unadorned, cloaked in the lowest of lights, nothing more than a dive bar for the mainly over fifties and whatever passing itinerant drinkers could find the place on the second floor of a half empty run-down shopping mall in Mar Vista. If you were an archaeologist, this was a place to dig up. I haven't been to Jumbos Clown Room in Hollywood, but have worn the T-shirt. Here they don't sell Lost and Found T-shirts. Yet. The Lost and Found is an unmediated experience. Like the Cabaret in the Cassavetes flick *Killing Of A Chinese Bookie*, a place so oddball and European, washed up on the west coast. Bars like these are an expression of the European diaspora in America, Kabaret Los Angeles, Angers Hollywood Babylon, the true bohemian underbelly of a city, hidden below and obscured by the 'Crooks and Angels' Los

Angeles we know and love from the movies – more *Carnivàle*, more existential, liminal and ephemeral, open-ended and without resolution, narrative, emotional or otherwise. Maybe Joe Fante was in on this, a bit player in a sadder place, refuges for unknowns and the want to be forgotten; only if you ask the dust will you hear their names barely whispered.

*Carnivàle*, a fictional composite of all this, a great circus romp, reworking *Freaks* into a celebration of misfits and entertainers in the dust bowl of the depression. Penny dreadful entertainment, democratic inclusivity when the circus came to town, and wherever it went, the only show in town. This packaging of gothic myths, remnant tales of European gods and other totems, drew on outsider weird comic book culture of the otherness that inspires prejudice, fear and the recoiling American identity we are more familiar with. A world more akin to the horror fantasy of Cthulhu than the greatest show on earth. *Carnivàle*, tapped into this rich seam of outsider stories and became the mother lode of first wave high production value cable TV serial dramas and box set fetish objects. Two seasons then cancelled, everything as it should be, up in the air. Modern freaks, and not in any sense in the minority.

With some effort my mind swims back into focus on the here and now, the memory tide of *Pacific Ocean Blue* ebbs, falls away; 'I was lost, but now am found, only soon to be happily lost again. . .'

The regular pool players brought their own cues in bags, sheaths. Now *that's* real. It's both *Bill and Ted* and *Cheers*, *The Simpsons*, the MidWest, the Wild West, post-war and *Happy Days*, like having your own darts back home. In post-*Happy Days* America, this 'for real' continuity with a tradition of community, social drinking, a place where locals belonged and therefore immortalised, is something hard to find on the coast – like looking for a handshake in a boxing ring, an unexpected beating heart dark and hidden in a town famously soulless, bright and shallow.

The Lost and Found is an opening scene of a movie, the end scene of a movie, as well as all the scenes in between. Of many movies. Maybe I should have Frank sit here, high in his cups and in good company, exchanging war stories with a played out old actor in a world where movies are mostly reruns or frachise entertainments. In a world where there is no money to make movies anymore – or pay movie stars – action and actors alike having evolved into CGI and Icon motion capture performances. Think Tupac performing on stage as a hologram at Coachella and throw that forward thirty years.

'And so with my pen I herald the end of the Lost and Found. I intend to write its death sentence, signed with a flourish in Courier Final Draft.'

'Right!' Tippins orders the bill. He hasn't read *Bindlestiff*, but nods at my rambling. When it comes to it, he will be the one to break it down, to run it through the movie magic software, turning pages into days, characters into call time schedules, all this without reading it.

A bar called the Lost and Found is doomed for all time. The movie is written in the stars, it's just a matter of time for it to fall to earth.

Sean throws a handful of bills on the bar, I haul myself up before Richard Tyson reappears with piss blooms on his trousers and the inevitable crushing farewell handshakes. We make our way to Sean's Range Rover.

What movie would this place eventually host? A redemption drama starring Mickey Rourke? Or a bittersweet romantic comedy about love and booze, featuring Steve Carrel, or a clever satire on Hollywood has-been's or never-were's starring A-listers on SAG rates? A Greek chorus of loveable rogues and their oddball truths in the face of the world, movie, Beckett-lite perhaps, or a straight up psychological horror movie? Most likely it will be an indie flick made for a few hundred grand with a happy hooker, some coke and a bag of stolen dollars. Pictures on the wall behind the bar of the stars, the reviews and, depending on how successful the film, photo ops. At a stretch, a little merch.

Don't ask me, I don't have the heart to write it.

Sean lights up a Marlboro Light. God love him.

I flash on a literary salon event in London, a city so remote to me in that instant I draw a blank remembering it in any detail. One city supplanted by the phenomena of another. A *White Review* event where two readers were telling their story in polyphony, (weaving in and out of sync with each other, a male voice chasing a female one, catching her up and then hers following his as reversed echo. . .) in which they called cigarettes 'tubes,' as a distancing device, as if the whole situation wasn't distant enough.

On the way out of the Lost and Found the last thing I saw over my shoulder was the barman serving drinks, charming a gaggle of cougar lushes. He's an older Channing Tatum, or Tatum Channing, I never remember which way round that goes, an older Channing Tatum in a world that didn't work out for him when the dancing ended, a guy who never wrote *Magic Mike*. In this parallel universe of Stories with a capital S where else you gonna get a job?

Sean takes a last drag on his tube, fires up the engine and we drive home.

Lost and Found.

# AS ALWAYS

*Chateau Marmont, Sunset Boulevard, Los Angeles, 2016*

The next morning I get a cab to the Chateau Marmont. Tippins is already at work, on set somewhere in the valley. ADs work themselves to death in this town, a life of feast or famine and when they are down, they worry themselves sick about their next gig. Average life expectancy of a Directors Guild of America assistant director is fifty-five. Directors? We hardly ever work and live forever.

Pride of place in the hotel garage is the owner's burgundy and cream Morgan convertible. I negotiate the super slippery polished flagstones without tripping and walk into the 1920s Spanish Hacienda styled open reception area.

'Nice to see you, sir, welcome back to the Chateau Marmont.' A beautiful, immaculately dressed Asian American man in his early thirties serenades me from behind the front desk.

'Thanks. Great to be back.'

Welcome back, now that's a line to savour, as you wait for your tasselled key. Last time somebody was stupid enough to put me up here was 2010.

'Room 26, we hope you have a great stay.' Ear to ear smile as he hands over the heavy brass key fob.

Sadly, he didn't say 'Your usual room @waynex', or 'Your regular suite' but that would come, the promise of an upgraded future welcome teases itself in that smile.

'Thanks, am sure I will as always.'

Weak. I've been here four times tops.

Weak, weak, weak.

He knows exactly how many times and who paid the bills, it's all there in front of him on his sneaky under-the-desk laptop. He glances back up at me. I smile like a Cheshire cat and head to the lifts. In my hand a real-life key which will open doors in an earthquake, unlike the credit card keys of most hotels that go south during power cuts.

'Enjoy' caresses my back through the foyer.

The solicitations of supermen.

As easily as that I was back on set at the arrhythmic yet still beating heart of old Hollywood. An illusion kept alive by the lavish, understated decor, stone floors and pillars, oak beams, heavy decorative carpet, and wall sconces with electric candles. 1920s Spanish colonial, a delusional fantasy that things here never change despite the drip, drip, drip, of corporate finance threatening that change is all there is.

You are both on and in Sunset Boulevard which leaves one giddy with self importance as you ascend in the mirrored lift.

*All right, Mr De Mille, I'm ready for my closeup.*

Lying on the bed, staring up at the rotating wooden blades of the ceiling fan, mind buzzing with white noise, my identity and immediate purpose were crushed and replaced by everything and everyone else who had been in this room, on this bed, in this hotel, in this town. Like trying to write with a Mont Blanc pen, thinking in the Chateau Marmont drew a blank. All you could think of, if thinking is the right word, was 'I am in the Chateau Marmont and look there's Ben Stiller's ninety-year-old dad Jerry, still doing lengths in the pool and there is the cottage where Keanu Reeves lived when he was dating David Geffen.'

Somebody bought me a Mont Blanc pen once, which came with its own bottle of obsidian ink that spilt all over my desk every time I unscrewed it. Or did I buy it myself at an airport? Perhaps I was that somebody? An airport is the only place in the world where it makes any sense to buy one. The only place in the world it also makes sense to buy other things like humidors and Rolex watches. I had to get rid of it. The pen literally renders you immobile at your desk, gripped between first and second fingers, more like a monkey's stick than a writing implement. My fingers sweated as I squeezed the shit out of it. Who uses a Mont Blanc pen? Odd, a Rolex is a luxury watch, but it has presence, has a pedigree, is reassuringly heavy on the wrist. It also keeps good time and value, so you always have emergency money, back-up funds on your wrist. Like keeping a packed suitcase in the hall by the front door. If you are the sort of person who values that kind of thing, or who has been 'on their toes' as a London gangster once described being on the run. Gangsters or refugees, a Rolex comes in handy.

I couldn't give away that useless bloody fountain pen, yet master of the universe brands must function normally in the hands of somebody – probably masters of the universe – a brand unto themselves, existing on an equal 'How to Spend it' footing with all the luxury items they surround themselves with.

I gaze out of the leaded period windows. The day passes.

Celebrities scuttle across Sunset Boulevard at sunset to buy booze from the bottle shop because the alcohol in the rooms is like joke expensive, even for them, as a point of principle, a sense memory of what things used to be worth before fame and money tinkered with the magnet in your compass.

Rip-offs instead of good deals, being taken advantage of,

where once things had been fair, brazen daylight robbery with everything charged to your room, your tab abused by acquaintances and friends alike. Whatever happened to going dutch? Everything is now on you. Routinely over-charged, obliged to tip large, these are just some pitfalls of the high life.

Tippins had once been in Shanghai on a shoot and got Shanghaied by some pimps who took his cards plus his PIN numbers to the ATM. Heavyset thugs with cheap shiny trousers that ran tight across their thighs, men who could do you damage. Tippins pulled his shirt cuff down over his 10k Rolex which they hadn't noticed or assumed was a fake. He'd only been in China an hour before getting hooked by a chubby looking student who took him back to a brothel and a better looking prostitute. He fucked her a few times and gave her some money to buy a new dress. That's when the heavies entered the room and cleaned him out. Later he asked them for some money to get a cab back to the hotel. They laughed, offered him a drink and a cigarette. This went on for hours. They let him keep his Amex after he explained there wasn't a PIN for it; you signed for stuff. They nodded, miming cutting off his hand, which cracked them up. Sean joined in. Sanguine at the fact they couldn't access his unlimited credit, they poured more drinks and asked him about life in L.A. Not such bad guys, finally they put him in a taxi. Back in his hotel room he cancelled his cards, put his Rolex in the safe, and after some online checks was refunded the 1500-odd bucks they rinsed him for.

6 p.m. and I pour a Stoli tonic from my contraband stash, ice on the house from the circa 1940 fridge, with a slice of stolen lemon from a tree in the hotel garden. I pick up the phone for room service and the pre-recorded voice sounds familiar. An actress I once cast in a commercial was the voice of the hotel. 'Hello you've reached the Chateau Marmont. Press 1 for laundry,' etc. The commercial had been set in a medieval village

and she had had to wear skimpy rags smothered in mud. Being the voice of the Chateau Marmont was a prestigious gig on some radars, something you put on your CV. I can't think of any other hotel in the world where this would be so.

I couldn't sleep, I couldn't think, I didn't feel like seeing anybody, lying immobile on the sofa. The room swam in front of me, an empty bottle of vodka on the coffee table. I was polluted with more than just alcohol, these random memories, vapour trails of thought; ambushed whilst drunk. I would never shoot the movie I was being paid to rewrite. This hotel torture, putting me in his place, killing me with other people's luxury. The exquisite pain of being amongst movie people, stars and those that make and trade them for a living. Play their game and just maybe, you'll get to play again, to stay here again.

*. . .we'll make another picture and another picture. You see, this is my life! It always will be! Nothing else! Just us, the cameras, and those wonderful people out there in the dark!*

Gloria Swanson. *Sunset Boulevard* right outside the window. Her words echoes, generated by the fabric of the place itself.

So it was with no little anxiety and trepidation that I came down the next morning for breakfast on the terrace, picking up pages of freshly printed script notes from the front desk. I take a seat. Sunshine, shade and acres of white linen. I open the Manilla envelope.

'Freshly squeezed orange juice, sir?'

'Yes, please.'

I read the notes from Tommy.

*Again, the New Orleans back story, it's too much, we get this guy is an anti-hero why make him such a loser?*

I'd kept this as one a few key flashbacks, to give depth, context, to Frank's journey. It's his hinterland.

*Flashbacks are out of fashion, bad scriptwriting.*

The waiter places a giant's glass of freshly squeezed orange juice on front of me. Almost a pint. How long did it take to pick that amount of oranges?

'Crispy bacon?'

'Great, thanks.'

The terrace is full of buzz, industry people, discrete breakfast meetings, everybody going to it with such verve and self belief. The terrace on which somebody probably did revisions to films like *21 Grams*. Or wrote *Crash*, a state of America movie in which Matt Dillon made a mini comeback. Race, class prejudice, murder, corruption; crackling dialogue right here on this terrace, by writers sipping this orange juice. From here the Hollywood imagination roams, not far, but sometimes it floats down from the terrace onto the streets of West L.A, and becomes infused with the dystopia of not being on the terrace, the terror of it. . .

'Your French toast, sir.'

Yeah and what about gallons of shit filter coffee you always serve with pots of cream that nobody drinks more than a sip of?

'Coffee?'

'Please.'

Tastes great after a litre of orange juice.

*Lose the following: The dog being winched to safety from the roof of a submerging house, following up the boy in the cradle winched down by the helicopter. The stand-off on the bridge, the sheriffs levelled shotguns, Frank and his baby, the bloated black body floating by in the river. Lose it. Don't. overcook. The set-up. Let's discuss where we're at with the budget and Frank later, I'll pick you up buddy.*

The budget had apparently doubled, which probably meant that Frank had been recast and I was out.

When will he pick me up? Tommy didn't say. Never does. It's a thing, a passive aggressive thing that winds the shit out of me. He never answers his phone and doesn't leave a personalised answer phone message. I'm left in a holding pattern here at the hotel. Without a car.

I look up.

Sir Ben Kingsley appears to be staring at me from an adjacent table. He's with a beautiful East Asian woman, well almost a girl, so his intense stare is something other than sexual, yet just as distracting. What does he want? A face that could be forty or four hundred, his eyes hollow, his body preternaturally thin. Meat puppet royalty.

*The stars are ageless aren't they?*

Thanks Norma, you're not wrong.

I sign for breakfast, charging it to the room, no cash needed here.

Back at my remodelled leather desk I spark up my laptop and cut the suggested scenes without hesitation, before falling asleep on the fresh linen.

# FUCK AMERIKKKA

*Bar Marmont, Sunset Boulevard, 2016*

'Your gin and tonic sir.'

I'd already had three beers and a bottle of sake at a Japanese place on Sunset, a late lunch or an early supper, before crossing the road back to the Marmont. I had been reading Kem Nunn's *Dogs of Winter* and was still surfing Heart Attacks, the premier California mysto surf spot, as I stumbled into the bar. It was 6.30 p.m. the witching hour for Industry post-work meet-ups. I'd had enough booze to distance myself from the world in a cosy redoubt of both mind and place. Me in the world as opposed to the world in me.

In America I always preferred to drink Tanqueray. Let the rest drink Grey Goose and Belvedere. America was also the only place in the world where I would order a Margarita. I have never been to Mexico but would probably do the same there. It's the weather, or something. The joy of your tongue chasing the salt around the rim of the glass, a playful American cocktail that also came in jugs. A little holiday innocence to temper the horror.

'Thanks, you got any peanuts?'

'We've got mixed nuts sir, I'll just get you some.'

'That's fine, thanks.'

Bar Marmont, two hundred yards down Sunset from the Chateau, was a funkier, younger spot than the terrace bar at the hotel but with the same prices. This was a place in flux, where the in crowd gathered, Hollywood understudies mostly, fresh faced English actors in the first flush of casting success, Juno, Maisie, Marcus and Ben, children of the British ruling class waiting in the wings. I'm free-styling here a little as there were virtually no lights in the place so you couldn't see shit beyond the table candles.

Jim Hawks and Tommy Adjacent sat opposite me in some kind of stasis whilst I had conversations with both the waitress and myself. As soon as I broke eye contact with her, Hawkes unfroze and was on me.

'Well @waynex, it's a privilege. I wanted to meet you to say, wow, what a great script, what a portrait of America that only an outsider could draw, wow man, I love it. The textures, pathos. The perspective is mind-blowing. A revelation to me and I was born in fucking Minnesota! Can't see the wood for the trees, right? A fascist dystopia? You got it. It's all just around the corner, man, meth, bikers, hobo killers, my journey across a broken country. *Land of Hunger* man, Chapeau. I love it, put it there.'

Chapeau? Well we were in the Chateau, I was surprised he didn't 'dig it'.

Jim Hawks holds out his hand. I don't want it, this palm turd offering. I hesitate a thousand years before taking it, finally gripping his clammy hand as hard as I can muster, but his smile doesn't waver.

'Thank you for your passion man, I know Frank is in great hands, it'll be great.'

I say that. Use the word great twice in one sentence.

'Lap dances with wolves. Right there. The Native American holocaust is very important to me, so cool that in a future-set dystopia this issue is present, in some ways resolved. I hook up with her, boom, save her from the hobo killer, who is for sure racist too, like those guys in the FTRA, see I already been doing my research, everything is lost, but not her, I save her. That's the movie. Fuck Amerikkka right?'

I smile, nod vigorously with enthusiasm.

It was Genocide not the Holocaust.

I am swamped by a vertigo that has nothing to do with heights, but everything to do with depths. I can't move, my hand grabs the arm of the chair as I descend as if trapped in a one-man Bathysphere.

Hawkes stands up, towering over me. Tall, skinny, bangles on both wrists, shades up on his forehead behind which lurks lots of cool hair. His time here is over, he's on a clock, another meeting, a 7.30, or maybe a date, or hot yoga. Denim jacket, a faded green checked shirt, both unwashed but aged perfectly, red wing boots the same. God knows what he had around his neck, I was surprised not to see a rabbit's foot. All he had to drink was tap water, so he was right as rain for any, or indeed all of these next possibilities, so many new doors for him to open.

It was only 7 p.m. I was loaded. I squinted up at his pipe cleaner profile, focusing on the gash of white teeth I assumed were still smiling in my direction I raise my arm with hand attached, Tommy's knuckles on my back prodding me up onto my feet.

Another shake. His eyes drilled into mine, he didn't need a camera to steal your soul. Like D. Day Lewis eating the furniture, this freak wanted to fuckin' own me.

'I can't wait to catch out!' A promise, a lie, a threat, who knew? His eyes snap away from mine. Tommy's lips close over teeth into a tighter smile, communicating *job done*, then out. I stare at Tommy, his mouth opens. I sit back down, sink down, surprised to find a sofa there to catch me.

'You speak to Forest?'

'Sure, called his agent straight away. I've known the guy for years. No problem. Happens all the time, budgets change, people change. He's fine about it.'

'Am I fine about it? Are you?'

'It was you who said how great he was in that other film. Shit, the only independent movie Forest ever made was *Assumption*. You see that? Me neither and nobody else. What do you care, you never met the guy? Forest ain't gonna starve, it's me and you who got to worry. Come on! 150 grand to walk away? Plus a writer credit on a $20 million movie? That's pretty fine. This film hits, you'll get to direct your London Jew film you've been talking about for years. That's how it works @waynex, you know that.'

I do, I do know that, and more. But what I know is sequestered by the booze, and I can't access it. The deep swell of the almost lysergic *sake* making a mystery of its whereabouts, shepherding my conscious mind, a rip tide pulling me away from what it is I do know. I sense that Tommy had briefed Hawkes on what to say, how to negotiate the *difficult Brit*. I felt that. I knew deep down that it wasn't Tommy but some Money who decided on calling the film *Land of Hunger*, somebody who had never been hungry in his life. But Tommy had, and I shouldn't blame him, even as the anger rose in my throat, I knew to tamp it back down. Hollywood is a self-styled liberal elite that benefits most from the pathologically unfair financial/economic system that is American capitalism today, but which leaps at the chance of making movies and money from movies set in near future fascist dystopias. Amerikkka the brave.

The sake reminds me of another America, summoning with great clarity a dive bar in Bakersfield, and a conversation about socialism with an oil rig worker who earns thirty bucks an hour on a field that yields in the high millions, and has seen two of his best friends killed by industrial negligence in the past five years, and countless other ex-workmates hooked on OxyContin and Fentanyl to manage the pain of accident and overwork for decades on minimum wages. Nationalise the oil industry? Hell yeah! Wage equality without health and safety corner cutting performance targets? Hell yeah, where do I sign?

The Tanqueray reins in the sake, tames it somehow and Tommy materialises before me like an apparition.

'You ever been to Bakersfield?'

'That redneck shit-hole, why would I ever go there?'

'So, here's the thing. . .' I consider telling him why, the planes of his face swimming in and out of focus, but decide against it. I wonder if Picasso ever painted this drunk.

'Shit you're right Tommy. Fuck it. Congratulations.'

I'll never forget the look of relief on his face, a friendship salvaged from the wreckage, steered back into charted waters and landfall in a country where everybody wants the same thing: success, peer recognition and the money, which is really the only thing, a golden key that in this magic land opens the locks to everything else. We lay the original thing to rest in these congratulations, the bad thing between us that neither of us wanted, but which now ruled us, so toxic we buried it.

'Fuck Jim Hawks mate!' Tommy raises his glass.

I'll drink to that. 'L'Chaim.'

We down our drinks, half of mine spilling down my cheek and chin, the opulent glass was too wide for my small mouth, pooling on the floor in libation for our waning friendship.

'You want another Tanqueray tonic?' But the moment was over, it was time to leave the scene and do the only thing we could do, and that was to move on.

The sense of expectancy I felt on the plane over had now completed its cycle, had exhausted itself.

'No I'm OK, thanks Tommy but I better go, the family's coming in tomorrow.'

'Say hi to the fam, yes, and let's celebrate before you go, it's a solid payday, the first of many, right?'

He hugs me as we spill outside. There are no witnesses to the biggest deal either of us had ever made in our lives. Tommy nervously checks the time on his watch, passing the valet his ticket. He has somewhere to be, they all have. I don't wait for the A8 to arrive on the street, released from a last embrace, I catch out of the Marmont on rubber legs, the sneakiest most godforsaken hobo in town.

# LAND OF HUNGER

**INT. COMMISSARY - EL SEGUNDO BEACH - DAY 2036**

FRANK shuffles inside. A big man but shy, he holds himself like a small one. With him is his dog, a frail old Labrador.

FRANK looks like a bum, a drunk, with unkempt hair, soiled clothes, big open high-top sneakers. He checks his watch out of habit, shakes his wrist. A delicate antique auto wind model, but it doesn't look like it's told the time in a long time. FRANK smacks his lips, opens the fridge door. It's not cold. He looks over at MR KIM, the skinny old Asian guy behind the counter.

              **MR KIM**
        Generator been out since
        yesterday.

FRANK grunts, picks a bottle of red from the shelf. The bottle has a hand-written label, it's local. He approaches the counter and

hands over some crumpled scrip notes. MR
KIM wraps the bottle in brown paper, hands it
back.

**MR KIM**

You got a letter this morning
Mister Frank. Post drop working
at least.

Mr KIM hands him the letter. Finger jabbing
at the postmark.

**MR KIM (CONT'D)**

That's two this year, both from
Detroit, Michigan. Very popular
man.

FRANK scowls, as in where the fuck else
would Detroit be. He doesn't respond, puts
the letter in his pocket. MR KIM comes round
the front of counter and feeds the dog some
treats. An antique jukebox sits silently
against the wall.

**MR KIM (CONT'D)**

When you going to fix it?

FRANK stares at the jukebox.

**FRANK**

Soon.

**MR KIM**

You been saying that for
months.

#### FRANK

Can't fix a jukebox without electricity.

#### MR KIM

New battery coming tomorrow.

#### FRANK

How about I come in on the weekend and look at it. Thing sits there long enough, I'll get to it.

#### MR KIM

You eaten anything today?

#### FRANK

Me? I'm just wasting away. Come on dog.

FRANK wanders out. The DOG hesitates, looks longingly at MR KIM hoping for another treat, then follows FRANK out.

                              **CUT TO:**

### INT. STORE - DAY - 2036

FRANK pushes past the crowd of men. We can hear the generator humming.

#### MR KIM

Here, I saved you some food, it cold but...

**FRANK**

Cold hell, I'm hungry.

FRANK unwraps a parcel of dim sum, eats it with his fingers. Palms one to his dog who gobbles it up.

**FRANK (CONT'D)**
(To dog)
Told you dim sum taste good, hot or cold.

**MR KIM**

You get bad news in that letter? You don't look so good Frank.

**FRANK**
(Eating)
Just news, person reading it choose what kind it is. Mm. Tastes good Mr Kim. You tell your wife from me.

**MR KIM**

Wife? My wife can't cook for shit. My mother makes dim sum.

**FRANK**

Well, you tell her, these shrimp balls are insane.

He pulls out the letter, carefully wiping his hands on his trousers first. It's even more crumpled than before.

### FRANK (CONT'D)
Letters are strange, they tell you some things, hide others. Was a time when there was no need for letters. You remember when you could talk face to face on the phone? Shit I half brought up my kids on that damn thing.

### MR KIM
Only time you need to worry about Frank is right now. My mother tells me that and she eighty-five.

### FRANK
That's some deep shit right there.

### MR KIM
You being funny?

FRANK shakes his head.

### FRANK
No sir.

He folds the letter and puts it back in his shirt pocket.

### FRANK (CONT'D)
I ask you something?

**MR KIM**

Sure.

**FRANK**

You like my dog?

**MR KIM**

Sure, I like your dog. Why?

**FRANK**

She too old to travel far, gets out of breath walking up and down the boardwalk.

**MR KIM**

Where you going Frank?

FRANK pats the letter.

**MR KIM (CONT'D)**

Detroit, Michigan?

**FRANK**

She likes you. You look after her for me?

**MR KIM**

Sure, you mend that jukebox. We got power this morning.

**FRANK**

Deal.

FRANK pulls the jukebox out from the wall and gets to work.

**CUT TO:**

**EXT. CHECKPOINT - DAY - 2036**

A line of what looks like refugees queue up outside the barbed-wire fence/checkpoint. Two very young looking soldiers are checking ID's. One of them hands back some papers to a frail looking old man.

**SOLDIER**

Sorry sir, says here you retired from active service in 1998. Our quota cut off is 2000. We let you in, what about the others?

**OLD MAN**

I served my country for twenty years...

**SOLDIER**

We all suffer, sir. With all respect, this isn't the same country sir, now move along.

**OLD MAN**

I got a purple star, injured outside Fallujah, came home and worked for KFC minimum wage fifteen years. I was a chef.

**SOLDIER**

Thank you for the story, sir.
Now move on.

**OLD MAN**

It's not a story, soldier.
That's my life.

He doesn't move.

**SOLDIER**

What's the difference?

**OLD MAN**

Move on where? Where exactly
should I move on to, sir?

An officer appears from the guardhouse.

**OFFICER**

What's the holdup here, soldier?

**SOLDIER**

Nothing to worry about, sir.
This gentleman just telling me
his life story. He finished now.

**OFFICER**

Move it along, soldier. Just
move it along.

The soldier turns back to the line, but the old man he was talking to has already shuffled away, another one takes his place.

**SOLDIER**

Papers please, sir.

CUT TO:

**INT. STORE - DAY - 2036**

Close up on finger pressing jukebox select button. Mr KIM chooses an old favourite, an old jazz track crackles to life.

**MR KIM**

Worth the wait, thanks Frank.

FRANK shrugs.

**FRANK**

Jazz.

FRANK leans down to his dog.

**FRANK (CONT'D)**

Now girl, you know how much we both like that dim sum. Well, here's where it's at, every day.
(Beat)
Don't look at me like that damn dog.

FRANK buries his face in the dog's ear, whispers, hides his tears.

**FRANK (CONT'D)**

You know I love you, and I be back, you and me come a long way together already, and this ain't the end of the journey, this isn't goodbye, no sir, it's just a vacation, something I gotta do.

FRANK stands up, hands the lead to Mr KIM. Digs around in his bag and hands him a dog coat, a tin bowl hangs from his backpack, he unties it.

**FRANK (CONT'D)**

She gets cold nights. And this here her bowl.

**MR KIM**

She be fine with me, you just come back, Frank.

**FRANK**

She'll eat anything, ain't no trouble, just sit her in the sun out front. Hates the damp, loves the sun. That's my dog. Now stay girl, stay.

WE TRACK IN ON DOG'S FACE AS FRANK SHUFFLES OUT THE DOOR.

**CUT TO:**

**EXT. CHECKPOINT - 2036**

FRANK approaches the checkpoint from the inside. He's the only one looking to go out, all the traffic is coming the other way. The SOLDIER checks his ID.

**SOLDIER**

You sure you want to go out into the public domain, sir?

(More)

**SOLDIER (CONT'D)**

It's dangerous, especially travelling alone. Corporate compounds won't take military, kind of a tit for tat retaliation. All you got left is the street sir, and that's no protection at all.

**FRANK**

Well, that's where I'm headed.

**SOLDIER**

You armed?

**FRANK**

Nope.

Guard pulls a face.

**SOLDIER**

Scrip ain't legal tender on the outside sir, nearest military compound east is Fort Irwin, you make it that far. Anyway, your funeral. Papers are all in order, says here you're some kinda hero.

**FRANK**

I look like any kind of hero to you, son?

After a long beat the Guard hands him his papers.

**SOLDIER**

Well, good luck, sir.

**FRANK**

Ain't no sir either. Now open up.

The guard opens the gate and FRANK comes outside and is immediately lost in the milling crowd.

**CUT TO:**

# ROADS TO DAMASCUS

*North-Western Iran, 2022*

A boot kicks through the embers of a dying fire.

Oily black smoke washes across the scene. Collapsed and collapsing ochre walls lie in mounds everywhere, obscene termite hills of bloody clay, ancient dust clouding above them. Breathe that in and its 'Mummy' time for you. Soldiers in uniform stumble, bent double like old men with walking sticks over their stubby, magically light ceramic assault rifles, hawking black phlegm, tears running freely down their cheeks, black mascara rivulets rendering them Alice Cooper lookalikes or Juggalo fanatics of the Insane Clown Posse. In the movie this overture features Twiztid singing 'We don't die' from a beatbox on the dash of an armoured troop carrier, channelling classic Vietnam films from back in the day, mixing up into full 90's nostalgia soundtrack as the camera pans across the landscape, revealing grunts digging in and digging the nihilism of the lyrics, on this their never-ending tour, joining in the defiant sing-along chorus:

> '*Axe murderers we don't die,*
> *Serial killers we don't die,*
> *Freaks of the night we don't die,*
> *We get high, we don't die.*'

The scene plays out/under/over this, the afterglow, the aftermath of an artillery strike/infantry firefight one, two combo; from the Pompeii poses of the dead soldiers dressed in a couture of burnt potato skin flakes, to the bleached bones of children whose soft flesh evaporated, (none on show today, this being a relatively minor and outlier skirmish, but these are connotative observations) leaving behind oddly out-of-place white skeleton fragments in the dirt; more gagging, more tears, more slimy, shiny, black snot frothing from darker clown faces. A buzzing in the ears, a drooping of the soul. A bad comedown, a drug without a half-life.

This is victory today, and it comes in many flavours.

A boot kicks through the embers of a dying fire.

'I mean that fucking fire had been going for thousands of years, right? Tended by generations of priests and we just put it out, extinguish it, just like that? And you think there is no consequence to this, no fallout, no payback? Shit, this may be a fucked-up country, but it still has its own karma, you know what I'm saying?'

Private Kenny Hatchet from Corpus Christi Texas. nineteen, white, skinny, weaned off a weekend meth habit during basic training, face weasel thin and scar-pitted, has always been prone to exaggeration. This fire had been going for perhaps fifty years, in a Zoroastrian temple founded a few hundred years ago and the two priests tending the fire had been evacuated the week before, along with the rest of the civilian population which amounted to around seventy-five people. After what happened in Homs/Aleppo/Raqqa/Mosul and the rest, both sides, reflecting the more patchwork topology of this war and its many tactical or humanitarian ceasefires, most parties to any given facet of each specific flare-up, allowed for the provision of civilian corridors of safety, at least on paper, that is until they didn't or there were errors.

In old war movies Kenny is the southern white trash kid who talks slow but stands tall, sacrificing himself for the usually better fed and educated northern officer type at the beginning of the third act. Like waiting for the black 'buddy' to die in most genre movies, Kenny had that sense of the foretold about him, had something of the doomed idiot savant about him and in his running off at the mouth. In other variations on a theme he's the platoon champion sniper, cradling his cherished heirloom rifle wrapped in oilskin, on account of all the racoons he got to shoot growing up, pinned down under heavy fire he would jerry up a mirror fragment attached to a wire on the end of the gun barrel, allowing him to see, if not shoot, round corners.

'It's written in American as well as Arab, look here. A Zoroastrian fire temple. Dar e Mehr. I heard of this shit before, was a tourist attraction I guess.'

Frank, an energetic black officer in his early thirties, holds up a broken fragment of signage. He's tall, a big man and his voice carries, piercing the outro of combat, reading what he can of the visitor blurb.

'It's Persian not Arab you heathen.'

Frank reads, 'Before entering the temple all visitors must take off their shoes.'

He looks around, scuffs through the ashes of the fire once again. The fire of war he had help make.

'No shit,' sighs Frank and throws the sign into the remaining corner of what once was a room, now a rubble triangle. In the middle of this space, in a pile of whiter, purer looking ash than the rest, lies a crumpled mass of bronze, a flat edge poking reflected dully. Amongst the dross this worked metal reveals it had once been part of a brazier. An iron spoke sticks out from this mess of bronze, and other spokes are lying in the ash.

The word 'archaeology' flashes through Franks mind, the first time he has any cause to think of it, with the sense that he is here making it for the future.

This according to Zoroastrian custom was the remains of a 'Fire of Victory', tended night and day by....

Frank stops thinking and responds to Kenny, an easier and more comfortable register than thought/reflection, and one that as an officer he is confident with.

'You talking shit, Kenny, a pile of shit as always.'

Frank walks away, out of this somehow claustrophobic room without walls, to face the sunset.

'Well at least we'll be warm tonight, heat not going out of that for days.'

Kenny keeps it up, all he really knows how to do is talk. 'The Koran says the Devil came from fire, Adam and Eve from clay. Allah said, *"What prevented thee from prostrating when I commanded thee?"*

He said: *"I am better than he: Thou didst create me from fire, and him from clay."'*

'The Koran my ass! Ain't no Koran in Corpus Christi soldier, just a load of sheep with real good hearing.'

'Heard that one before, sir.' Kenny smiles nervously, lights up, match flaring against the fast fading sunset. The rest of the squad have gathered in the ruins, drawn by the smouldering fire.

Sinclair, all freckles on milk skin under red cropped hair, a country boy, as far as the warrior stereotypes go, squats alongside a much darker Madero, Mexican, female, short and muscled like a bull, peeling valuable Kevlar body armour from a corpse. Companions of Ulysses. Two sides of an American coin being spent frivolously in the deserts of wherever.

To consecrate a 'Fire of Victory' you needed to blend sixteen different types of fire, including fire that comes from lightning and the fire from a funeral pyre.

Madero fingers a hole in the Kevlar. 'Where they get this shit? Brand new and useless.' There's a hole right through the middle of the breastplate, her finger wiggles out the other side in disgust. She chucks it back on the corpse.

'Fake fucking Kevlar. Keep it.'

'On your travels across the River Styx.'

'Private, dispose of that corpse right now!' bellows Frank from outside, now distracted by messages on his iPhone.

'What and where the fuck is the River Styx?'

Kenny drags the body out of the temple and ditches him by the side of the road. Puts the broken Kevlar vest over his face, makes the sign of the cross and bounds back to his spot by the fire. Frank sits off to one side, an officer alone with his responsibilities.

'I'll have you know we got a well-stocked library in Corpus Christi, yessir.'

Frank loses his patience. 'Kenny, just shut the fuck up, time to eat and get some sleep.'

'Come to think of it sir, I am hungry.'

Each type of fire is consecrated separately before being mixed together, this process can take up to a year. There were nine of these super fire temples in the world, all at least 250 years old. Now make that eight. Types of fire. Think about that, like types of snow. You have to look to see it. Different physical qualities, colours, temperatures, not just fire, but an intensely observed phenomenon. Different metaphysical qualities.

Bravo company, 1st Combat Engineer Battalion, dig in for the night at the Takht E Soleyman fire temple in Western Azerbaijan, in north-western Iran, not far from the besieged city of Tabriz. Spillage from the fighting in Syria, which has doubled back into Iraq and on into Iran, an endless chase, the splinters of one insurgent/terrorist/freedom fighting group becoming the nucleus of another, a war characterised by shifting allegiances, the ebb and flow of munitions, sporadic firefights, sequences of precision extraction and insertion, miraculous appearances and disappearances. An overextension of logistics provoked by rapid advances in technology. In reality, the most overdeveloped army in the world chasing its tail, chasing the fire that won't be put out, the unquenchable fire of human agency.

Kenny was a long way from home, but as he would tell you himself, Corpus Christi was a fucking shit-hole, life in or out of the army just as FUBAR as it ever was. He still flinched when the 'copters came to Evac them, he'd been flinching since he could remember, an outgrowth of childhood 'shying away from', an aftershock hangover of his meth anxiety, now just how he was wired, raw, sensitive, the antennae of his survival instinct.

He was a twitchy motherfucker.

Previously Kenny had been in wannabe Alt.Punk band The Scarecrow People. He played bass because it was simple to learn and he dug the low notes which drowned out his tinnitus. Tinnitus caused by being hit upside the head throughout childhood; the sound of silence for him was hissing feedback. They played mostly Depeche Mode covers, daring to play a few of their own songs usually early on in the set to an empty room. Corpus Christi audiences were hard as nails, ultra conservative, who still ate freedom fries in 2020, a grudge held over from another war, so mostly they just stuck to the chord changes they were addicted to.

Kenny kept a journal, something he had seen somebody do in a movie, and he thought that was pretty cool and amongst other things he wrote lyrics in it. It was in his kitbag and every day he put something in it, a drawing, a poem, some sentences. 'A record of who he is,' he would say to anybody who cared to ask. 'You wanna know more about Kenny Hatchet, then read this.'

He never actually 'said' any of this because nobody ever asked, but it's what he felt. Kenny inscribed himself into each day that passed so there would be a record of him in the world is also what he would never say, but still. . .

He had been a vet long before he joined up, had all of those syndromes, all of that apartness, going into the marines; the army was a perfect fit for fucked-up teenagers. From the PTSD of childhood to that of combat, the same ringing in the ears, the same wariness of respite. Made him a good soldier, he took to it like a fish to water.

Warmed by a dead fire, stripped down to T-shirts, they ate supper. A black billionaire Boys Club T, lettering in red, a Trump/Pence 2020 campaign T, raggedy and almost worn out on white. Various sports T's, all faded colours and cartoon sports mascots. A Vegas resort T. An odd intrusion of off-world differentiated personalities, a scene that Kenny would later draw in frames for a comic strip of his tour.

Kenny rips the top off his MRE ration, peers inside like it was Christmas morning and he a child in a family that wasn't the one he came from.

'Meals refused by the enemy.' Kenny licks his lips. 'It's mac and cheese and look some of that new Perky Jerky.' He eats quickly and without pleasure with his fingers, chewing over the caffeinated beef.

'They gave us Prevetin so we could fight, fuck and hell knows what all night long, then do it again and again till we drop down dead and then they just resupply the equipment with new recruits instead of the other way round. Hitler had 'em all hooked on it. Maybe that's what they put in Perky Jerky, a kind of watered down meth. Shit, they probably got their own labs making the shit.'

'Shut up and eat,' comes from the gloom.

'Funny they wean me off that shit in basic, only to deal it back to me in combat.'

The others eat, as night shadows fall on the ruins, they eat and look out through the now clearing billows of smoke. Mostly they can tune out Kenny, aided by post-combat zone out.

'Fire worship oldest form of worship there is. Makes sense, right? First guy to make a fire, shit he woulda got a lot of pussy. Predates all organised religion, it all comes out of the fire.'

He rekindles a small fire in the ashes of the old one. Low guttering flames, as there is too much ash for this fire to take properly, poorly fed as it is with the cardboard packaging from their ready meals, a sickly fire.

Kenny talks too much and he's happy to tell you why that is. Way he tells it he kept his uncle alive one winter when they were out hunting and got caught in a snowstorm. The weather broke and his uncle got knocked down by a falling branch. Drifting in and out of consciousness and with a broken leg, Uncle Pete was in a bad way. Kenny 'kept me alive by talking me to death' is how he liked to tell it ever after. The storm passed by dawn and Kenny could see they were only a hundred yards from their truck. He was eight. The talking habit took root.

Madero, eases down next to him, decompressing herself around the fire. Kenny keeps talking, offers a cigarette. Madero shakes her head and starts rolling a joint instead, Kenny barely misses a beat.

'I hear this whole valley is cursed. Whole patrols gone missing up in the mountains. It starts with electrical interference, their phones go dead and then, nada, they gone. We seen some spooky stuff, right? What we think are men, sometimes children, out beyond the perimeter but when the patrol goes out, nothing. Kurds, Iraqis, Iranians, Syrians, nobody strays far from the road now, probably why we caught them here, all that space to hide in, to disappear into, shit, why else they trap themselves here?'

Kenny shrugs, pokes a stick in the fire to light their smokes.

'Where you hear that anyway? I ain't never seen shit like

that, ones I kill, you better believe they stay dead.'

'A farmer we interrogated in the last village, perhaps he was trying to spook us.'

'Sell it to Hollywood.'

'They be making films about this war for years to come.'

Night falls and the light from the meagre fire dials up in compensation, its dark audience thickening.

'You tell me you ain't superstitious, not just one bit? You ain't feeling it in a place like this, the cradle of civilisation we're blasting to hell? Man, I feel like a baddie in *Raiders of the Lost Ark* or some shit like that.'

Madero shakes her head, but her eyes remain agnostic. She closes them and draws deep on the joint which she passes silently to Kenny.

'Shit don't give him the J, don't do it!' somebody shouts out from the darkness.

Madero smiles, almost giggles, but says nothing. Kenny tokes deep off the joint and passes it back.

Other soldiers have just finished piling the remains of at least sixteen enemy fighters in a pile and covered that pile with bricks to mask the smell. They slump round the perimeter, smoking silently.

Respect for the dead. In whose army? From severed Argentinian heads held aloft at Goose Green snapped on a Polaroid and flashed from a wallet in pubs down the years ever since, to the viral videos from the first Iraq war, respect for the dead had long been out of fashion. King Darius had been here before them, trail-blazed and marked all their cards, him worse than any tin pot General Buck Naked or even Pol Pot himself. This war had its camera ban and social media blackout, leaving it to memory however false, and hearsay, that plus battlefield mementos, to write this chapter of man's inhumanity to man.

Stay alive by any means necessary, kill or be killed, move on. Do it in numbers, stacking the odds. No duels, no bravado, let the tech do its job, enable it to protect yourself. Remember, you are just the flesh in this war of tech and materiel.

Kenny has by now had a few hits off Madero's joint. Kenny shouldn't smoke.

'Sergeant from Pensacola told me they all seeing snatches of the same vision, like the combat, the constant hiding, the shit food, the dead it's all fucked up their minds. Like the angels our soldiers swear they saw in the First World War, I read a book about that. An army of the dead, an armoured division of the dead, Revolutionary guard from the first Iraq war, maybe back a ways to the Iran-Iraq war, but led by ancient warriors, kings, under a black flag. With every death this army gets bigger, no matter whether you Sunni, Shia, Jew, Christian, American, this army ain't choosy, you just gotta be dead. He interrogated one guy, he wanted out, wanted to be taken out, Guantanamo, we still got that? Or some shit like that, somewhere safe, gave up his whole outfit, he just wanted out. Can you believe it? Got spooked somehow. Kinda makes sense though right, some *Game of Thrones* shit right there, white walkers an' all. . .'

Madero was no longer awake, had the ability to sleep through anything, the muscles in her legs locked like land buoys keeping her afloat. A dead spliff hanging from thin lips, pursed in whatever form of half sleep this was.

'Build a wall to keep the Wildlings out.'

Kenny toys with a piece of paper and a photograph he'd taken from one of the dead. A scrap from the Koran, found folded in the boy's pocket next to the photograph of a pet dog.

'Build a wall. How was that for you? Work out good?'

The body was about seventeen years old. He worries the two objects like beads, staring at them long enough they make him get up.

'Problem with a wall is, what goes up must come down. Its destruction is right there in its foundations. As it goes up, easy to imagine it coming down. Like a red rag to the bull of fate.'

By the only remaining standing wall of the temple are two guards on duty, sitting behind the tripod of a M249 rifle. Kenny approaches them. One of them is Arabic.

'You want a smoke?' He pulls out two crumpled cigarettes from a soft pack of American Spirits and hands them to the soldiers.

'Combat ciggies, all crushed and bent out of shape, but they still smoke.'

The man smells the cigarette with distrust.

Kenny shows him the pack. 'American Spirit. Additive free. Yeah, I know. Bit like the barbed wire being recyclable right?'

The man blanks him. Kenny shrugs, hands him the scrap of paper. He lights them both. The man coughs, not used to this brand of cigarettes.

'Can you read this? Looks like Arabic. The writing, can you read it?'

'I guess, give me a minute.'

They smoke, the man slowly reads and translates, 'He said–'

Kenny jumps in, 'Who said?'

'Allah. Just listen or forget it OK, I'm tired.'

Kenny's fingers zip his mouth. 'OK, OK I'm all ears.'

The soldier shrugs his shoulders and continues translating.

'Allah said to the angels, Fall prostrate before Adam. They fell prostrate, except Iblis, he's like Satan, OK?'

Kenny nods, 'Satan, sure.'

'Iblis refused, was too arrogant, and a disbeliever. "O Satan, what prevented you from prostrating before what I created with My hands? Are you too arrogant? Have you rebelled? Iblis argues that he is better than Adam. "You created me from fire and created him from mud." Allah was angry, "Therefore, you must go down, for you are not to be arrogant here. Get out; you are debased. Get out from this, disgraced and expelled. If any of the other angels follow thee, Hell will I fill with you all."

'It's from the Koran, part of the story of the creation of Iblis, how he ended up in hell.'

Kenny nods his head thoughtfully. . .

'This Iblis, he reckoned angels were better than man, right? But man was Allah's greatest creation, better than any angel. I like it, brings the Archangel Gabriel down to earth that's for sure. "Hell will I fill with you all". He wasn't messing around.'

The soldier hands Kenny back the crumpled piece of paper. 'Where you find it?' finishing his cigarette with a cough against the back of his hand.

'A seventeen-year-old boy soldier carried it around with him, maybe give him courage against devils like us. Now he dead. That's too bad. Here.'

He hands the soldier the rest of the cigarettes and goes back to his pile of rubble. Madero has gone and the fire is almost out.

Frank calls in their Evac on his iPhone after determining that the area can only be secured until daybreak. Their transports out of gas are being disabled with small charges, flashing briefly but thankfully not loud enough to wake the dead.

Kenny has been drawing, lit by the torch from his helmet. He copies out the crumpled piece of paper from the Koran, then throws it on the hot ashes, it flares and is ash within seconds.

'Makes perfect sense. Perfect sense. We're here, we arrived, with that pile of corpses.'

Sinclair wakes up cold and puts his combat jacket back on. To himself and anybody else near enough to hear he says, 'Shit was just getting to the good bit.'

And then to Kenny, 'The fuck you talking to Kenny?'

'Who you talkin' to? Its early checkout time, we turn to ash when the sun comes up.'

They both get up as the sound of helicopters approaches. Searchlights laser down harsh trippy gazes into the destroyed temple and surrounds, it's Evac time and everyone scrambles for the choppers. Under the harsh green phosphorescent light, they all look undead. Kenny scratches his arm, then the side of his face; an invisible itch, the meth itch he grew up with, a habit that returns now and then, in times of stress or in the aftermath of exhilaration. He is one of the last to tumble up inside the helicopter, Frank reaching for his hand and pulling him in.

This is victory today, and it comes in many colours.

\* \* \*

*El Segundo, 2036*

Frank sits on the sand, a bottle of wine between his legs, the crashing waves noisy but regular, a rhythm he can understand, one that comforts him and that he can rock to. He sits between rusty tank traps that line the low tide mark, refracting, disorganising the rolling breakers at regularly spaced intervals. His dog watches him, anxiously, not at all reassured by the pounding waves.

Frank waves the bottle towards the sea, pouring a libation onto the sand.

'The road from Damascus is a long and winding road, a long and winding road, yessir!'

He fishes inside his pocket for the crumpled-up letter, hesitant to unfold it he mumbles, drowned out by the sound of the waves.

'We got all the time in the world, we can talk all night. Yes we can Sarah.'

Frank drinks deeply, clears his throat, trying to focus on the words, his hand bringing the letter first close to then away from his eye. Beyond the tank traps the inky black hulks of derelict ships shade in the horizon. Abandoned at anchor when oil prices hit a number either too high or too low. Too high to buy, too low to sell.

'Update. As you can see, I haven't stopped drinking. But I'm done gambling, yes ma'am. Cut that right back to the point where I don't need it and it sure as hell don't need me anymore. Planning on using the same technique with the drink too, so watch this space, watch this space.'

He squints at the letter, scared to read it straight, he would rather spy it askance, through split fingers.

'Could've sent my boys to college. Ivy League, Stamford, all them fancy places, take your pick, price is right. Work hard, put some away, build your life and pass it on. This here was America and money talked.'

Frank reads a little more, every paragraph costs him an effort of will not to look away. Eventually he looks out to sea. His hands shake with the weight of what he hasn't read but has scanned anyway, knowing the signs to look for on a page, the shapes of letters and the sentences that contain words like grades and school team, girlfriends and accidents, although how he knew how to decipher this was a mystery. It was all there, the boys' achievements at school and in sports, their growing up, in a place where those things still kind of mattered. He folds the letter and puts it back in his pocket, half read yet fully understood.

'You know I lived here five years, and never once been in the sea.'

Frank stands up and looks beyond the waves. He strips off as methodically as any ex-marine would, and runs into the water, past the old danger signs and the tank traps. His dog gets up, barks, skirts the water, worrying the tideline, scared of it, back and forth, forward and back, a lunar dance. She barks her anguish, backing off and coming forward again to the edge of that abyss, hard-wired not to cross the edge of her primal fear.

# ESCAPE FROM L.A.

**EXT. DOWNTOWN L.A - DAY - 2036**

FRANK surveys the scene with alien eyes. Homeless people line the streets, zonked out in the blistering heat. Time-lapse photography as the street folk keep pace with the sun's shadow as it glides across the street; a mass migration to keep in the shade. Sequence shot like a nature documentary.

**An armed gas station.**

From a watchtower a bored looking guard covers the pumps with a machine gun.

**The bus stand for Tijuana.**

White and black families wait in the heat, babies in pushchairs, a cross section of the migratory lives that populate new southern California, a constant tide of humanity and goods. They all board the bus, squeeze past

the armed guard and give their tickets to the
Hispanic driver. Bursting at the seams the
bus pulls away, groaning under the strain,
thick black diesel smoke pours from the
exhaust, revealing FRANK entering the canteen
across the street.

**INT. CANTEEN - CONTINUOUS**

FRANK approaches a canteen, he looks like he
needs the restroom.

> **SECURITY**
>
> This ain't no compound,
> customers only. If you got
> cash money, you a customer,
> otherwise you ain't.

> **FRANK (WHISPER)**
>
> I just need to use the
> facilities.

> **SECURITY**
>
> Customers only.

> **FRANK**
>
> You got staff toilets?

> **SECURITY**
>
> Employees only. You're gonna
> have to leave.

> **FRANK**
>
> I need the toilet, sir.

The SECURITY GUARD pushes FRANK down the
short flight of stairs. Behind the glass
the diners look away. FRANK stumbles away,
towards a grocery store.

                                           **CUT TO:**

**INT. GROCERY STORE - CONTINUOUS**

The place is empty as are most of the
shelves. FRANK walks up and down the aisles
looking for the toilets.

                    **MAN**

    Can I help you, sir?

FRANK comes up to the till. The man's hand
reaches under the counter.

                    **FRANK**

    Please man, I gotta go.

The MAN pulls out a shotgun, levels it at
FRANK.

                    **MAN**

    I believe you do, sir, but not
    here, now get out!

**EXT. ALLEY - CONTINUOUS**

An exasperated FRANK runs into an alley and
takes a dump behind a garbage dumpster. A
security car rolls by, flashing its lights as
FRANK hauls up his trousers and runs off.

                                          **CUT TO:**

**INT. PAWNSHOP - DAY - 2036**

FRANK is at the counter. There's a small quiet queue behind him. He takes off his signet ring, passes it across. The PAWNBROKER eyes the ring.

**PAWNBROKER**

Fifty.

The PAWNBROKER looks at FRANK, back down to the ring in his hand.

**PAWNBROKER (CONT'D)**

That ain't gold.

**FRANK**

That's my daddy's ring, was his daddy's before him.

**PAWNBROKER**

The story doesn't make it worth more than fifty bucks, unless you want to try and sell it to a library. What about that watch?

**FRANK**

It broke, besides it ain't for sale. I'll take the fifty.

FRANK stares the man down as he takes the money.

                    **FRANK (CONT'D)**

I'll be back for it.


                    **PAWNBROKER**

That's what they all say. Next
please.

**EXT. APARTMENT BLOCK/DOWNTOWN - NIGHT - 2036**

FRANK rests in the doorway of a gutted
downtown apartment block. He watches the
street, witnesses a crack attack.


TRACKING SHOT ON A METH HEAD AS HE/SHE
PERFORMS CONTINUOUS SOMERSAULTS DOWN THE
CENTRE OF THE STREET, HIS/HER UNCONTROLLABLE
ENERGY AND STRENGTH BURNING STRAIGHT FROM THE
PIPE.

                                    **CUT TO:**


**EXT. APARTMENT BLOCK/DOWNTOWN - NIGHT - 2036**

CARS COME AND GO, RICH WEST-SIDE COMPOUND
KIDS COME DOWNTOWN TO SCORE. AS THE CARS
PULL UP DEALERS EMERGE FROM SHADOWS, SKIP,
SHUFFLE, STROLL OVER TO THE CARS. TIME-LAPSE
PHOTOGRAPHY AS THIS SCENE, THIS SEQUENCE
LOOPS, LAYERING THE IMAGE WITH REPEATING
AFTERBURNS OF ITSELF, LAYING DOWN THE
TIMELESS PATTERNS OF STREET LIFE.


**INT. 24/7 - NIGHT - 2036**

Sound of a hyper game show/talent contest
from a screen below the counter. FRANK stands
behind a grill. The server takes his money

and pushes a four-pack of toilet roll and a tube of toothpaste through the hatch. The server goes back to watching his show.

**EXT. L.A - NIGHT - 2036**

FRANK walks east through the city towards the sunrise. Sporadic sirens wail near and far, as he leaves L.A behind him.

**CUT TO:**

# CATCHING OUT

*The Jungle, 2036*

Heading for the hills, Frank finally disentangles himself from Los Angeles. Almost dawn and he spies the flickering lights of a camp rising before him, from its roots in an unfinished highway underpass it sprawls up the side of the hill behind it, down into the gully beyond and back up again, drawing him onward. Backed by the rising sun, dotted with campfires, it forms a strong silhouette, the timeless, ragged outline of human settlement.

Frank sweats, he's not used to walking far, his heart pounds, and he gets dizzy tying up his shoes. The closer he gets to the camp his eye picks out the details, the place strewn with makeshift habitation, markers of our persistent occupation of the planet; cardboard boxes, packing crate lean-tos, tarps strung between scrawny trees, sheets made into awnings, abandoned cars, sometimes one on top of the other, somehow welded into a single space. And the signs of our persistent ingenuity: rolls of photo-sensitive foil laid out over the roofs/tarps and rigged up to mini generators. They glint, reflecting the early morning sunlight. And all of this strung with intermittent light panels.

Ingenuity. Reminds Frank of his tours of duty. Make do, makeshift, make it home. First people he sees are two meth heads sprawled under a dead tree, broken pipes at head and feet funeral gifts for the yet to be dead. Frank walks through the camp, nodding at the few people who catch his eye, taking his bearings, looking for a place to perch. A mother stirs a pot on an open fire, her kids sit on an upended packing crate watching a small flickering screen. One of the support struts of the highway is decorated with a beautiful charcoal drawing which reminds him of old hippies and far-out cults from TV shows. A lion attacks an antelope, the action taking place in 3D, so you have to move around the concrete to see it all. The predator and her prey. Funny how concrete rots just like anything else, underneath the charcoal the surface seethes as if an injured animal itself.

Higher up on the hill is a more organised looking part of the camp, a proper Hobo Jungle, where you get a sense of a pecking order amongst the backpacks, the pitched tents and space between each. Frank stops in front of a grizzly looking white man in his mid-sixties, wearing a checked shirt with braces, and sitting in front of a small electric ring burner boiling water for coffee.

'Sun's up, coffee's up,' the old man says, pleased with himself.

'You got a good spot here.'

'Can see the whole damn place. I was watching you winding your way up here. Who you looking for?'

'Always seek the alpha male, the leader of the pack.'

Coughing out a laugh, 'Where you learn that shit?'

'Marines. Counter-insurgency training.'

'No shit. And you think that's me?'

'Well, you the only one making coffee.'

'Sit down marine. Wanna cup?'

'Sounds good, smells good. Columbian?'

'Nope. Nicaragua. Dealer I know brings it in cross-country.'

'See, you're connected, I knew training would prove useful one day.'

He sits and they drink the coffee.

'What's your name, boy?'

Frank bristles but replies flatly.

'Frank.'

'Frank. Is that it?'

'Franklin actually. My mom wanted me to have a name that would look good on job applications, get me noticed.'

'Did it?'

'Joined up when I was seventeen, never applied for shit. Just walked in off the street, they were hungrier for me than I was for them.'

'War always hiring. And now we're here. All chewed up and spat out.'

'I'm just passing through. Lived down on the beach last few years.'

'Vets compound?'

'El Segundo. Mostly raw recruits and old men, but we got along, regular air drops, scrip, hell, we even got post.'

'I heard. Easy street.'

Frank swats a fly from his face, mops his head with a handkerchief.

'Who all these people anyway?'

'Here? We got all sorts.'

'I see that.'

'See them kids over there?' He gestures with a stick. Two young men fast asleep, another flies a rag kite with the intensity of a kid playing a computer game.

'Spent two years selling ass on Sunset, smoking meth, now just here to play it out. Kids like that suck your dick, steal your shit, wash your car, kill you, it don't matter. What about you?'

Frank doesn't rise to the bait, just flat eyes him, dismissing his manner as just an old man's defences. 'Was thinking of catching a train.'

'Bet you never done that before.'

'Not without a ticket.'

The old man laughs.

'That's a good one, ain't heard that before.' He turns back to the fire, stokes it.

'Ain't been no passenger trains for must be ten years. They don't want people moving about I guess. You got any skills Frank, apart from counter-insurgency training?'

'I fix things. Was an engineer back in the Corps. Engines, electrical, you name it, if it broke I fix it.'

'Shit, you must be rushed off your feet. Well, I'm riding north to work the fruit farms. Stay in camp longer than a few days you seize up.'

He taps his head.

'Hard work but it pays hard cash.'

'Sounds good.'

'Was a time it was seasonal, but now, well, just runs on what they call cycles. You on drugs?'

'No. I drink some.'

'You mind Mexicans?'

'Nope.'

'Don't suppose you do.' Larry squints for a response out of the corner of his eye. Frank finishes his coffee, chucks the grounds into the fire, doesn't give him the pleasure.

The old man draws a rough map in the dirt with his stick.

'All right then. Here's where we at and this is where we're going. And here is where the train goes. Los Angeles to Bakersfield. Getting busy again. We used to say if you can't catch a train here, then you can't catch a train period. You ever heard of the Tehachapi loop?'

'Nope.'

He draws a circle in the dirt. 'Freight train averaging fifty cars will cross over itself on its way to Mojave.'

'Like a dog chasing its tail.'

'There will be a month, six weeks work there picking fruit if you want it. Strawberries mostly, they ain't invented a machine yet can pick them without squashing the shit out of them.'

'How much they pay?'

'Around three bucks an hour, plus scrip for the subsidised canteen and store. Eight hour shifts. Get to save forty-five bucks a day if you smart. It gets too hot, we work nights. Same money.'

'Three bucks an hour? When I was a kid, we earnt more doing a paper round.'

'Where you been boy? It sure must be cosy in that compound. Out here we got devaluation.'

The old man gets up smartly, rolls up his solar panel, packs his pack tight, bags up his garbage. He stamps out the fire leaving a dark chocolate circle on the hillside. Like he was never there, or just a rock that rolled away.

'World gone to hell in a handbasket, in case you hadn't noticed.'

The old man hawks and spits, 'For what it's worth I don't leave no mess.' He shoulders his backpack.

'Names Larry, but people call me Trainwreck.' He holds out a bony, liver-spotted hand.

Frank surveys the other homeless, strewn all the way down the hill, listless under the now already hot morning sun. The camp looks more like a fly trap than a place to live. He aches all over but feels the need to keep moving, but also a strange fear, one that makes him want to leave this place as quickly as possible.

He stands and takes Trainwreck's hand.

'Pleased to meet you.'

'Now we done exchanging pleasantries we got somewhere to get to.' Larry strides off down the hill, Frank follows, energised to find himself back on a mission, comrades of a few minutes and a cup of coffee, freshly minted in the currency of what happens next.

# PARALLEL LINES

*California, 2036*

Frank lies wheezing on the floor of the boxcar, trying to catch his breath. The old man just sits there, gets his roll out and smokes a cigarette.

'You're out of shape. Give yourself a heart attack if you don't watch it.'

Frank looks up, panting. 'I'm OK, I'll be fine. Long time since I ran anywhere.'

'Better rest up. In the morning we switch trains at Bakersfield.'

Frank lies down. As his eyes get accustomed to the dark, they rove around the interior walls of the boxcar discovering strange drawings and graffiti. 'Shit, just like that Lion and the Antelope, back at the camp.'

'Yep. Cave painting is what that is. "I was here", RIPs, meet ups, jokes, warnings. These wagons are a noticeboard, an obituary and a confessional. Hobos been doing this since, well since before it went to shit for everyone else. We had a head start.'

Frank reads out some tags, the names of past travellers.

'Colossus of Roads, Short Track, Gooseberry Johnson.'

Larry smiles. 'Yep, that's a good one. He must have loved gooseberries. Everyone thinks they special, we all do, it's our nature, keeps us going in hard times. Brings comfort. That someone will see our mark, that we are known in the world, our existence isn't devoid of meaning. Shit like that.'

Frank sits up on his elbow, wanting more. Larry doesn't disappoint.

'Got mine right after I crawled out of that wreck. Eighteen people died the day I survived, crawled right out of a car much the same as this one 'cept it looked more like a busted squeeze box full of ripe tomatoes. Shit, I scrawled my tag all over the Eastern seaboard that summer I was so jizzed up.'

'You think you deserved to live?'

'What kind of dumb question is that Frank?'

'That piece of luck, it change your life Larry?'

'Well, it sure made it longer.'

Larry hunkers down in his roll, turns over and is immediately, efficiently asleep. Frank pulls his coat around him, fidgets with his back to the wall of the car. His first night as a hobo and he can't sleep. He watches the flicker of the world passing as it reaches him through the slats of the boxcar, a few distant lights passing and sounds far and near, animal, locomotive and just the plain sound of the world at night.

\* \* \*

A soft light fills the boxcar. Frank comes to, still sitting there, pulls himself up, all aches and stiff joints, rubs his knees for they hurt the most. The train is barely crawling along. Larry stands in the doorway, all supple, legs splayed pissing into the wind.

'They say after you piss out of your first boxcar you're hooked. Nothing like it.'

Frank joins him in the doorway. Frank pisses. They both

laugh, shake it out, pull the door shut and sit back down at opposite ends of the car. Larry throws Frank a hard biscuit and a bottle of water. The train picks up speed. Time passes.

'Time we were getting off.'

'How you know?'

Frank cracks open the door of the boxcar as Bakersfield approaches.

'Body clock never failed me yet.'

'So, what do we do now?'

'We don't want to get out of the yard, just change trains. We gotta jump down, find somewhere to hide out until a Mojave bound comes through.'

Larry grabs his pack, waits for the train to slow at a bend then chucks it and follows it out of the train. A parachute jump from five feet. Frank panics at being left alone, this old man moves too fast, he's either here or somewhere else, with nothing much in between. Frank grabs his bag and jumps without thinking about landing.

They only have to wait an hour before another train approaches the bend, slows and Trainwreck spots an open door. Second train jumped, Frank now sits with his legs swinging from an open door catching his breath. Reminds him of a dawn helicopter ride from another lifetime. Being out in the world brings back memories. Smells brought on the wind, movement, noise and colour, clears his head of the stale habits of the last ten years, letting the genie out of the lamp. His mind wanders.

They pass through a huge wind farm on the plains of Tehachapi. 'You seen this?' Frank calls over his shoulder.

'Yep, pretty isn't it? All that juice powers the compound up at Fort Irwin. Twenty-four-hour power. Imagine that.'

Larry reaches in his pack for a drink, pulls out a half bottle of bourbon and takes a pull.

Frank turns and automatically eyes the bottle.

'For the rest of us it's the stone age with a few miracles sprinkled on top. You want a drink?'

'No, thanks.'

'Looks like you got the shakes.'

'It's cold.'

Frank gets up with no small effort and takes the bottle, takes a hard pull and hands it back. He sits down, looser in himself and closer to the old man. Larry wants to hear more, and somehow Frank feels comfortable telling it, rubbing his knees, massaging his story into life.

'Finished my tour back in '22. Had a train wreck all of my own.'

'Operation Syrian Unity. Figured as much. You get injured?'

'Not till I got home. Brought it back with me and passed it around.'

The old man drinks and passes what's left to Frank who finishes it off, an unsatisfying mouthwash cap sip, the same little disappointment he experiences after every empty bottle followed by a spike of needless anger, but instead of throwing the bottle out of the open door, he passes it back to Train-wreck, who shakes it out and puts it back in his pack.

'All I can say is after all the yesterdays I had, tomorrow is still waiting for me, and that's as good as it's got any right to get.'

'OK. I like that.' They share a smile.

'See that up there?' Larry gestures at a drawing on the wall, a weird chalk squiggle of a wizard with a huge white beard. Words tangled up in the beard, like twigs and leaves reads:

'*SHORT TRACK IS A DEAD MAN.*'

'Short track. Friend of mine. Found him in a car like this one, with his throat slit, all bled out like a punctured swimming pool, and he ain't the first. Somebody been on these trains killing hobos for the past fifteen years, maybe more. Killer's one of us too. Me and him been shadowing each other for a lifetime it seems. He leaves his sign. Like a spell, a hex on the next is what we call it.'

Trainwreck gestures to the chalk Wizard.

'Rest of us leave ours. An invisible test of wills. Sometimes I see someone and think to myself, is that him, the angry drunk, or him there the lovesick one, or him, the silent drifter. Can drive you crazy thinking about it, him being one of us.'

'Nobody looking to catch him?'

'Who cares? A hobo killer? Doing what's left of society a favour.'

'That's cold. Where I grew up as long as black men killing each other it didn't even make the news. Whites killing black, much the same.'

Larry nods his agreement. 'Was one hobo, Bozo Texino he tagged himself, drew a face under a wide-brim ten-gallon hat, like we had in the movies when I was a kid, back in the day. Well Bozo Texino, he set out to trap him, even addressed the jungle up at Britt, appealing for hobo unity whatever that is. He caught out that night, with a round of applause and some empty promises ringing in his ears. Nobody ever saw him again and to this day I swear the hobo killer was in that audience. Probably the man who clapped the loudest. They even made a film about it, about the myth of Bozo Texino. Well, weren't no myth, just flesh and blood like the rest of us, just another dead hobo is what it was.'

Larry gets up and faces the chalk wizard, traces his hand over his beard.

'Hobo just a word now, anyway. I spend most winters up in Canada with my sister. Husband a big shot in what they call gene splicing. Stamping butterflies, I call it, he hates that. I get my own unit, even has a shower. Shit, ten years ago I'd of caught out within the week. Nowadays come spring she has to kick me out. I hear the whistle, tracks run right past her house, sometimes it half scares me to death. Was a time I didn't need to hear it blow twice.'

They both look outside., transfixed both by the rhythm of the train and the open mesas and rolling hills of northern

California framed in the cinema screen of the open boxcar door.

Later and the last of the sun slides across the wooden planks of the floor parsing time like a sundial. Trainwreck rummages in his pack and gets out an old paintbrush, threadbare bristles more like a stick than a brush, and a small bottle of white paint. He gets up and daubs his mark on the wall. Frank stands and watches.

'There, there's my tag, so that hellhound will know I seen his and for sure one of us following the other.'

On the wall underneath the wizard are chalked the parallel lines of a train track, but one rail is all twisted and broke, sleepers scattered like pickup sticks, breaking the parallel.

'Don't know why I still do it. I ain't ever gonna catch him. Habit I guess, like biting your nails, or cocking your leg.'

# THE EARTH IS BROKEN

**INT. BOXCAR - NIGHT - 2036**

A man stands by the open door of an empty boxcar. An inky silhouette of a man fashioned from a pipe cleaner. He drinks, a demijohn hanging from his little finger. The stars are out; he talks to them, and to the emptiness in between.

          **HOBO KILLER**

    They said this country was
    built on hard work and
    integrity and worshipping God.

Beat. The surface of a lake rushes past, reflecting the starry dome overhead. The man drinks, drool and wine flies from his chin.

          **HOBO KILLER (CONT.)**

    That's lies, a fairy tale for
    children. America made by men
    out of murder, mayhem, slavery,
          (More)

### HOBO KILLER (CONT.)

and oppression. Stealing and
killing and raping is what
forged the United States and
fear fed the engine. Still
does. It's a runaway train of
bad things. You can make it
spit you out, make it hate you,
because it has the fear inside
itself. Everything does. You
can get away, be independent
of it, but it's tricky, there
is always a price to pay and
the blood and glory of it all
entices you. Blood calls to
blood. But if you try to deal
in it, trade blows with it,
then it eats you up again. Like
an abacus, the whole starry
whorl is an accounting, we are
all beads strung on it, one
side or another. Added up to
its glory or deducted from it.
Get off the train, stay off the
train, diminish it by one, by
one, diminish it by one.

CAMERA pans down to reveal HOBO KILLER is
talking to a DEAD MAN who he holds up by his
collar, black blood seeps onto the floor of
the train and out of the car, whipped away
like ribbons in the wind as the train rattles
through an empty ravine. The HOBO KILLER lets
go of the body and it disappears out of the

open door as if it had never been, and the pipe cleaner man is alone again.

> **HOBO KILLER (CONT.)**
> America hates that, it hates losing you, one by one I deduct from its terrible glory.

**CUT TO:**

**EXT. FREIGHT TRAIN TERMINAL BAKERSFIELD 2036 - DAWN**

'THE EARTH IS BROKEN' by TIM BUCKLEY MIXES UP OVER:

FRANK and LARRY watch the freight trains come and go through his marine issue night-vision binoculars.

NIGHT-VISION GOGGLES WATCH A SWITCHING YARD.

A long freight liner pulls away as they run for an open boxcar.

BOOTS CRUNCH THE LOOSE GRAVEL.

We catch up with the train, running parallel, huffing and puffing, we grab hold, just make it, throw the pack in first, before disappearing into the open wagon. The yard recedes into an inky blackness as we catch out...

# FRUIT PICKERS

*Monsanto farm complex, 2036*

Frank and Larry line up with other workers to enter the Monsanto farm complex. Heavy security scrutinises paperwork and then they are sprayed and scanned. This is called the induction process. This is more Agro-Military than the smiling farmhand leaning on his pitchfork drawn on the company logo, backed by a naïve sketch of an adobe ranch house nestled in the lee of rolling hills.

White, Mexican, black, all are scrutinised the same, fit and able, no drugs, no previous Monsanto convictions. Larry has a good record, but the clerk asks him pointedly if he's still up to it. He laughs this off, with a 'You wanna arm wrestle?' line and the clerk hesitates a beat but signs him in and Larry and Frank shuffle forward. All accepted workers sign a six-week contract and are issued dungaree-style work clothes, assigned a bunk in a long row of container-like cabins, and the evening off. As ever there is a company store which gives you credit against your paycheck, all transactions digitally processed via your ID card which hangs around each worker's neck.

The novelty of a bed is too tempting for Larry and Frank and they turn in early.

Over the next days they work side by side in fields full of strawberries. It's back-breaking work, but repetition gives rise to rhythm, which both helps the time pass and eases the working of the body. They are all picking huge, almost cartoon perfect strawberries. Frank sweats, but a clean sweat not a booze one. He looks up upon row after row of workers and feels good. 'Robots can't pick soft fruit,' he thinks. Even genetically modified ones.

At dusk a field kitchen feeds them and a crate of beer does the rounds. No liquor allowed on the farm, but plenty of cold company beers. Larry slakes his thirst.

'Best beer of the day, the rest pale incrementally.'

Frank sips a can of Diet Coke wishing there was something else in it. After the boxcar whiskey he hasn't touched a drop, trying to repair one of the many promises he has made and broken to himself and everybody else. He daydreams about booze, the uplift it gave him, the bitter taste of it, but filled the hole with hard work and easy talk.

A group of Mexican workers sit at the next trestle table, silently drinking beers.

Frank gestures towards their neighbours. 'Know what these guys call us? Los Belitre.'

Larry finishes his beer, reaches for another. 'What's that mean?'

'Rogues, scoundrels.'

'Mexican bastards.' Larry salutes the puzzled looking Mexicans.

'Sticks and stones old timer. I learnt that. Day we met you called me boy twice in the space of ten minutes and had something worse on the tip of your tongue like you was rolling around a sweet you didn't know whether to suck or spit out.'

Larry almost chokes on his beer.

'Bad habit I guess. Was twenty years old before I realised

'Damn Yankee' was two words. Times change son, people rarely.'

'In Syria we had names, all kinds of names. Towel heads, Hajjis, camel jockeys, white boys called 'em sandniggers thought it was all right to say that in front of me, all sorts of shit, same as back in Iraq, Vietnam, hell even World War Two I guess, and on and on. Ignorant just the same. Didn't matter what name it said on your dog tags, or what name you was called, by the end of your tour you was either alive or dead.'

Larry nods his head, wipes beer froth from his scrawny beard. 'Where I grew up white families been killing each other since the Civil War, some before that. What side you was on more important than whether you alive or dead. What surname you carried marked you one or the other.'

'Feuding hillbillies. I watched the TV shows.'

'Oh yeah, well I hope that was entertaining for you'ns. I came home, only job for me was down the mine working alongside my dad. I seen the men we buried in Iraq, bulldozed right over their trenches. Not a single fancy pants engineer had to get out of his vehicle. Not one. Sent us Appalachian boys in to cover it up and not a once did I complain. A week underground and I cleared out. Was like I was the one being buried. Foreman called me a coward. Daddy laid him clean out. They put him back on the late shift for his trouble, which ended up killing him.'

Larry finishes his beer, opens another in the grip of a sudden thirst. 'They only recovered forty-four bodies from the trenches. We burned the rest in the desert. The experience kind of opened up my horizons, you could say.'

All of a sudden, they arrived where neither aimed to be, a place too serious, a place too personal. Frank had nothing more to add, not even something like 'That was a long time ago.' For in his face you could see it sitting there like it was yesterday. Larry shifted in his seat, lit another cigarette buying time for it to pass. He offered one to Frank.

'You know Mojave Indians call white men beaver eaters.'

They both laugh gratefully.

'Now you know the black man doesn't do that.' Frank winks. Gets up, peers out into the gloaming across the open fields. He stretches.

'Today I'm tired. Deep down physically exhausted. Been a long time since I felt that. Man it feels good.'

Frank closes his eyes content.

\* \* \*

And so six weeks pass.

# TOOTH PICKERS

**EXT. MOJAVE PARK CITY - DAY - 2036**

Classic small-town America, but with a self-conscious ersatz feeling. A town of nothing much but a mixture of fake and fading memories. That plus a lot of security.

PAN off a 'HARVEST FESTIVAL' banner onto FRANK and LARRY sitting on a bench eating super-size Gen-modded corn cobs.

              **FRANK**

    You like these boiled or
    barbecued?

              **LARRY**

    Boiled with butter, black
    pepper, salt. Stick a fork
    in one end, eat them like
    popsicles.

FRANK picks at his teeth. Kids are riding on a miniature old steam train from the gold rush days. Families of migrant workers stand watching.

**FRANK**

Older you get, more the corn gets stuck between your damn teeth.

A TROUPE OF MOJAVE INDIANS PERFORM A RAIN DANCE IN FRONT OF RUGS LADEN WITH BASKETS OF OVERSIZED PRODUCE: MAIZE, BEANS, PUMPKINS, ETC.

**CUT BACK:**

FRANK and LARRY have finished their cobs and are both sitting there with toothpicks in their mouths, LARRY rolling his back and forth across his top lip.

**LARRY (CONT'D)**

This is better'n TV.

**FRANK**

Beats Thanksgiving that's for sure. When you ever watch TV?

LARRY shrugs.

**LARRY**

Just a figure of speech I guess.

**FRANK**

When the hurricane hit in '22 it took out the electricity.
(More)

### **FRANK (CON'T)**

No TV, no nothing. My wife had
to phone her sister in Florida
to find out what was going on
from her television, and I
mean what was going on in her
favourite TV shows.

FRANK laughs at this memory.

### **LARRY**

You was married? Kids?

### **FRANK**

Six and more weeks we worked
together you never asked, and
I never told. Two boys. Ain't
seen them in ten years. You?

### **LARRY**

Nope. Never did. Thank God.
Got hitched some, but it never
worked out, I always had the
itch to move on.

FRANK goes back to picking his teeth, LARRY
turns back to the show.

### **FRANK**

My wife drowned saving my
youngest. I couldn't save her
because I can't swim.

**LARRY**

A marine who can't swim?

FRANK nods.

**FRANK**

I skipped swim qualification week. Pulled a few strings, shuffled some paperwork. Besides they was sending us to the desert.

**LARRY**

Shit.

**FRANK**

I survived because she made me save the boy. Her relatives came and took the kids back east. Detroit. I drank. Their aunt sent me letters. Now she's dead.

**LARRY**

Your wife die knowing she saved your boy?

**FRANK**

I believe she did.

LARRY watches FRANK, there's nothing to add. They get up, start walking to fill the silence.

KIDS HOOT WITH JOY AS THE TRAIN BLOWS ITS
WHISTLE AND CHUGS PAST.

**FRANK**

Maybe they should get
themselves some miniature hobos
for the train set.

LARRY smiles.

**LARRY**

I hear they running freight
again from Portland on across
to Chicago. Food one way, steel
coming back the other. That
near enough to Detroit.

**FRANK**

Don't know if I'm ready yet.

**LARRY**

None of my business, just
saying. That what you wrote?

FRANK looks down at the postcard in his hand.
They stop outside the company store.

**FRANK**

Ain't had a drink for more than
five weeks.

**LARRY**

You wanna turn up the last
American hero, is that it?

**FRANK**

I'll settle for sober.

**LARRY**

Go ahead and post the damn thing.

FRANK goes inside. LARRY rolls a cigarette; watches truckloads of workers come and go. FRANK comes back out.

**LARRY**

You set?

FRANK nods.

**FRANK**

Don't even get to lick the damn stamp no more.

# TWO HANDSHAKES

*California, 2036*

A few hobos, transients, squat round small fires, waiting to catch out. Larry has made a pot of coffee. Frank can't settle, shifting his weight from one foot to the other, itching for his ride. They both finish their coffee, chuck the grounds into the fire. This is a parting of the ways, one that was always coming, but now it's here, imminent, it surprised them both and gave everything a strange clarity. The distance of future time was already between them.

'Where you headed?' asks Frank, a little too loudly.

'Mexico, I reckon. If I can get across the border, I hear they set new fences, but I always managed it across before. Farms down there hiring, fancy myself a warm winter. You do me a favour?'

Frank nods, washes out his canteen, rolls his bedding, reties his boots, with a simple matter-of-fact pleasure. If somebody from before met him now and said, 'You've changed Frank, something's different', it would be this, a rediscovered economy of movement, a younger man's bones.

Larry passes him a small box, wrapped up in a handkerchief.

'What's in it?'

'Family mementos, letters I sent to my mother, and hers to me when I was overseas and the years after that before she died.'

'Why you give them to me?'

'You're a family man, Frank, you had more of it than I ever did.' Larry's arm sags, as if he assumes the gift will not be taken, and now he wishes he never got the damn thing out of his pack, that it was a bad idea in the first place and he couldn't wait to stuff it back into the end of his roll.

'You only going to Mexico.'

Cosmic silence.

'How about you look after them for me until we meet again? If that makes you feel any better. Don't seem right to throw them away.'

This last remark a challenge, an acknowledgement of the irreversibility of change, of their separate fates, that has crept up on them, found them out, a response to it, a stubborn small bravery in the face of the immutable.

He almost forces the box into Frank's hands and goes back into his pack for more.

'And here, take these.'

He gives him a bag of paint marker pens. Frank takes it all in silence.

'Leave your mark, I'm done leaving mine. Take 'em. Mixture of indelible ink and paint sticks, work on most surfaces, paint, rust or just cold steel.'

A big moment, of goodbye, recognition of the fact that the passage of time creates intimacy whether or not you are looking for it, the beat between before and after, a shearing away of one from the other, that is also the moment we are witness to an unbreakable connection, and then it's gone in a rush of vertigo, this brief glimpse, flash, onto the quantum history of us.

'Like big cats spraying trees in the forest.' Frank's right there, turning towards what's next. He retrieves his night-vision goggles from his kitbag.

'Take 'em, go on. Help you catch the train home.'

'This cat getting a bit long in the tooth.' Larry warms himself by what's left of the fire, his face gold.

Frank remembers another long-ago fire, one he put out, somehow connected to this one. He holds out the goggles, Larry can't resist, his eyes light up, bright with something, he takes them, fumbles them into his kit to get them out of sight.

'I got 'em off a guy in first recon, combat marine coming off his tour. First time I used 'em was the day I met you. Call it a fair trade, if it make you feel any better, and I'll keep the letters add 'em to my own pile.'

There's nothing else.

They shake hands.

Frank turns and heads for the tracks.

And the cosmos plays us this...

> *'Why don't you work like other folks do?*
> *How the hell can I work when there's no work to do?*
> *Hallelujah, I'm a bum,*
> *Hallelujah, bum again,*
> *Hallelujah, give us a handout*
> *To revive us again.*
> *Oh, why don't you save all the money you earn?*
> *If I didn't eat, I'd have money to burn.*
> *Whenever I get all the money I earn,*
> *The boss will be broke, and to work he must turn.*
> *Oh, I like my boss, he's a good friend of mine,*
> *That's why I am starving out on the bread line.*
> *When springtime it comes, oh, won't we have fun;*
> *We'll throw off our jobs, and go on the bum.*
> *With a of the 1961 Freedom Riders version thrown in*
> *Hallelujah, I'm a-travelin',*
> *Hallelujah, ain't it fine?*
> *Hallelujah, I'm a-travelin',*
> *Down freedom's main line.'*

— 'Hallelujah I'm a bum' – Industrial Workers of the World, 1908

*Oregon, 2036*

This song and a dead man's sleep deliver Frank to Oregon refreshed, yet he hums and sings the chorus to himself as he walks away from a train yard just north of Eugene bringing the dark of the night before into the bright daylight of the morning after. 'Hallelujah I'm a bum'. It feels right inside his head, a cosy ear-worm, 'Hallelujah Bum again,' as he finally heads east, a leaner man, taking evenly spaced strides and breathing easily around the cadence of the refrain. 'Hallelujah give us a handout, to revive us once again'. . .

It's almost dusk and a rare autumn shower passes in a flash, illuminated by a corridor of sunlight, leaving him soaking wet, but the thirsty earth dries within minutes. Frank looks around as if somebody has played a trick on him, he flashes on the water balloon ambushes of his childhood, laughs out loud from the fresh shock of memory, as his clothes start steaming. Up ahead there is what looks like a mom-and-pop's gas station. Behind it a grain silo rises above a stand of trees. Piles of tyres, huge five foot across ones are stacked up on the fore-court. As Frank approaches a man appears from inside, hunched behind a rusty looking double-barrel shotgun.

Automatically Frank drops his kitbag and raises his hands, this is how you do it, always has been, it's automatic. On reflection he realises the gun probably won't work and after a beat lowers his hands.

'Place looked deserted.'

'Well it ain't. What you want?' An old man, not much older than his gun, skinny, white, worn jeans and a worn out grey corduroy jacket. Probably harmless but also desperate in some as yet indefinable way, which potentially makes him something other than harmless.

Frank takes it easy. 'I was just looking for a place to dry off, change my clothes.'

'This ain't no motel. Besides, been shut ten years.' The shotgun droops, just from the weight of it, the uselessness of it.

'Well, I'm sorry about that, I can get changed in the woods.' He turns to move on, behind him the old man keeps talking.

'Japanese were our last market. Our soft white wheat was good for making their noodles. Demand nose-dived after the meltdown, and their population just went tits up. Lead run out of the Jap's pencil. Our final export destination. Bushel price hit the floor.'

Frank stops, turns back to him.

'You were a farmer?'

'What's it look like to you? Gas and tyres. Sold 'em to all the farms round here. See that big five-footer over there? Grain elevator takes four of them, five grand each back in the day, that's good business.'

'We had tyres like that over in Syria. Big-ass tyres.'

'Ethanol prices went through the roof after you lot fucked that up, but without a federal subsidy to replant with soy, that's all she wrote round here.'

The old man spits, but finally puts the shotgun down on top of a rusty gas pump.

'You look hungry. You hungry?'

'Yes sir.'

'Well come on inside and get out of them wet clothes. Name's Welt, Nathan Welt.' He points to a fading sign above the station. 'Welt and Sons gas and tyres. That's me. Never had any kids but they say it looks good on a sign.'

By the time Frank has dried off and changed, the old man's cooking noodles over a gas stove. Hundreds of packets of Japanese noodles line the shelves of what once was an office.

'Name's Frank, never had a sign, but I got two sons and I'm heading east.'

'Shit, that's a short story.'

'You don't want to hear the long one.'

Nathan Welt raises an eye, turns and places two bowls of

steaming noodles on the table. He sits, bobs his head down into the bowl and starts slurping. He looks up through the steam, gestures the chair opposite with an as yet unused fork.

'Take a seat Frank, this is our wheat right here. Japanese sure did love it. Got enough to keep me going until I check out I reckon. Sprinkle a little sachet on top, you got pepper flavour or regular miso, soy sauce, low sodium soy sauce here, the blue one.'

He throws a handful of sachets across the table.

'Low sodium soy sauce. No shit.' Frank smiles, starts to laugh.

'100% American wheat, Jap noodles. Go figure.'

'You ever get sick of eating noodles?'

'Yep. I dream of steaks, yes I do.'

A gently rising laughter fills the room as they slurp the soup and wind noodles onto their forks.

'You looking for work?'

Frank nods, slurps some more.

'If you heading east, I hear they paying good money to clear the roads coming out of Omaha, Nebraska. Feds still in charge down there, been fifteen years, they figure it's safe enough to go back in.'

'I seen that figuring method up close. It don't figure.'

Nathan Welt shrugs. 'Man's gotta work.'

'I'm good with my hands, fix almost anything.'

'Well, that shotgun you so scared of a while back ain't worked for years, you reckon you can fix that?'

'You think you gonna need it?'

Nathan Welt doesn't answer but pulls a face, sticking out his bottom lip and bobbing his head forward a little like a tortoise.

'Some people dream of noodles.'

Frank smiles. The shotgun sits by the door, he picks it up, an antique, full of rust and wear. He breaks it, eyes both barrels then goes out for his pack, gets out some tools and a bottle of oil wrapped in a cloth. The old man clears the table. Frank starts breaking the gun down and cleaning it, as the old man makes coffee and smokes.

'This gun got a story?'

'You ever come across one that didn't? Just depends whether the story is behind it or yet to happen. That shotgun was my grandfather's, he used it for killing rabbits and scaring off people he didn't like of which there was a lot, mostly folks he owed money to.'

After Frank is done they come outside, he hands Nathan the shotgun.

'Only the right barrel works, other one almost rusted through, likely to injure you.'

'Single barrel doubles my ammo.' Nathan Welt pushes his bottom lip out again, stubborn, facing what the world hands him like a tortoise, slowly, but with purpose going forward.

He loads up and fires at a rusty silo, the recoil and surprise almost knock him over. With a big toothy smile, he reloads the shotgun, takes aim. The fun of shooting something takes years off him.

'I reckon it's still got a few tales in it. Thanks fella.'

Early morning finds Frank all packed up and ready to leave. Nathan Welt has made chicory coffee. They drink it at the table.

'You welcome to stay a few days in the back there, more'n welcome. Ton of things you can fix round here, trouble is I can only pay you in noodles.'

Frank smiles. 'Thanks Nathan, but I got a train to catch.' They come outside.

'Nearest train station is past Snake River, by the Oregon border. Indian territory, thirty miles or so east of here, got an Indian name I don't recall. They ain't that bad you humour them, besides now they holding all the cards.'

Frank smiles. 'All good things come to those who wait.'

Nathan shrugs, bobs his head in agreement. 'Frank. You take it easy.'

They shake hands and Frank lifts his pack back up on his

shoulders, walks off down the road. Shading his eyes Welt watches him disappear around the first bend.

'He got a train to catch, now that's funny.'

But the old man doesn't smile, he shuffles back inside. Smiling is what you do or don't do when other people are around. His eyes fall on the shotgun by the door and then the half empty box of cartridges on the table. Probably his last, he thinks, making a mental note to keep a couple for himself should the need or desire ever arise.

Frank shakes his head, mumbling to himself as he goes, about who holds the cards, the cards he held, Kenny way back and his Indian shape shifting tall tales, under velvet African skies spangled with silver stars...

# INDIAN TERRITORY

*'In the time of the Seventh Fire'*

*Nebraska, 2036*

*'I did not know then how much was ended. When I look back now from this high hill of my old age, I can still see the butchered women and children lying heaped and scattered all along the crooked gulch as plain as when I saw them with eyes still young. And I can see that something else died there in the bloody mud and was buried in the blizzard. A people's dream died there. It was a beautiful dream. . . the nation's hoop is broken and scattered. There is no center any longer, and the sacred tree is dead.'*

— Black Elk

From 2020 escalating attacks on Bud, Coors Lite and other beer delivery convoys to the liquor stores of Whiteclay, Nebraska, resulted in the deaths of a number of drivers, natives and police. The years after Standing Rock saw the standoff between Native America and both federal and local law enforcement evolve into a war of attrition played out in the glare of social and mainstream media. In 2028, armed with Chinese automatic rifles and high explosives a band of Lakota and Cherokee warriors burnt out the town in the space of three hours. All of it. The fourteen residents of Whiteclay who had sold 13 million cans of beer to the reservation annually, were either elsewhere or were incinerated. Two Sioux died in the inferno, blowing themselves up in their eagerness to eradicate this genocidal killer of their people since the nineteenth century. The place now simply doesn't exist, scorched earth lines either side of the new asphalt road leading to the old Reservation border as if wrought by natural disaster. By this time federal administration was in disarray and local law enforcement ill equipped, underpaid and unwilling to deal with a heavily armed and increasingly militant Native population. National guard and some locally stationed military reserve units withdrew east, re-deployed to protect the fragile economic infrastructure of New East makeover cities like Cincinnati, Columbus, Cleveland, Detroit and Chicago. 'Indian territory', as was, expanded to fill the void.

After the destruction of the Dakota access oil pipeline, First Nations across the Midwest had become well organised as political, and later potentially military forces to be reckoned with, backed by the DGR (Deep Green Resistance) who proved to be more than the loony eco-left Facebook pussies we all took them for at the time. The goals of the Red Power movement of the 1960s, viewed of at best as 'of its time' and dormant for well over sixty years came to fruition.

With more and more players on the field everything became harder to call. By 2030 the Black Hills were de facto once again occupied by plains tribes. Original land rights devolved to the plains Indians including upriver water rights that would come to dominate the political economies of the South-West for years to come. Boundaries of reservations across Oregon, Wyoming, Nebraska, Montana and the Dakotas ceased to have any meaning. The land was there for the taking. Poor tribes that had for years resisted the offers of compensation for their sacred lands got them back as what remained of the Federal Government no longer had the resources to pay. Mindful of pre-colonisation inter-tribal conflict and wars between tribes, cross-tribal relations, mutual casino ownership structures, investment oversight committees had as of 2036 maintained the peace, and the First Nations flourished.

Most of the mines had been bankrupted in 2028 by the final devaluation of the dollar. Fracking had long destroyed the viability of deep seam mining, before world recession, the sidelining of OPEC, knocked the price of oil to below $15 a barrel. A new Renmimbi backed currency came too late for these companies to resist their expropriation. The tribes closed the mines for good. Now the Black Hills generate 70% of Native wealth through a string of casinos that entice the remaining white wealth of the eastern seaboard and the new Eastern (global) money that had flooded Florida.

The silk roads of antiquity once again switched polarity, flooding the new world with goods and money. Wages and employment took a huge hit, but there was money and all you could do was follow it.

The wealth from gambling, drugs and alcohol isn't wasted, it gets re-allocated. Lifting a whole set of peoples out of poverty this way solves some problems but not others, or at best it just shifts these problems around. But new wealth, in a continent that has undergone devaluation, chronic loan defaults and an end-of-empire ennui, speaks volumes. History picks its winners, and after 400 years of oppression, native America had finally weathered the storm of White colonialism. The circle of the hoop was almost whole once more.

Where once hardly anybody spoke it and it was hardly taught in what few schools there were, Lakota is now the primary language for 70% of Oglala Sioux now living on lands that have been re-extended to the original borders of the 1866 treaty and beyond, some of it paid for with hard cash. There is even a sophisticated drug and alcohol rehab programme for Native peoples called the Red Road and its chain of high-tech sweat lodges extends from Idaho to Iowa.

Life expectancy for native peoples increased by ten years after the collapse of Federal America, men from 44 to 54, women five years longer. Child mortality rates also decreased. This was in part thanks to the closing down of the uranium mines, and the donation of anti-radiation drugs by the revitalised ANC Revolutionary Government of South Africa. The Oglala Sioux had been drinking irradiated water that had come down from the hills, full of discarded minerals and runoff from the mines themselves. What was once invisible became visible, and out of this the future is made.

For what was left of the tribes, Turtle Island has got its mojo back. This was indeed the time of the Seventh Fire.

> *'It is this time that the light skinned race will be given a choice between two roads. If they choose the right road, then the Seventh Fire will light the Eighth and final Fire, an eternal fire of peace, love brotherhood and sisterhood. If the light skinned race makes the wrong choice of the roads, then the destruction which they brought with them in coming to this continent will come back at them and cause much suffering and death to all the Earth's people.'*
>
> — The Seventh Prophet

# LUCY LOOKS TWICE

*Pine Ridge Oglala Lakota reservation, South Dakota, 2036*

"Remember the online computer game *World of Warcraft*? *WOW* as it was called. They stopped updating it when the internet fragmented, when it stopped being a world wide web. What was left of the game ran locally on rogue servers hosted by players. Before that they had eight million people by the nuts paying ten bucks a month. It was 'the subscription model that became the rulebook for late cycle capitalism'. I read that in a magazine someplace, although I can't remember where I would have been where they had magazines.

Players who had to go to work, or who were planning a holiday, farmed out their characters to workers in cyber cafes in places like Seoul, Bangkok, Jakarta, who would play the game for you, keeping your levels up, keeping you in the game 24/7. You gave them access to your avatar. Attributes, skills, special powers, guild membership, levelling up, was the key to success in this world, your avatar and her role in that world demanded constant attention. You had to keep up. The game was a full-time job, not just a pastime. In some places it was the main source of employment, replacing call centres as an important part of the final economy. Playing games for other people. One cyber cafe in Seoul was raided by a gang from a rival cafe, the victims not even knowing they were in a gang until the cold steel of this other gang's machetes and pistol barrels were thrown down on them, forcing players at gunpoint to transfer the wealth of the game, a real-world holdup for unreal gems, in-game weapons and spells that don't exist. From then on most of these places got security, and serious players took out in-game insurance.

The internet came to the Rez when I was a kid, paid for by the Four Winds Casino, and my neighbour had an old computer they took from the mobile dentist after it shut down when the Federal Government ran out of money. Her mum had been the receptionist. The computer was her payout. She had no use for it, so we played on it, and it kind of dulled you, zoned you out. Fucked the pain away, my mom used to say as she played Peaches in the kitchen. 'An oldy but goody,' she said when we asked her what that shit was.

We played *Warcraft* two years straight, from age fourteen through sixteen. I'm kinda kidding but to be honest it ate up a lot of time, time when all the changes were happening outside; hell, us Natives were finally levelling up in the world and I missed most of it playing *Warcraft*.

Inside the Reservation time had been frozen for generations. The collapse of the Federal Government was the first thing to affect us, as we depended on them like an addict does a dealer. Other than those who developed the casinos that is, which created a few millionaires, which is a strange and wonderful thing let me tell you. Rest of us was Federal handouts through and through. Dependent, subdued, 'they go us on the bottle' as the old 'Red Power' braves would tell us if we ever listened. We rarely did because we knew it and was ashamed of it.

Instead we suffered withdrawal symptoms, some of us played computer games, whilst others got angry and organised.

Then we took back the Black Hills without a bullet being fired as they used to say, which was lucky because we didn't have many bullets. Then along came big agro making offers, hell, Chief Little Crow said it was treaty time all over again. Always somebody wanted our land, land that wasn't ours is what they never understood. In fact, they had made us like them by making us think we did own it. More than anything, more than English, more than Jesus more than America itself, owning things, owning land, what's mine and what's yours, this, this dividing up of the world was a devil unto itself. And to be honest, the seed of it was in us already, perhaps always had been.

We were just kids playing *Warcraft* when all of this was happening, kind of depressing to miss out, looking back on it. One night, on what they used to call Indigenous People's Day, which had replaced Christopher Columbus Day, (this was the type of symbolic shit we had managed to pull off back in the day), my brother Chaska came to the trailer. He was *Akichita*, a 'New Brave', rode a horse he called 'big dog'. There is a Lakota word, 'ShunkaWakan', but big dog is better. It's what we called horses when we first saw them when the Spanish came to America. My brother lived in an eco-Tepee whatever the fuck that was, but that night he came into the trailer with enough energy likely to light the whole place up. New tattoos, a brand new page of history across his back and running up and down his arms, the occupation of Wounded Knee, Lakota with AK's, a brand new pickup truck that was half a horse, or that's what it looked like dancing in the flame light as we dragged him out to the barrel fire, orange tongues licking each and every tattoo, bringing the story to life as we twisted him this way and that to see more, to read more, to ask him all kinds of shit. He laughed, pushing us away. He wanted to speak to Mom. Dad came round later that night, or maybe it was an uncle, wearing an old Pine Ridge Pumas T-Shirt. They both loved basketball so this detail doesn't help me remember which it was, but he was drinking, and I remember my brother knocking the beer from his hand, looking at him worse than any white man, worse even than the last county sheriff. Chaska means eldest son and it was sad because he didn't have any younger brothers just us two girls.

My uncle or father spat on the ground, said something like 'New brave? Think you're better than me, better than your elders? You're no more than a boy scout. You think teaching our people to speak Lakota, to ride horses, and how to use a bow and arrow is going to make any of this any better?'

He was drunk and twirled around gesturing the whole shithole of a place. I remember exactly what my brother said, in all of this story which is pretty vague, my memory must be shot to fuck, but I do remember exactly what he said, because it was so unexpected, I thought he was just going to beat this old man, because my brother has a flaring up type of anger, and even if this old man was our father he deserved it, he knew who his son was (or his nephew), but instead he just put his hand on his chest, on his heart which I think is on the left, he put his hand there and said without any anger in his voice, 'But it changes everything here.'

Then he winked at me and walked away.

Two days later Whiteclay burned to the ground and my brother was dead. Ten years later most of what my brother said has more or less happened and he never lived to see it. I close my eyes and all I can truly remember are those tattoos leaping across his back in the flicker of the flames, and how that must of been how they looked when he burnt to death.

A few months after that things changed. One night me and Sally Ann sat and watched the *Warcraft* movie trilogy. Back to back. We had been smoking, *Sho'-Lah*, I think this was one of the first times, perhaps because of how sad I was after my brother died, maybe not, there's a million reasons to smoke Ice not all of them good. Those films made me so sick I couldn't look at the game again. I was all *War Crafted* out.

So we stopped. We came outside. I learnt to ride and took up Lakota language classes aged sixteen. Damn hard for a baby to learn to talk, you try it at sixteen. Two years later I had my own trailer and was working at the casino, speaking fluent Lakota to the Chinese, Anglo and Russian customers who found it charming and tipped accordingly, Google translating the shit out of all of it on their fancy intranet devices.

One story from those growing up years stays with me and goes to show that even the time-wasting parts of your life have stuff to teach us. I think you can't waste time, if you sift through it enough. For me the story that stands out is the *Warcraft* funeral story. I still tell people it now though the game itself is pretty much history. So when I tell this story it's like a myth, a fantasy I made up, even though it's true, it did happen, and the people I tell they look at me like, wow you crazy meth head. Well they may be right, but hey, use your imagination to see beyond that.

Anyway, a long time ago...

A *Warcraft* player from Norway died in real life, in a car crash. Trying to imagine Norway, its people, its roads, it's countryside from the Pine Ridge reservation took a lot of effort.

Most of her friends were online, in the chatrooms and community spaces of the game. She played it A LOT. I wonder who the other three people in her car could have been, real people. Anyway, they survived, she didn't.

All the players in her clade decided to hold a funeral for her in the game, to bury her avatar. Her boyfriend in real life had control of her account and gave permission for the funeral to go ahead, he gave them her codes, same as you would do when farming out your player. He was happy to let her die in the game, which is pretty cool of him, not to want to take over her attributes, or even keep her as a reminder, or even worse sell her as an ongoing avatar. No, this guy did the classy thing. To let her die twice and be done with it. I never asked if he was in the car when she died, if he was one of the three others. Maybe he was driving, that would be my take on it.

The funeral was to be held by a big lake. No weapons allowed, they had to be stashed, time locked, at a stipulated distance. It was to take place on 4th March 2006, so this is like way back in time, when my mom was young in the slow time of the reservation. We were invisible to the outside world. Back then it was boom times elsewhere but the same fucked-up times on the Rez. Through *Warcraft* you learn about things like Norway and car crashes and boom times. I first heard this story twenty years after it happened, it had become part of the mythology of the game.

The dead Norwegian had been an officer in a horde guild on the Illidan shard (now that's funny, shard/shards). Sorry this is all tech talk, if you don't play you don't know or need to know, because for most people it's pretty lame.

Her boyfriend posted all these details about her. He wanted to share that with the people she played Warcraft with. In real life amongst other things, she loved waterfalls and walking in nature, because that's what they've got in Norway I guess. Here I'm surrounded by it too, but I don't walk in it, it's just a huge fact all around me and it sits there watching us mostly. Sometimes I think it judges us, sadly and blankly, and I feel in the wrong sometimes looking out at it, which is an odd way to feel about animals, hills and open prairie. All the bigwig elders and youth workers, and tribal minded people say we have to reconnect with nature, before the seventh fire. Crazy old folks and their past, dances and costumes, stories that went nowhere but had cool names in them and all the corn you could eat come Indigenous People's Day.

The funeral was to be held at Frost Fire Springs in the land of Winter Spring. This is a contested area of the server, so there was no overall control by any one horde. Neutral territory. Like how the open plains were back in the day, owned by nobody, shared by everyone. I never believed that, not with the history we have to live with. How far back you gotta go for paradise? In *Warcraft*, this place was like happy hunting y'all. That I do believe because I've been there since. An opposing alliance Guild called Serenity Now saw the notice posted for attendees to be respected and left alone during the funeral. It also read that there were to be no weapons. So what did they do? They raided it killing everyone and taking all their shit. How cool was that? People lost their shit, there was a *World of Warcraft* wide outrage, comments, posts and all that, how could you do this, it breaks all the rules. Life has these big moral rules, but a game? It can only have the rules of the game itself, how to play the game, not our life rules put into the game.

Made me think that most *Skah* people see us as ghosts in their world, avatars from a game nobody still played, nor abided by any of its rules. White people who liked us were mostly no better, they imagined us as more noble than we could ever have been, in a fantasy no less complex than *Warcraft*, but one designed to allow them to pity us, leftover spirits that we are. Pity let them rule us, protection, preservation let them own us, own who we were all the way back. We were their *Indians*. Proud remnants of a culture that saw all the shit come down the pipe, that's how they played us, they played us heroic. Well that's not me or anyone I know. You wouldn't want me or anyone I know as your avatar, no sir.

Serenity Now weren't done with just stealing all the enchantments, weapons, gold gems and armour of the mourners, they celebrated it in a posted video of the raid with a comments stream about how great they were. Now that really got them noticed. They got millions of views on YouTube, became the superstars of the whole fucking game. Then they disappeared, as quickly as they had arrived. Account closed. 2006. Boom time heroes.

I came out of that game and found all the other kids my age could speak Lakota, could ride horses, went camping in tepees, and the two-bit two trailer tied together casino that flooded every time it rained was now on a building site for the soon to be reborn Prairie Wind Casino complex. The New Braves had triumphed in the real world like Serenity Now had done in *World of Warcraft*. My brother had died making it so. And that made our family something to be proud of. We became visible; Turtle Island heroes in the time of the seventh fire if you know all your cool Indian shit. I had a lot of catching up to do in the years that followed.

My best friend is called Sally Ann, we grew up together so her story is my story except she hasn't got a Lakota name, just a white one, that plus her stripper name Lap Dances with Wolves which makes her sad whenever she takes a break from being angry. She's twenty-two and I'm twenty-three. Older and wiser.

My name is 'Lucy Looks Twice', namesake of my great-great-greatest-grandmother, daughter of Black Elk, whose words they stole which they call translated and made into something else, the words they wanted to hear, which we had to take back, which took many winter counts, so that Black Elk could finally speak once more as he does today.

I had stepped from one game into another, and this time I was playing myself."

# AMBUSH

**EXT. SNAKE RIVER PLAINS - DAWN - 2036**

FRANK wakes in his bivouac, a spider drops on its thread, dangles over his face. He eyes it, rolls over to avoid breaking the thread and gets up. He looks out over a river valley. Fording the river, we see a band of Coos First Nation Indians, throwing up spray as they go, riding a mixture of horses and quad bikes, they come up the bank and straight at us. They circle FRANK laughing and shouting, eventually after they have had their fun, the leader, on a quad bike, rides up to him.

                **COOS LEADER**

    Xchiichuu ye Iluwechis?
    Xchiichuu ye Iluwechis?[1]

---

1. Xchiichuu ye Iluwechis? Xchiichuu ye Iluwechis? (How are you? (Literally) How is your heart?)

**FRANK**

What?

The Indian points at FRANK, then places
his right hand up by left side of his face
whilst signing left with his index finger,
he draws his hand across his eyes, bringing
the hand down in front of his face with
the index finger raised. FRANK shakes his
head. The man hands him his canteen. FRANK
hesitates. The man rattles it. FRANK takes
it, drinks. Immediately coughs and spits out
the contents.

**COOS LEADER**

Nii luuwii[2]

The other Coos laugh at this.

**FRANK (CONT'D)**

Whiskey? I don't drink.

The young COOS INDIANS find this very funny.
FRANK hands it back to him. He passes Frank
a second canteen. Frank takes it, opens it,
smells water and drinks deeply. He hands it
back.

**FRANK (CONT'D)**

Thanks. Any idea where I can
catch a train round here? I'm
headed for Nebraska.

He tries to sign train, and point east.
Kindergarten stuff.

---

2. Nii luuwii (Not so well)

**COOS LEADER**

You don't speak Coos, you can't sign. Damn I knew it, he speaks American!

His buddies all laugh. FRANK smiles.

**FRANK**

You got me.

**COOS LEADER**

You want a lift to the trains? Sure thing, brother, get on...

# LAP DANCES WITH WOLVES

*Nebraska, 2036*

A trailer park like any other, twenty miles from the Pine Ridge Rez, as was. Deserted strip malls rub up against bleak open prairie, an open wound of refuse and abandoned vehicles snakes like a useless border between what was once town and what has always been country; a topological suburbia to the great Mesas that lie to the north, themselves an overture for the Black Hills, and all that once contested American heritage.

A post-western landscape.

A wisp escapes the hole as the glass bowl fills up with dense white smoke, to be sucked through a half full bong of Red Warrior and out through a straw, from where it sweetly vacuums into your lungs, and back out of your mouth and nose in ropes of white candy. You tingle, you feel lighter, a better you. The real you, breathing in and out, blowing clouds.

Sally Ann, A.K.A. 'Lap dances with Wolves', sits peacefully smoking on the steps of her mobile home, staring out at the distant pines, on a pale hill spotted with trees across the turnpike. Hot hands and cold feet, her tongue explores each tooth, an expert of every gap, an explorer across ridges of eroded enamel, flicks across each crater, each crumbling molar. Never had money for dentists in her family when America was on its feet except one time a free trailer did the rounds of the parks and malls, and almost immediately a queue of thirty, forty folks lined up for the free treatment, everything from fillings to root canals, but sadly no cosmetic work was what she remembered her mum saying. Sally Ann parses out this story as her tongue checks out the heroic teeth left in her mouth and the soft pits of those already repossessed.

She is two thirds Lakota Sioux and has found her post-American dream in a glass meth bong. The only one for sale since Oxycontin lost its license. Methamphetamine. Long after the Tweaker Nation hashtags, blowing clouds, meth, Tina, Pookie pipe, Ice smoking ampersands, Tumblrs, Periscopes, Snapchats and Instagram stories had vanished, the drug itself remained, offline, here in the desert of the real.

Flash on the back story...

In 2016 Oxycontin had been upgraded to a version that contained 'abuse deterrent' technology. A pan-American epidemic of opiate, mainly Oxycontin overdoses threatened Pardue Pharma with existential threat lawsuits plus the loss of their licences. 'Contin' is short for continuous (snappier no?), Oxy was the only drug that continuously released opiate over twelve hours. So you could take a big hit all at once without having to interrupt your sleep or work. The original one-hit wonder, except it wasn't and if you needed to take it more often, then what made it any different from cheaper generic opiate delivery systems? And if hundreds of thousands of Americans had OD'd on it because their doctors were pill farmers, or pushers or scrip sellers, then the least they could do was stop addicts abusing their instructions by snorting it or jacking it up. Now when you crushed the pill it turned to an unusable gummy gel (Pardue Pharma eventually lost their license in 2022 and besides by then generics had ripped their profit margins into single billion-dollar shreds). In the regulatory and litigious meltdown that accompanied the rapid shrinking of federal jurisdiction, meth emerged as the most adaptable, most small scale survivable entrepreneurial drug success story in the history of America. The devolution of economic power made meth the cheapest way to fuck the pain away, and by a long shot the most honest. Meth millionaires didn't endow museums the world over and there never were any crystal meth philanthropists.

Three nights a week Sally Ann strips at the casino. A couple of bowls makes this sufferable, even getting finger fucked through her bikini in the back of a leather banquette by whoever stuffs the right amount of currency in them first. A tingling low level and abstract meth horniness becomes a cloak of protection in this environment, protected by the spell of the smoke, shrouded in vapour where nobody really touches her, in the cups of her sex magic.

'Lucy Looks Twice' shares her shift. As per her name she would flash her eyes back at the customers over her shoulder on the runway to make the point. Sally Ann didn't like the fact her best friend allowed her Lakota name, her true name, to double up as her stripper one, but never said anything to her, she kept that observation to herself.

Lucy pulls up in her twenty-year-old Nissan Juke.

'Hey Sally Ann.'

'Hey, Lucy.'

'You ready for work?'

'Unpa?'

'Sure.'

She gets out of the car, Sally Ann scoots up on her step as Lucy sits down next to her, passing her the pipe. Lucy fires up, rolls the bulb and takes a hit. She talks as she breathes the smoke back out, a rope of frayed cotton wool snaking up into the sky, quickly dissipating above her.

'I ever tell you how I managed to learn Lakota, what the trick was?'

'Never did, although I was surprised, pretty jealous too to tell the truth.'

'This shit. This shit gave me the focus, allowed me to read, take it in, concentrate, 'cos I figure all those computer games we played growing up, they fucked with our minds, unwired them, made us stupid, some government plan or just a happy coincidence for the fuckers. . . but smoking this? Brings it all back home. . .'

'Didn't help me any. I can't speak more than ten words.'

'Well maybe you just might be shit at languages.'

'Probably. You ever read about how learning a language rewires your whole mind? They reckon there's a virus in the Bible makes you stupid too. Like literally a virus, just saying or reading the words fucks with your sine, sine, wiring.'

'No shit. Thank God we ain't never read it.' They both giggle, Sally Ann rolls the last hit from the pipe, her left eye twitches and she rubs at it, rubbing the twitch out.

She blows fat O's in front of her, signalling nothing.

'You mean synapsis?'

Sally Ann's eye has stopped twitching. 'Yeah, that's the word, the Bible fucks with them.'

'Huh. Explains a lot you think about it.'

'Well I guess it's time to go to work.' Sally Ann cleans the pipe out and puts it in her handbag. 'Omnakhiya.'

'Holy pipe.' Lucy stands up, stretches tall and yells a war cry.

'You crazy bitch.' Sally Ann laughs, gets up and joins her, both of them howling at the distant hills and the trees.

# AMERICAN SPIRITS

*Oregon to Idaho, 2036*

A goods train cuts through an open plain bordered on both sides by forest. Seen from behind the treeline it flickers past, black and gold livery arrested into consecutive frames between the trunks of the trees. An armed guard sits on a flatbed, smoking, legs dangling. He raises his hand to shade his eyes, eyeballing the Coos warrior band weaving in and out of the treeline. He waves to them, wishing he could have as much fun. Eventually the train and the Coos converge at the Oregon border yard.

Frank is riding shotgun on one of the quad bikes. The guard now up on his feet whoops the posse on, especially the horses which are not so common a sight, and they wave back at him.

The Coos are picking up a delivery from the depot. Jerry cans of ethanol, a consignment of irrigation pipes in sections that they lash to a trailer behind one of the quads. Smaller items go into the horses' saddle bags. Frank watches all this commerce, appreciates and absorbs the energy of it. The leader pulls up alongside Frank.

'Guard here will let you ride, next stop is Boise Idaho.' The man chucks up a package which is caught by the guard, who nods, pocketing a carton of American Spirit cigarettes.

'Thanks, appreciate it.'

'You ever back this way, come up to the Rez, north of here maybe fifteen miles. The Three Rivers Casino is open for business. We got slots working, card tables, dancing girls, shit there's even a museum.'

'Damn. I stopped gambling too.'

'Too bad.'

'Way too bad.'

They shake hands.

Frank gets up on the train. The guard smokes and they watch the Coos take off. As the train pulls away they both whoop and wave as they disappear back into the forest, caught up in the energy of the moment, the kinetic excitement of being in the world.

Later dozing under the stars Frank thinks of the tin box Larry gave him and he retrieves it from his pack. Before reading one of the letters, he thinks whether Larry had told him he could read them or not. He flashes on the old man dead, keeled over in a row of strawberries or other fruits and catches his breath. The letter was dated March 2, 1991.

*Dear Mom.*

*Thank you for the parcel it got to me right before the invasion started, so I shared it with my squad, made me the hero for the day, although I was the only one to enjoy the pickled walnuts! As you may have seen on the television it is all over now and not many of us have been killed or injured. I'm safe, although I cannot say the same for the Iraqi boys we have seen here. Just to say the marines and our air force were too much for them and leave it at that. Scariest thing here is the desert and all the burned-out vehicles, especially at night. A mess which will take somebody a long time to clean up, thank God*

*it won't be me. This place gets under your skin. They are aiming to send us back to Saudi soon and in another month or so I will be home. Hope you are all keeping well, love to Lauren and thank her for looking after Elvis. Seen a few big snakes over here, one time on patrol one fell out of a tree, made my sergeant holler and almost shit himself, but I paid him no mind, snakes never scared me none, was a funny moment actually and I scored me some tough guy points with the rest of the boys for not screaming. Tell Dad his little man is hanging in there, funny to hear he called me that, I love you all,*
   *Larry x*

The address on the envelope was Sago West Virginia, a name he had heard of before, but where or for what reason, he no longer had a clue.

*Boise, Idaho, 2036*

*"We are all born from the same celestial seed;*
*all of us have the same father,*
*from which the earth, the mother who feeds us,*
*receives clear drops of rain,*
*producing from them bright wheat*
*and lush trees,*
*and the human race,*
*and the species of beasts,*
*offering up the foods with which all bodies are*
*nourished,*
*to lead a sweet life*
*and generate offspring..."*
— Lucretius (11, 991-7)

The outskirts of Boise, Idaho. Rows of mostly derelict houses, boarded up, abandoned cars, litter in the streets, some kids playing out. An almost pastoral scene from the last seventy-odd years of inland American. Life away from the coasts, where the fallout from recent changes is harder to discern. Lots of broken stuff, from potholes in the roads to boarded up shops and sagging chain link fences protecting nothing very much. A place where you expect to see dogs in packs around bins, or in the scrubby non-spaces under flyovers.

Frank approaches the porch of the first house that looks like it's occupied, in as far as he can tell a poor white neighbourhood. He rings the bell which doesn't work, then knocks on the door, which rattles. A woman finally answers.

'Yes? Can I help you?' A middle-aged woman, not taken aback by his being black, nor poor, her eyes direct and clear.

'You got anything broken, needs fixing?'

'You a comedian mister? I ain't got any money if that's what you after.'

The woman looks cold.

'You cook? I could do with a hot meal.'

'Heater's broke, been broke since last winter. You fix that I'll make you something to eat.'

'You got a deal, just show me where it is.'

Before she opens the door, she hesitates. 'No funny business you hear?'

'No funny business, none whatsoever.'

Later Frank sits at the kitchen table eating a plate of food. A man comes in the side door, he must be the husband.

'Who the fuck is this?'

'He never said his name.'

'Name's Frank, sir.'

The woman shrugs, they both watch Frank as he finishes up his food.

'Where'd he come from?'

She shrugs again, Frank says nothing.

'He mended the heater. Said you'd do it months ago and I'm

sick of freezing to death.'

'Well, you better eat up and be on your way mister.'

'Took him ten minutes. Then he fixed the bell.'

The husband walks to the front door, goes outside and rings the bell. 'Honey, I'm home.'

His wife laughs nervously, places a plate of food for her husband on the table, tops up Franks plate too. Frank looks up.

'Was just loose wiring, panels up on the roof working fine. Most things go wrong with electrical are just that. I always say that loose wiring made some people a lot of money.'

Frank gets up and faces the husband. Frank is nearly twice his size.

'Everybody told we gotta keep buying new shit when something broke, even when it ain't, it ain't broke, instead they say it's out of date, which is bullshit. Although there are some things you can't fix.'

'Like what?' The man looks up from his plate as his wife tidies away Frank's.

'You ever seen under the bonnet of one of them electric cars? Need Inspector Gadget to fix that. Shit, cars like that don't need no bonnets, no point looking inside unless you a robot.'

The man stares at Frank.

'Sorry, I get carried away when I have an audience.'

Frank picks up his pack.

'Good food ma'am. Thank you.' He nods at the husband who is still eating, having opened himself a beer from the fridge.

The woman follows Frank to the door.

'Thank you, mister.'

Husband comes onto the porch, beer in one hand and the other high up on his wife's arse, eyeballing Frank as he walks down the road, shouts after him.

'Whole town's broken, you could spend a season here for sure.'

And sure enough he hasn't gone more than half a mile when he sees a frail looking old man up a ladder struggling with a huge grey tarpaulin snagged on the roof of a barn.

'You want some help with that?' Frank shouts.

As soon as you know it he's fixing up some broken rafters, stapling heavy PVC over the gaps in the roof. The old couple watch, wrapped in rugs. The barn is their home, the house behind it derelict for some reason. The woman cooks over an open fire. He sleeps by the fire that night after the old couple go to bed, exhausted from telling him their list of ailments and the irregular supply of pharmaceuticals, since the country hit the skids.

The following morning finds Frank with his head under the bonnet of an old Chrysler truck. A fourteen-year-old boy sits in the cab watching him, rolling a spliff. The air has a chill in it, a proper late autumn chill.

'You can turn her over now.'

The boy starts the engine, it splutters and dies. Frank adjusts something, gives the boy the thumbs up and this time it works just fine, turns over chuckling to itself without Frank having to do anything more.

They sit together in the cab, warmed by the engine and sharing the joint.

'Where you from?'

'New Orleans.'

'You there when it finally went under?'

'Got back just in time.'

'Back from where?'

'Syria.'

'Where the hell is that? Nebraska?'

'No, it ain't in Nebraska. Hell, you smoke too much boy.' He starts laughing.

'What's so funny?'

'Nothing son, nothing at all.'

The boy hands him the joint. Frank sucks hard on the spliff, the smoke curls out and shrouds his face.

'Good shit. You grow it?'

'Everyone grows it, no need for dealers round here.'

He passes the joint back to the kid, relaxed and a little buzzed, first time Frank has smoked for a long time. The radio plays some country music, they nod to it.

'Time for me to move on, you drop me at the train depot?'

'Sure, you tell me where Syria is,' the now serious looking boy asks.

That night Frank hunkers down in a hobo jungle by the freight yard. Without full-time security the transient have moved in full-time and the camp has put down roots. Fires dot the landscape; freight trains pass in the background. Security comes and goes with the trains, not looking for trouble. If you could take the cold they turned a blind eye to riding the open flatbeds, just stay away from the closed boxcars.

Frank checks the groups huddled around the fires, their faces, the way they hold themselves revealing who they were and what they are now: hobos, vets, women, children, orphans, men wearing ruined suits. An old hobo deals an invisible hand of cards, the hand that life dealt him, an endless hand of patience. A middle-aged man in a crumpled suit is delivering something approaching a speech, or an old-fashioned talk, but he has no audience, and on closer inspection was never looking for one.

'They gave us freedom right from birth, from the get go. This here was the land of freedom. Set it up as the bright shining city on the hill, well turns out we didn't want it. Can't eat dreams, but they can eat you. Eat us all up chasing them, and when we all caught up, when we make it, Poof! It's not there anymore, probably never was, it was just a bright shining lie, is what it was.'

Frank finds his way through the jungle, picks his path down towards the tracks. A freight train blows its whistle. He runs past a group of young hobos who are roasting rats on sticks by the fire. He remembers visiting a fairground with his father as a child. The train slows as it negotiates the yard. Effortlessly he jumps up onto a flatbed, after throwing his pack up first. Down below and blurring with acceleration two young hobos make fully clothed love by the dying embers of a trash fire. They writhe and groan, laugh and gasp. Behind them the broken man is still talking, rapping almost to the soundtrack, his themes twist and turn in on themselves, repeated, looped, occasionally new words creeping in, renewing his sermon. Flecks of white spittle worked into the corners of his mouth, where they harden. The wet mouth, making all of it too soft, almost fungal.

'Only freedom people want is the freedom to fuck, we are all slaves to the genetic impulse, yessir.' He lubricates, jaws working themselves too hard.

The train pulls out of the yard and Boise behind it. Frank huddles deep down into his coat, his back up against a wooden crate.

The train passes a lake, sunken telegraph poles staggered along the shoreline, mesmerising Frank into counting them as they flicker past. A light rain starts to fall.

Later Frank wakes, as if on cue as the train enters Wyoming. Just like Larry did, he senses when to sleep, when to wake, when it's safe to do one and timely to do the other.

*South Dakota, 2036*

As Frank travels east autumn has outstayed its welcome in the woods he walks through, tired browns and faded russets, and yet some bright yellow splashes, tell their new story amidst the reliable grammar of evergreen. Shades he's never seen or taken notice of before. The cold somehow intensifies everything, gives shape to smells and heightens colour. Tree sap, earth humus, the piss and shit of wildlife, the smell of rain, rain in the air, rain on leaves, rotten woodland, the almost obscene smell of undergrowth, soil, root and leaf.

He gathers fern for kindling and sets a small fire. The clouds of smoke, he breathes in, nose tickled, he sneezes, so unlike the chemical fires he's used to. The fire takes, he sits, warms himself by protecting its little flames, now adding some bark and dry moss and the fire grows, crackles warmer. It smells good, he lies down and listens to a river nearby.

The next morning the woods are disturbed by a gang of teenagers fucking around with sticks, smoking pot or meth, expending a lot of nervous energy. The presence of girls amplifies this energy, making it more reckless, more dangerous. The cold keeps them moving about. One of them, a gangly youth in a loose-fitting combat jacket, gestures for his friends to shush, he's spotted something. He calls them over. He's spotted Frank.

Through the trees they spy on him in his boxer shorts, washing in the river. His clothes are all laid out drying on the rocks. On his body we see faded combat tats for the first time. Black on brown they resemble a strange mottling, a camouflage across his chest and upper arms.

The gangly youth, natural leader of the gang comes down into the river, the two girls and three other boys hang back by the treeline.

'Yo! Fuckin' tramp homo!'

Frank looks up. The other kids hide behind the trees, suppressing their laughter.

'Jeez man you're polluting our river.'

He is no more than seventeen, but wild beyond his years. There is a sense of threat, the girls hang back, nervous, like they've seen it all before, their guy is getting nasty. The other boys are nervous too, knowing they will have to back him up or else. Frank continues washing. With his back turned he speaks low and slow.

'I'm just washing my clothes son, that's all I'm doing, you leave me alone and that's all this is, a man washing his clothes.'

'You see a man here Jonesy?' He points with his stick. Jones slopes down from the treeline.

'Hell no all I see is some crazy naked-assed cold as shit bum, you?'

'Shit, I want to say, I want to say,' the skinny leader is running this one through his mind...

'Say what?' They start circling Frank, combat jacket drops his stick for the knife in his back pocket.

'In school we were told not to say it...'

'We're in the woods, so damn well say it!'

'All I see is a... nigger. A nigger bum!'

Frank continues to wash his clothes, he doesn't give a fuck about that word.

One of the girls has had enough, she wants more pipe. 'Come on Pete, leave him be, we gonna smoke that pipe or what?'

It seems saying the word for these white country kids, breaking this taboo, has both released them from a residual obligation but at the same time nothing changes. None of them move.

'Nigger!' The knife catches the light, the word bounces off it. Repeating the word has the effect of hastening what comes next. The second boy spins round and lashes out at Frank with his stick, hitting him across the shoulder. Frank doesn't resist.

'You done kid? I suggest you done. You with the knife, I say you especially done.'

The boys giggle nervously, the girls cry out. Frank's energy doesn't match theirs, this unnerves them.

'No, I guess I ain't done,' and he comes at Frank with his blade. The girls scream, stick boy falls backwards into the water, the classic backup coward. Words were a game, the taboo broken was enough to satisfy them, but it has pushed the boy with the knife too far, unbalanced him into a different future.

Frank moves super-fast, pulls some serious special training

type move on the knife boy, snapping his arm like a twig. His friend runs away, back to the treeline where the girls cower. The knife boy starts blubbing, flailing about in the shallow water. Frank now holds the knife and stands over him naked.

'Get away from me! Who the fuck are you mister?'

'I'm just a black man washing his clothes in the river. Now get the fuck out of here.'

The kid scuttles back to his friends nursing his arm. As they disappear back up the hill, we can hear them cursing Frank, threatening retribution.

'My arm you crazy fucker! Crazy mutherfucking tramp. . . I'll get you, you bastard!'

The woods return to silence, Frank to his washing, but his eyes bright, senses alive to what may come next out here in the wilderness.

Frank walks through the bleak, open Nebraska landscape. A cop car appears on the horizon, comes slowly, silently towards him. He looks left and right, there's nowhere to run, just the road bringing the cop car to him. He puts down his kitbag. The cop flashes his lights, cycles the siren, pulls up. The cop, white, early sixties, gets out slowly and approaches Frank, his hand resting on the butt of his sidearm.

'You the vagrant who attacked this here kid?' He gestures to the back of his cop car.

'I ain't no vagrant. I was minding my own business. You beat a naked man with a stick there gonna be consequences. Besides, this one here had a knife.'

Frank holds out the knife to the cop, handle first, who takes it, and shoots a look over his shoulder at the kid in the car, shakes his head and turns back to Frank.

'You break his arm, mister? It broke in three places.'

Frank just stands there, swats a fly from his neck. The cop is sizing Frank up, he still hasn't moved his hand from his gun butt.

'Come over to the car, sir.'

'You a real cop?'

'Sheriff, Kadoka county. Conagra pays the bills but I ain't Corp, if that's what you mean. Come over to the car, sir, nice and slowly.'

'Shit, that's old school. I get to spread 'em? You gonna frisk me? Ain't seen a real cop in years. Let's do this.'

Frank picks up his bag, nice and slowly and steps towards the car, hands where the cop can see them. The cop's hand exerts less pressure on the gun, is just resting there, he's made his mind up. In the passenger seat we see the kid nursing his broken arm. Frank makes big eyes at him. The cop gestures him to get in the back.

Behind bars, Frank sits at a small wobbly table. He puts his palm flat on it, moves it about to see where the wobble is coming from. Frank takes out a piece of card from his pocket, folds it over methodically and wedges it under the wonky leg. He places his palm back flat on the table to test it.

The sheriff has been watching Frank through the bars of the cell, now he comes inside.

'Looks like we got us a handyman.'

'I always get the wobbly table. Especially in restaurants, follows me all around the world.'

'You been all round the world?'

'Some of it. More like there and back as opposed to all around.'

'Huh.' Sheriff sits down opposite him. Lights himself a cigarette, offers Frank one.

'Never did smoke cigarettes. They'll kill you.'

The other man nods his head as he takes a long drag.

'Slow enough so you can make the arrangements.'

Sheriff takes out Frank's wallet and looks through it.

'Frank Baptiste. These your kids?'

'Yessir. They older now.'

'Where you headed?'

'Detroit, eventually. Where my boys at.'

'You walking there?'

'Some of it. Got a few things to do on the way and besides need time to think what I'm gonna say I ever get there.'

'You see service?'

Frank fingers his dog tags.

'Marine Corps., sergeant, first combat engineers. That's how come I seen some of the world. Syria, two tours, 2020-2022, sir.'

The cop hands Frank back his wallet. 'Engineers for shit! In the second Iraq war if you wanna call it that, for it sure wasn't no Viet fucking Nam, we sat under tarp for three weeks waiting for replacement parts, that never showed up because the computer lost the order, like they was Fed-exing us fishing rods. Never did see no engineers. Played ball for near on a damn month. That was my war. Lieutenant, 24th infantry.'

'We got better since I guess. If it's broke, we fix it. Sir.'

'That right? That how come you broke the kid's arm?'

'Marine Corps martial arts training programme is how, sir. Had some of that Israeli badass shit in it too, can't remember the name of it.'

The sheriff grins, 'Kid picked on the wrong fucking tramp I guess.'

'Shit we been through, pissant fool thinks he can call me that? Fucker needs his mouth washed out, sir.'

'No doubt.' He gets up, picks up his smokes from the table.

'I'm just holding on until they stop paying me.'

'That may be the case, but somebody got the trains running, must be fixing something. Indians seem to be fixing a lot of stuff too. Can I use the toilet?'

Sheriff gestures to the open cell door.

'It's in back. When you done I'll give you a lift to the county line.'

***

They drive in an easy silence until the sheriff pulls over. Frank gets out, grabs his kitbag from the back seat. The sheriff opens his window and hands him a package wrapped in tin foil.

'Here. Turkey and tuna. What you call surf and turf. Wife makes 'em every day and every day I throw them away.'

'You should tell her not to bother.'

'Don't have the heart to. You ever asked yourself where they get all the turkeys and all the tuna from?'

'Nope. Maybe she trying to poison you.'

The Sheriff shrugs. 'That kid got two older brothers and a mean father.'

'Told you I'm heading east, besides you're the sheriff round here right?'

'You damn right. Take it easy soldier.'

He turns the car around and drives back the way he came.

*South Dakota to Nebraska, 2036*

Lucid dreaming. Frank opens his eyes, above him the twisted pipe cleaner branches of a tree against a grey sky. He's unsurprised to see it's still raining, after the dry heat of the conjured desert. When his wife died this was how he talked to her. Not just in his head, in the frenzied monologue of grief, but in willed dreams, from which he woke refreshed. Dream yoga. He'd looked it up online, that's what they called what he did. The rest was talking to yourself like a homeless person. He may have been homeless, but he could close his eyes and return home. He conjured his own back story. How he managed it he had no idea, maybe trauma triggered it, he'd never had dreams like that before the war, or maybe New Orleans herself, the drowned city had remade him this way; the river, the bridge, Kenny, his wife, the dog, his kids. Like a river, memories flowed easily through him, but in the end there was no nourishment to it, all his dreaming left him fuzzy headed and hungry.

He reaches into his pack and takes out Kenny's journal, starts thumbing through it. Terrible lyrics scrawled in minuscule handwriting, alongside some passable drawings of the squad, capturing them as they were fourteen years before in Syria and Iran. The first war with a camera ban took us back to drawing. Memories of other battlefields, further back in time, drawings glimpsed on the History Channel growing up. Official war artists. Courtroom sketches of defendants. The odd timelessness of this style, never quite in or of the moment.

The things we draw are not the things we take photographs of. Inadmissible in a court of law, which was of course the whole point.

The next page unexpectedly taken up by a three colour drawing of a desert cactus. No drawings of a soldier standing precariously on a pile of corpses holding up two severed heads, smiling for the camera, managing a precarious V sign with the fingers of one hand without dropping the head, quite a feat. Nobody smiles for the pencil. But for the camera, you can lose your head for the second it takes to click, to depress the shutter, the adrenalin God rush of killing can affect your judgement, but to pose for this over time is something nobody has done, neither Hannibal Lecter, Adolf Hitler or Idi Amin.

When you write down what people are thinking, or draw what people are doing, you immediately reinvent them in the image of, from the perspective of, you. That's undergraduate sociology: participant observation, which makes of the world an infinite fiction. Ask one hundred people to draw a man playing a piano and you would think that all the drawings would have something in common. Pianos and the men playing them. Unless you asked people who didn't know what a piano was. Or a man. Then you would get some odd drawings. Ask the same people to draw an old lady being attacked by a man.

This time you wouldn't expect to get as much commonality in the results. The people doing the drawing are in the drawings. All drawing is to some extent a self-portrait. A portrait of what the person asked thinks about, what they have experienced, of the thing he or she has been asked to draw, write, paint, photograph. These drawings are little autobiographies, especially in the details.

If you catch with words some of the thousands of thoughts, flashed images and sound memories we all experience, generate, every second then they read like the presence of an author, of somebody outside the mind it is trying to illuminate. We all have these thoughts, we live in a stream of constant references and lucid dreams, and fantasies, alliances, self-delusions of grandeur, or self-hating complexes which make us see ourselves as we are not. We all live like this every second of every day and night, it's staggering how we do it.

We know this is how we are. By glimpsing how a character, a person interacts with the world, in attempting to communicate this, the act of doing so, of being witness, creates a fictional gap. Reading it makes this gap bigger. Then you have to imagine, you have to try and glimpse all of this without it being said, without insight, you have to dream being Frank. Take away the lucidity of prose, take away the book, the words and what do you have? There are only scenes, like in the movies. A place we know is not real, but which tricks us into experiencing it unmediated. The most mediated of art forms, the most literally contrived and one involving hundreds of conspirators – cast, crew, producers, the culture, ultimately the audience – has as its ultimate conjuring trick the flicker, the darkness between frames, the Meth/Emeth Golem moment where life is breathed into death, where the immobile moves, where stills become movies, the screen a living mirror to our lives, our shadows thrown on the cave wall, this joyous flicker.

Kenny's drawings were snapshots of the people he met, the

places he'd been and the thoughts he had in one image. At the Zoroastrian temple, he reimagined the original fire cradled in an elaborate bronze brazier, rendered with an almost graphic novel like hyper-realism. For him this scene was something out of a comic, a fantastic comic. As he said himself, 'Shit's like *Raiders of the Lost Ark.*'

Franks thumbs the next page, a pencil drawing rubbed into the page so hard it almost tore through it, a charcoal outline of a burnt corpse, the Syrian armoured car driver he named Darius. As if drawn in the burnt detritus of the subject, human soot or some such. After a while of this lucid dreaming Frank's migraine comes on, as it always does, so he closes the journal, his hands sweating on the bloodstained bindings, and slides it carefully back in his pack. *Blood, sweat and tears* he thinks as he hauls himself up from under the tree.

The rain has finally stopped, so he gets going. His headache fades. After an hour of walking through the big country, he comes upon some deep ruts in the open plain, seemingly age old, Neolithic marks on the earth, ley-lines that seen from the sky would reveal some pattern, some design. They ran east-west and Frank remembered something about the Oregon trail in the 1800's, and sure enough he finds some old rusty sign pointing this out, but it had fallen over in the brush.

He's heading east, against the grain of the wagon scars, away from that story, or at least back to where it started. He walked between the ruts, felt them under his boots, paused and looked and thought. Parallel scored lines in the earth, rolling out from the east and flaring west, deep in places and filled with rainwater. Something Kenny would have drawn, those wagon wheel ruts, protected, placed under a charm by the thousands of dreams riding them, Kenny taking his time thinking on it all, riffing on this rich psychic space and making them all wait in the truck, disinterested, sweating under the hot sun until he was finished.

# GIRL ON A BRIDGE

**EXT. BRIDGE - DAY - 2036**

SALLY ANN, twenty something, stands on a bridge overlooking an empty highway. She's tall and skinny with long jet-black hair. She teeters on the river side of the railings. Old Nike trainers sit by her feet on the edge of the bridge, her toes curl over the edge. Her black flag of hair blows out behind her in the wind as she leans forward, a figurehead on the prow of a ship, her fingertips on the railing just stopping her from falling.

FRANK steps onto the bridge. Stops and stares at the girl. He doesn't trust bridges.

**FRANK**
What you doing, girl?

She looks across at him.

**SALLY ANN**
What you doing, tramp?

**FRANK**

Crossing the bridge.

**SALLY ANN**

Well I'm the girl on the bridge so it's up to me whether you can cross it or not. Don't come a step closer.

She leans further out.

**FRANK**

Pretty dangerous leaning out like that.

**SALLY ANN**

Yes it is.

**FRANK**

You ain't gonna do anything stupid are you?

**SALLY ANN**

Maybe. What's it to you?

**FRANK**

Why you want to do that?

**SALLY ANN**

You ever been bored, mister?

**FRANK**

I have, sure.

He steps towards her.

> **SALLY ANN**
>
> So bored that you don't feel alive anymore, that your life is just a memory. Feeling that you wouldn't mind dying, to end the boredom of it all? Before you even forget you were ever alive? Just to see what happens next?
>
> **FRANK**
>
> I seen what happens next, enough to realise being bored probably ain't all that bad.
>
> **SALLY ANN**
>
> Where you see that? Dead hobos by the side of the road, sliced in half by passing freight trains?
>
> **FRANK**
>
> Huh, maybe. I never seen anyone kill themselves though.
>
> **SALLY ANN**
>
> Is it still tough being black mister?

She leans back a little watching him.

**FRANK**

From where I'm standing it
looks pretty tough being white.

**SALLY ANN**

I'm not white, I am two thirds
Lakota Sioux.

**FRANK**

Everybody got a story.

**SALLY ANN**

You know the life expectancy
of a female on the reservation
back in the day was fifty-two.
Shit, men died at forty-four.
They say it was Uranium from
the mines flowing down from the
Black Hills. We took back the
Hills, what's left of them.
Now we live longer. Longer for
what I don't know. Now that's a
story.

FRANK turns to his pack, undoes it and reaches inside.

**SALLY ANN**
(NERVOUS)
What you got there?

**FRANK**

You hungry?

He brings out the sandwiches wrapped tightly in tin foil.

**FRANK**

These a day old, but you look like you need a meal.

**SALLY ANN**

Oh my! Tramp food. Looks like I'll throw myself to my doom another time.

She grabs her trainers, wobbles on the edge, FRANK rushes to help and manages to steady her, hauling her up over the rails. She fixes her wild hair and stares him down, her eye twitches, she rubs it and it stops twitching.

**SALLY ANN**

You didn't save me you know, I do this all the time.

She eyeballs the two packages in FRANK'S hands.

**SALLY ANN (CONT'D)**

Roadkill! Mmm. Rabbit or hedgehog?

**FRANK**

Tuna or chicken?

She looks hungrily at the food shaking with adrenalin.

**SALLY ANN**

Tuna.

He passes her the tuna sandwich. She slumps down against the railings, her adrenalin fled. They sit side by side. She takes a huge bite from her sandwich. FRANK smiles.

# TURTLE ISLAND

*Nebraska, 2036*

Frank sits on a deckchair in front of Sally Ann's trailer taking in the view of the park. Some dogs scratch about, in one corner up by a rusting but functional natural gas tank a few families live, you can tell by the washing lines strung between trailer and post. Down by the road there are youths on pushbikes and a man working under the bonnet of an old pickup. Mixed Indian mainly, some whites, no blacks. She comes out, swallowed up in a big duffel coat and sits on her steps next to him.

'You smoke?' She offers him her pipe.

'That shit? No thanks.'

'What type of goddamn tramp are you?'

'Don't drink neither.'

She goes back inside and returns with a can of Coke and a bottle of beer. She hands him the Coke.

'Coke in a can. Lemme see.'

He reads the words on the can. 'Made in India.'

'They sell it up at Pine Ridge. Beer you have to buy at the casino, ditto spirits, they're still illegal on the old Rez. Meth you can get anywhere.'

She takes a deep draw from the bottle, followed by a hit from the pipe.

'After they burnt down Whiteclay it was better for mixed bloods to move out of the Rez. They didn't trust us not to drink amongst other things. All my life I dreamt of moving away, leaving the reservation in the rearview. Didn't expect to get kicked out. Assholes. Plus, you can still see it from end of the road, which annoys the fuck out of me.'

She points in a vague direction behind her trailer, her thin arm corded with muscle.

'My best friend Lucy still there, we work together. Lives in a brand-new trailer, has two kids in school, regular electricity since they built the solar power plant, a Chinese water purifying thing that means we get less cancer and they even got a new hospital and a, what you call it, a walk-in health clinic. Place is a paradise on earth. She's pure blood Lakota, trace her family way back past the movies and only has one name, Lucy Looks Twice.'

Sally Ann chuckles, a private joke between her and her pipe. 'Still works as a stripper though, same as me.'

She breathes in, long, deep and even, as the meth bubbles through the water, cleansing itself up into her lungs. It pulls her away right into it, like she's already inside the pipe, at a place where she wants to be, needs to get to and is now being breathed back into herself somehow, making it, getting there, hitting that sweet home run.

She exhales. 'This bother you?'

'Nope, not as long as you ain't gonna attack me or any shit like that.'

'This? This just smooths out the day, my problem is I get drunk too quickly, I get all red-cheeked then pass out.'

'How the West Was Won, I guess.'

'That's funny.' She coughs, dry, high in the throat.

They drink and watch the sunset. She talks. Frank unrolls

his pack and falls asleep at some point, but Sally Ann smokes some more and watches some more sky, sitting there on her three-riser step, blanket wrapped around her shoulders, lone night watch on her reservation.

In the morning she wakes him with a gentle prod of the toe and a plate of scrambled eggs. His nose wakes first, she has drizzled Tabasco all over them.

One eye opens. 'Where you get sauce like that? Ain't seen that even in the company store.'

She shrugs, 'I take it from work, they have boxes of the stuff.'

'Huh. Hot sauce, perks of the job.' He sits up, takes the plate and eats. 'You not hungry?'

'I already ate. Come into the trailer for some coffee. I get that too. Toilet, showers is over there,' she says pointing to an uneven row of Porta-loos.

After he washes Frank comes inside and sits at a tiny counter, drinking and enjoying the smell of coffee which fills the space. Sally Ann is getting changed behind a curtain that divides the trailer.

'You never told me your name.'

'You were too busy talking. Frank Baptiste, born and raised in New Orleans.'

'The place that drowned.'

'Yes, it did. Second time for good, more dead in it than alive. Was a man down there, young and clever, he developed an app for your phone that tracked the corpses buried in cemeteries, so when the floods came back, and the bodies floated off they could be paired back to their graves. Paired back to their graves. A clever guy, made a fortune.'

She comes out from behind the curtain, head first, a surprised look on her face.

'Now nobody tracking anything back, it all gone.'

'You OK?'

'Yeah, sorry. Now I'm the one talking too much.'

She comes out wearing jeans and T-shirt, cherry red roll-neck jumper combing and re-combing her long ink black hair with meticulous attention, then braiding it.

'People sure do make money out of the strangest things. I hear droughts get so bad in the south-west you gotta drink your own piss from a bag that turns it back into water. African guy invented it, just a bag with some chemicals in it, saved most of Africa I guess, must have made a million outta that, must have.'

Frank has been watching her fix her hair, not listening at all. He's deep inside, and to get out he has to sing, so he raps from memory, mostly under his breath, Lil' Wayne, the bard of New Orleans.

Sally Ann looks and feels like she's in his space, not the other way round, a feeling of trespass. She needs to reclaim the present, burst the bubble of his past.

'Lucy picking me up soon, my car still broke, we got the early shift at the casino.'

Frank comes round, rotates back to the world.

'People wanna drink at eight thirty in the morning?'

'It open twenty-four hours, so there's no early or late, just rollin' shifts for the guys come off the 'copters and planes from all the time zones they got left.'

Frank shakes his head. 'Lucy Looks Twice, you told me about her.'

'I did?'

Frank nods. 'What she look twice at?'

'Everything. So you better watch out. You see these states around here, Dakota, Lakota, Nakota, all names of the original, OG Indian gangster women. This whole land is a matriarchy, a patchwork quilt made and named by women. Shit, now we got all the jobs, all the qualifications, we own all the uprivers they got left, but it was only when the fucking casinos turned up that the men sobered up. Foreigners still want to deal with the men, the elders, so once again we get fucked, and here I am in a beat up old trailer not even on my own land, taking my clothes off for money and drugs.'

'You been smoking, already?'

'You the one rappin' to yourself over the age of forty. I never had no reason to hate on a black man, don't get me started.'

'Looks like the white man was the problem around here.'

'So, you ain't totally ignorant. "How the West Was Won", you said it. Now they gone and lost it again, and for good, which I guess is progress.'

Frank finishes his coffee. 'You like being a stripper?'

'That's an arrogant question because it contains its own answer, and nobody answers for me, nobody. I'm not a whore that's what you thinking. Only extras I do are hand jobs and you can feel my pussy, but only through the bikini.'

Frank wipes his hand across his face. 'How old are you Sally Ann?'

'Twenty too many questions.'

'What car you got? What's up with it?'

'Chevy sitting out on the street. Hasn't run for six months, probably dead, I'm a stripper not a mechanic, I ask any of the dumb fucks around here they'll want blow job for just looking, so you can try and steal it but…'

'If I can fix it up, get it going, you give me a lift?'

'I got the day off work tomorrow, where you gotta get to?'

'Two hour drive I reckon, we could go in the morning, you'll see, somebody I got to visit.'

She frowns at him. 'Friend or foe?'

Frank looks at her. 'Where he's at it don't matter which.'

'Don't get all mysterious on me, I don't like mysterious men, I like straight up and down fellas, ones you can read like a postcard.'

'How many you ever met like that?'

'I stopped looking.'

'Now how about I fix that car?'

# KENNY

**EXT. MILITARY CEMETERY - DAY - 2036**

A derelict military cemetery. They pull up in SALLY ANN's beat up old Chevy.

**FRANK**

This is it.

**SALLY ANN**

I hate wide open spaces.

She still has her hands on the wheel.

**FRANK**

Well then you live in the wrong place. Come on.

FRANK gets out of the car and pulls out a crumpled-up map of the graveyard from his backpack. His finger pokes the page. SALLY ANN nervously leaves the car.

**FRANK (CONT'D)**

Says here he's in row sixteen, grave number twenty-three.

FRANK leads her through the lines of gravestones, some broken, others missing. She hangs back, smoking cigarettes nervously.

**SALLY ANN**

I don't like graveyards, spook the shit out of me.

**FRANK**

Only the other day you was looking to be lying in one.

**SALLY ANN**

Shit no, we burn. My friends will build a pyre for me.

**FRANK**

That the old Indian way? Thought most of you was Christian.

**SALLY ANN**

It ain't Indian, it's from *Warcraft*.

FRANK looks at her but she's not forthcoming. He goes back to his search, finally finding the grave he's looking for. It's a little crooked, but still standing. The grave has a Wiccan pentagram symbol on it. Painted pebbles lie on the top of the grave, and the rusty casing of a rifle round. We read the inscription:

**KENNETH T. HATCHET. PRIVATE US MARINE CORP JUNE 2 1999 - AUGUST 12 2019. OPERATION SYRIAN FREEDOM.**

FRANK picks up a pebble, a message is painted on it in white nail varnish.

**C/U INSCRIPTION READS: 'LOVE YOU FOREVER MOM'**

### FRANK

Told you I'd come. Just taken me a while is all.

FRANK sits down, his back resting on the gravestone. He fingers the shell casing. SALLY ANN sits down too at a distance, smoking.

### FRANK (CONT)

A lot of shit hit the fan since you gone. Anyways, I never figured why they buried you in Bumfuck, Nebraska, but here you are yessir. You lucky not to come back, you know that. If you could see me now Kenny. What nigh on twenty years do to a man. The power of nature, you were sure right about that.

### SALLY ANN

Was he a Methodist?

FRANK starts laughing, he can't stop. She looks annoyed.

### SALLY ANN (CONT'D)

I say something funny?

### FRANK

No girl, he wasn't no god-
damned Methodist.

FRANK stands up and throws the casing into the trees.

### FRANK (CONT'D)

Kenny was a pacifist amongst
other things.

### SALLY ANN

What's that?

FRANK pulls himself together, points to the Wiccan symbol above his friend's name.

### FRANK

He didn't believe in killing
people.

### SALLY ANN

Then why he join the marines?

### FRANK

Now that's a good question.
He grew up in Corpus Christi.
Tough place for a sensitive
kid. Maybe he was looking for
a way out, from the drugs, the
boredom.

**FRANK (CONT'D)**

Ring any bells? He was nineteen and he'd read all the books in the library. He said that once I thought it was a joke, but he looked at me dead straight. 'You ever seen the library in Corpus Christi?'

**SALLY ANN**

Jumping off a bridge a hell of a lot simpler way out you ask me.

**FRANK**

Kenny here wanted to live, wanted all of us to live. He believed in Mother Nature, in the natural magic that surrounds us all but that most of us can't see. You see any magic?

**SALLY ANN**

Mother Earth is a demanding bitch, I know that.

**FRANK**

He believed in Wicca, that's what that sign there stands for. We got Christian, Jew, Muslim and we got Wiccan. Probably some Methodists here too somewhere.

### **SALLY ANN**

>Just ways of tagging the dead,
>like you said, they got an app
>for that.

FRANK takes a bottle from his pack, raises it to his friend's grave.

### **FRANK (CONT'D)**

>I stopped drinking, but that
>doesn't mean you have to.

He pours the bottle in libation over his friend's grave. As FRANK talks to KENNY, all the joy seeps from his face.

### **FRANK (CONT'D)**

>In a parallel universe you
>standing here and I'm lying
>where you are right? You sober
>and I'm dead. Never understood
>that until now. One of us dead,
>one still alive, just not in
>the same place. In this place
>we had another storm down in
>New Orleans. They stopped
>naming them you hear about
>that? Now it's just numbers,
>long numbers, or they square
>'em to the power of, if you
>follow me. Because, because
>they infinite, tornadoes,
>hurricanes, electrical,
>whirlwind,

(More)

**FRANK (CONT'D)**

twister clusters, we'll never run out of numbers for them, but they might just run out of people to number them. That storm took everything away from me Kenny, like you were taken away. Newspapers called it K2, sounded snappy, they liked that, it fitted in neat with the rest of the news...

**SALLY ANN**

You angry at a hurricane Frank? It just nature, like your boy here said, ain't nothing to be crazy at.

**FRANK**

You ever heard of the ancient Persians?

**SALLY ANN**

Nope, never did. This another trick question?

**FRANK**

Had a king called Darius, his army, stretch from horizon to horizon. Took a message weeks to get from one side of it to the other.

FRANK stands up now and gestures at the expanse of the cemetery.

### FRANK (CONT'D)

He was invading Mesopotamia, to capture Babylon. You know where that is?

She shakes her head.

### FRANK (CONT'D)

Well Darius, he knew where it was. On the way there he came to this river, wide and deep, now I've seen this river same one now as it was then. The Euphrates. EU-PH-RA-TES. His men couldn't cross it, couldn't ford it, couldn't bridge it. So he decided to punish the river. He set his men, his engineers, to divert the water, to humble the damn river before his mighty army. Took him almost a year but he did it and when his army crossed the dry dusty riverbed they spat and laughed on their way to capture the finest city in the world.

### SALLY ANN

Guess he had issues.

**FRANK**

That's how I feel about the world, need to change where the river runs.

**SALLY ANN**

World's always been full of angry men.

FRANK runs his hand over the gravestone.

**FRANK**

You too young to have a family I remember you telling me that. Had a world of pussy waiting for you when you got back home, a world of pussy. Dammit boy you had some sass. And you saw it all coming...

He head hurts, he clutches it. SALLY ANN looks scared.

**SALLY ANN**

Hey you OK? Don't scare me Frank.

FRANK rocks to and fro clutching his head, his migraine out of control.

**SALLY ANN (CONT.)**

Frank, come back.

**EXT. RAQQA SYRIAN DESERT - DAY - 2019**

FRANK drives the Humvee along the banks of the Euphrates. His squad survey the landscape, scan the horizon, everybody singing along to the music except KENNY who sits sullenly withdrawn, drawing in his journal. The radio plays an old hit, BONEY M 'By the River of Babylon'.

>                **FRANK**
>             (sings)
>        When we remember Zion. Yeah,
>        yeah, yeah, yeah, yeah.


>                **MADERO**
>        What a voice Sarge, what a
>        voice.

CLOSE UP ON: Kenny's sketchbook as we see him trace the silk roads, ancient trading routes between the Near and Far East along the arteries of rivers. He looks up and through the window sees the body of a woman, floating bloated in the river, a baby's hand appears wrapped in her undone headscarf which is snagged on something, holding them both there in the water. Kenny tries to speak but is drowned out by his buddies singing. He turns back to his drawing. Nobody else saw a thing. He draws.

**EXT. CEMETERY - CONTINUOUS - 2036**

FRANK sits by the grave, tears running down his face. SALLY ANN looks spooked, she can't handle this. FRANK is now drinking from the bottle.

**FRANK**

Everyone else was singing along, 'cept you, just scribbling away, intent on something.

He takes out Kenny's journal, thumbs to the page he's after. A picture of what looks like a woman drowning, holding up a baby for rescue.

**FRANK**

How you know that Kenny? How you know to draw this? Who is she? You knew who you was drawing? How you know?

He places the journal, open on the page, onto the grave, holding it down with the pebbles.

**SALLY ANN**

Come on Frank, let's go, come on.

**FRANK**

I was driving, wasn't paying enough attention, been up three days, everything dancing up in my face, my world was blurred, jagged. Was never gonna see no RPG, barely make out the road. Maybe you should be with him, with Kenny, he about your age.

### FRANK (CONT'D)

Should be me in that grave, not you.

He gets up, walks away, she follows, pulls him back. Takes the bottle from his hand, smashes it.

### SALLY ANN

Now don't pull this shit, don't pull this shit damn you, you as good as dead like this Frank. Look you can stay awhile, help fix up my place like you did the car. Hell you can sleep inside, it starting to get cold. . .

### FRANK

That boy would have made you happy. Had a good heart. You hear that Kenny in your pagan heaven, it's a paradise right, a, a what you call it, a Valhalla?

### SALLY ANN

Why you save me back there on the bridge? Why you talk me out of it? Damn you Frank!

SALLY ANN storms off back to the car, gets in, lights a cigarette, wipes her eyes and starts the engine. FRANK approaches at his usual slow pace. She hits the wheel in frustration but doesn't leave. He leans into her open window., calm, measured, back to his usual self.

**FRANK**

Can you swim Sally Ann?

**SALLY ANN**

Swim? What the hell you talking about?

FRANK gestures swimming with his arms.

**FRANK**

Can you teach me how to swim?

# PLANET EARTH

*Nebraska, 2036*

The Snake River flows onto the plains of north-eastern Nebraska. Rivers flow immune to those that use and or abuse them. They just are, in the way all of nature is, until they are not. So full of being in the world, rivers are blind to us. We look at nature as if into a mirror yet see no reflection. So the hate is also ultimately fear. Nature shocks us, especially after it has been damaged, it tears away our self-confidence with its indifference, the blasted ridge tops of Appalachia are witness to that.

Perhaps the fury of Darius has something to do with this, how dare the Euphrates flow so high and so wide thwarting the aims of men? Xerxes, his son, (a family it seems with water issues), had the Mediterranean whipped for its sheer audacity at interfering with his plans to invade Greece.

For years we agonised over climate change and the weather, but the real swerve ball turned out to be space weather. A solar flare, or to be more technical a coronal mass ejection (an explosion of electromagnetic power) emits radio waves that took out our GPS accuracy in 2024. For a week. GPS is a weak signal, so the receivers are tuned to enhance receptivity, leaving them open to being flooded, fried by the stronger radio waves caused by the coronal mass ejection.

GPS systems across the globe were affected. Galileo in Europe, Glonass in Russia, Compass/Beidou in China were late to the game but were also were taken out by the flare event of 2014. This led to investment in Eloran systems, based on WW2 technology, which simply emitted a stronger signal with less need for hyper sensitive receptivity. Korea/Russia/China/UK were all investment players in this technology and reaped the financial benefits post-2024.

NOAA (National Oceanic and Atmospheric Administration) space weather prediction centre, funding slashed in 2017, failed to predict this 'triple X class' event, as it had done the X class event in 2014. Despite the fact that 2024 aligned exponentially with the eleven-year cycles of solar events prior to it, and having seen an escalation from A, B, C and M classes of event on a scale it had come up with and monitored. (Each class being an exponential power of ten bigger than the last, similar to Richter scale measurement.)

What with the erratic and attention-grabbing climate changes here on Earth, space weather watch took a back seat. In 2003 the highest ever flare was recorded at X28 when the sensors monitoring it blew. In 2024, there was no scale for it to be measured off.

Exotic minerals trading on the markets of the new silk road countries like Kazakhstan, Turkey and Uzbekistan, was mostly automatic and had been the object of a craze of trading in the early twenties. After the stalemate of western military adventures in Syria/Iran/Iraq saw a rise in get rich schemes for the bi-coastal retired, grey hair, live long, wealth pools of North America, not to say an ageing and also wealthy Chinese middle class, who all focused their portfolios (or had their portfolios focused for them by fund managers) too narrowly and fell foul of so many million mistimed computer trades. Worse, but echoing, the Ponzi schemes that bedevilled post-Soviet eastern Europe during the noughties, wealth was literally reamed out of this east/west cash nexus overnight.

Power outages, the internet and satellites all recovered in a matter of days, falling back on more secure systems, but the automatic financial trading system and the GPS generated time stamps needed to approve automatic transactions, matching trading orders, syncing stock markets and baseline prices across the globe suffered severe disruption, triggering what amounted to a flushing of wealth and savings out of one economy and into a series of others.

Independent fund managers flew by the seat of their pants having mostly never invested in the backup systems of traditional financial and banking institutions. It took almost a week for them to haul, piecemeal, everybody out of the cloud. 'Three nights that shook the world' or 'Time sabotage' were the two scripted titles of films that never got made due to the collapse of multi- media financing and the final proof that the subscription model explosion started by *World of Warcraft* was at an end. And then some.

This space weather induced financial crisis resulted in a haphazard redistribution of wealth that finally tipped the dollar over and over-inflated currencies across the resurgent silk roads, with its own concomitant effects that we are still living with today.

The dream of having our credit card records wiped by one of these space weather events, a neo-hippy liberal fantasy of the noughties, sadly didn't come to pass.

Solar flares: loops and arcs of flaring gas, pouring up and out of the sun, plunging down and back into it. Solar prominences that can be seen from Earth, plasma ropes weaving themselves in and out of the suns umbra. The power of a billion hydrogen bombs, pouring out of the sun and towards us.

Beautiful.

That's nature. A transcendent cosmic phenomenon.

But one without agency. Unlike us, such fragile beings so full of agency, always busy mitigating our precarious existence. In works of magical fiction, it's just this agency that we impose on nature in order to allow us a level playing field with all things cosmic. Think of Treebeard stomping all over Sauron's Orcs in *Lord of the Rings*, or the darker more mystical world of Robert Holdstock's *Mythago Wood*, an eschatological attempt to fuse our destiny with that of the planet, an almost transcendent sexual fusing of 'all things' from first principles; human/natural/animal/vegetable neither one within or without the other. This 'Gaia' is the product of our hubris.

In subtler works of philosophy we witness attempts to give us a less precarious existence by seeking ways to understand and curtail our super powers of agency. By making us 'of Nature', equal to but not above the droughts, the storms, the cold, the heat of climate dystopia; only then can we enjoy, reap benefits from embracing our fragility.

So the river flows, and we rassle with it.

Sally Ann teaches Frank the basics of swimming breast stroke in the Snake River, where it flows slow, almost back on itself in the lee of an oxbow lake. Framed by oversize but mostly broken wind farm sails, his efforts are basic, animal, repetitive. In the best sense of the word Frank is experiencing being.

'That's it Frank, you floating, that's half of it, not to be scared of the water, to relax, to let it flow around you.'

Frank floats for a beat, then subsides, coming up spitting and swearing. Two of the nearest windsails let out a rusty groan and start moving, catching his eye.

'It's fucking cold.'

'Most people learn to swim in the summer.'

They are both in underwear plus Sally Ann has a T-shirt on for decency, the scene more like an accidental falling in, than any conventional swimming lesson.

'I been in the sea once, and that was a lot easier, not to say warmer. But I got to learn.'

She shows him again the simple frog like movement of the stroke, her bare arms and legs forming a blurry white cross under the dark olive waters. Frank's attempts are invisible save for his head bobbing up, chin and the whites of his eyes pointing up to the sky.

Finally, she gets out and wraps herself in a Prairie Wind Casino towel.

'Why Frank? Why you gotta swim? Most kids on the Rez can't swim, why is it so important?'

He stands, preacher deep in the water, and tells her.

'I was a fat kid, never learnt to swim because I was ashamed of taking my clothes off.'

He laughs at this. 'My wife died in New Orleans because she couldn't swim. Saved our baby though, passed him up as the water surged around her. Minute I had him safe in my arms, she was gone, like she was never there. I learn to swim it's for her. They invent a time machine I dive in and save them both, or go back further in time and we both take lessons before we have any kids.'

There is no comeback to this answer, just the piercing dark eyes of one who knows, and the creaking whoosh of the stop-start wind-farm.

'Come out now, Frank. Come out.'

Back in the car, wrapped in blankets, heater up full, the cold has shaken Sally Ann loose, her voice rising above the squealing of the worn-out alternator belt. Frank shaking so hard his teeth click and rattle.

'Not as cold as it used to be, hell, Snake River was frozen over six months of the year when I was a kid, we poked holes in it and fished. All round here has changed. You laugh at me for hating wide open spaces, but you know what, you know what I read? Indians used to live in forests, us Oglala, east, up in Minnesota when it was full of lakes and forests. Only came out on the plains some hundreds of years ago. More likely to paddle a canoe than ride a horse. Stepping out onto the plains was the first step towards the slavery of the reservation.'

'You sound like a politician.'

'Yeah that's Lucy's brother, the one who died, he told us that when we were kids. He said things for people to remember. Full of shit, maybe, but you know, some shit changes, other shit don't.'

'How all that help you now?'

Frank has warmed up enough to drive, puts the Chevy into gear and they move.

'It's genes stupid. For instance, you wanna lose weight, still the 5 and 2 diet the only way, that's because our genes still think we're hunter-gatherers. We're programmed for feast and famine. We had a lot of that recently right, so it must be good for us somehow. All these plains, they ain't natural, plains for grazing, for cattle and you know who brought them west. Weren't here before, the whole land changed for them dumb cows. Have to dig ten feet for water you can drink, the soil so alkaline. I don't know what that word means but it's what I read. These rivers, Niobrara, Snake and all the other tributaries of the Missouri, they had to run their cattle point to point between 'em, like climbing branches of a tree all the way up and west, so they would make it to the coast. Cattle drives, just like in the movies. Indians lived by the rivers so that collision was always gonna be head on. You can still see the marks they made coming down the riverbank, but only when the water low in summer, it risen so much these last wet years.'

'You ever see the old TV show *Planet Earth*? Was on BBC America back in the day.'

She shakes her head, lights a cigarette with a shaky hand, three rubs of the wheel, flame, smoke, inhale.

'Kenny had it on a drive, we watched it. Best natural history programme ever made he kept saying. Whole amazing planet we had, jungles, deserts, animals coming to the river like you say, coming to drink. Birds, lions, giraffe, little things too, like mice, insects. In big close-up slow motion, camera on an eagle they did that too, drones filming hyenas chasing antelope. You interested in this stuff, should watch it.'

Sally Ann shrugs. 'There's nothing natural about history. Lucy's brother said that too.'

That night, by a communal fire in the trailer park, Frank opens up as if he had just been baptised. Sally Ann, on the other hand, has gone quiet, she had spent herself on the journey home and now this unasked-for intimacy has confused her, and she aches for her meth pipe to smooth everything out, at the same time as being annoyed that she doesn't just go and get it. Something about Frank has messed with her mind.

Frank feels the need to restart conversation and rummages for something that will open her up again.

'Met some Indians, back in Oregon, Coos Indians they called themselves, talked to me in their language. Chief made signs at me. The others thought it was funny. You know what this means?'

Frank repeats the sign, hand drawn across his face, the index finger pointing down.

She frowns, tries to recall.

'Black, white man. The pointy finger is the giveaway.'

She smiles.

Frank smiles back. 'First time I been called that.'

'Ain't nothing a black man could do to an Indian a white man didn't get there first I guess is what that means. You either a friend or just another white man. But you have the option.'

'He gave me a lift on his quad bike.'

'Yeah, casino Indians got all the toys, for sure. Now the

Feds mostly fled back east, it's a growing business. You know they fly Chinese in on helicopters from New York or Chicago I believe. No shit, right? Even some worth cookies from Detroit got money to gamble. This country getting back on its feet!'

'Detroit, that's where I'm going.'

'I read about it. Only city without a curfew. Must be some fancy people live there, real fancy.'

'My boys are there.'

'Well you better spruce yourself up Frank, that city got ideas above its station.'

Frank flinches, as she wraps herself tighter into her blanket and disappears into the flames of the fire.

# SMOKE SIGNALS

*South Dakota, 2036*

*'My nation in your history textbooks, they were little more important in the history of Canada than the buffalo that ranged the plains. I in your plays and motion pictures, and when I drank your fire-water, I got drunk very, drunk. And I forgot.'*

— Chief Dan George, 1967.

The 2000's, boom time for the FNC's (First Nation Casinos), giving them, unknowingly at the time, a hole card for the all-in poker game that followed the financial, political and cultural meltdown of the mid 2020's.

First Nations, a subset of humanity that time but not Facebook forgot. The Vietnam War was the last time we used them as a metaphor to explore our own discontents. The sheet upon which we projected our ills. Dustin Hoffman as Little big man, the Forrest Gump of *How the West Was Won*. You can make this up and we did. Native Americans came to represent an innocence lost, an American spirit we had betrayed (not by killing and corralling them, but bizarrely doing the same elsewhere). They always stood for something missing in us, it was never about them.

And when I say 'us' or 'we' here I mean America or as some would have it, Amerikkka, not the European 'me' nor the global other, 'us', but them, the remnant other, a hegemony in freefall: America the brave.

*The stallion skittering across the rain-soaked highway, disorientated, rearing in fright at the cars, the endless cars barreling past, the rain, the expanse of tarmacadam barely controllable under his rider, Kirk Douglas, the last cowboy, unable to cross, crucified on the highway. Platonic counterpart to the last Indian, these images are cinematic gold, Lonely are the brave, lonely are the braves. . .*

In the early twenty first century The Indians of Standing Rock were inundated by the fleeing liberal elite, the young but cowed white American dogs of the last Clinton debacle, confederates of the last age sequestered in the declared safe spaces of social media, in effect a virtual liberal resort/reservation overlaid onto a real Native American one.

Pipeline duly approved in 2017, it never got underway. The 3.8 billion to make it so had gone south. When the shit hit the fan for the rest of 'us' some Nations had a head start. War, ruin, unexpected dramatic changes, reverses in polarity, all of these things and more were to come, and when they did, amongst other deleterious effects, gambling soared.

From a single chambered bullet in a six-shooter, bets taken on a hand spinning the barrel in full view of the audience, like making a big deal of showing what you're doing in a magic show, the hand somehow grows in size as it spins the barrel before placing the gun to the temple and pulling the trigger. Click or death, climax, anticlimax, big death, little death. When the veneer of normality is removed, when the curtain is ripped back, when comfortable lies evaporate, we gamble, we party. Babylon, Berlin, Saigon, Beirut, Tel Aviv, Cape Town, and Pine

Ridge. We fuck, we party hard. It's in *Star Wars*, it's in our genes. By 2036 the new normal found the FNC's riding high, as the United States waned, her flag spilling stars like coins, the New World became the happy (ish) hunting ground for what was once the Third World, and for the rag tag bag of planet wide elites that always have and always will survive the churn.

2036. The Pine Ridge Indian reservation was busy, but a little run down. It had had an investment upswing, but now the profits were falling back into fewer pockets.

The Prairie Wind Casino complex had an Indian theme straight out of the 1950's when it opened in 2019. A kitsch retro style accommodating to the hegemonic demands of how 'Indians' were seen, in what was still the United States of America. Concurrent with Tiki bar culture, and an extension of the fifties nostalgia that persists and enjoyed a MidWest revival after the election of Trump in 2016. Cut to twenty years later and the place feels doubly tired, exhibiting a series of stereotypes that history has almost, but not quite, out-run. So we have pretty squaws serving drinks, fake totem poles holding the place up, gaudy portraits of proud Sioux braves, even a history of the Lakota people mural between the card tables and the slots. Left to right Wounded Knee and Custer's last stand play out on the entertainment stage alongside Standing Rock and the burning of Whiteclay. They even put on 'the first Thanksgiving', every First Nation's Day celebrations. Puritan costumes, hats and bonnets run up on the sewing machines of the Rez alongside native 'fringe dresses' and bead chokers, chest pieces and armbands. In white face the kids from the Rez would play the Pilgrim children, the odd Polish, Romanian immigrant cast as the adults; these were the last ghost dances, performed nightly and with matinees on the weekend.

> *'But in the long hundred years since the white man came, I have seen my freedom disappear like the salmon going mysteriously out to sea. The white man's strange customs, which I could not understand, pressed down upon me until I could no longer breathe. When I fought to protect my land and my home, I a savage. When I neither understood nor welcomed his way of life, I lazy. When I tried to rule my people, I of my authority.'*
>
> — Chief Dan George 1967

America last, America last.

The annual dance in the sky which heralded twentieth-century-style Thanksgiving, hadn't taken place for ten years as the only aircraft are military, federal, foreign or corporate. Those that still celebrate are old and do it alone. Family doesn't travel anymore. The fly over states are now the centre of a country that rotted from the coasts inwards. The kids don't come back for the holidays, the lucky ones are home already. As the coastal boom collapsed and the rivers ran dry they fled east, mostly by car, on foot when the gas ran out, rewinding the dream all the way back to its source. Some made it to NY and others boarded boats to Europe, the people smugglers making their last fortunes, that's how far the American dream imploded, a black hole tucking itself in, the new world collapsing back on the old in a seamless origami-like gesture of defeat.

The chance for solipsism/reflection that the holidays gave the bi-coastal elites, the novels, magazine articles, blogs and movies expressed through the eyes of this phenomenon had become a marker, a tree ring time stamp for this post-Thanksgiving world. Those art forms shrank so rapidly as the new economic model's vacuum shrunk themselves around whatever new realities pertained, that you couldn't find a movie, novel, sitcom, etc. about going home for Thanksgiving after 2020/21. It ceased to be a meme.

So now holidays are FaceTime events for those with jobs in the corporate/military/security industries and access to the net, plus the high liberal elite based out of the last off-shore hold outs of the social media empires that heralded the destruction of an economy was still predicated on the extraction of the surplus value of labour, but this last time without the labour.

'What do people do?' graffiti appearing all over the continental United States as the street expression of this high and post Marxist practical observation. We can and do starve. Automation, of production, transport and algorithmic data gathering, not artificial intelligence, was to prove our Achilles heel, the spreadsheets and efficiencies of production that decide all of our futures. We can and do protest. Biological AI, 'thinking robots' were still the stuff of rumour coming in on the transports from South East Asia and most of that cloaked by diplomatic immunity. We can and do wreck. In these gaps the lucky ones thrived/survived albeit radically reconfigured. We work, where we can we work.

2018–2030. Trade wars, restrictions on travel, the closing of borders. In short order. The rise of the black economy, high-tech drone smuggling and old-fashioned people smuggling fills the void. And where did the people smugglers come from? They must have had other jobs before the collapse, they seemed to just appear out of thin air, summoned by demand. People so flexible, so adaptable that when that opportunity arose, they took it. This is what people do, this is our neo-Darwinian existence.

Casino kitsch is what's left of Thanksgiving, sports, Independence Day and swearing allegiance to the flag, the American tradition. Things recede with speed. Remember when shops, stores that have been there for ages close and became a new coffee bar, or a deli, or a coffee and vinyl shop, and nobody can remember what was there before after about a week? This is our aphasia, an inability to maintain the past in the face of the ever-present.

If you want to know what America was like, then Prairie Wind Casino complex and others like it are the places to visit. The difference now being the people: the dealers speak Lakota, the punters mostly Russian, Yoruba, Uzbek, Hindi, Indian English, Kazakh or Putonghua (Mandarin).

Outside the helipads that service them. Traders, (of goods, not currency or stocks), soldiers, diplomats, accountants.

The parking lot is full of pimped Fords, Chevy's and Mustangs, plus a gaggle of quad bikes for the youngsters. Indians are nothing if not conservative when it comes to transport, in fact the casino car parks serve as de facto transport museums for the brand names of neo-Liberalism.

'Well lookee here Marge, a 1976 Grand Cherokee. Got a 4.2 inline 6 AMC engine if I'm not mistaken.'

Downstairs is the strip club. More nostalgia, like the inside of a tepee nobody ever lived in but the shape of which we are still familiar with. The bass line hook of a sixty-year-old Depeche Mode hit reverberates up the stairs. Gehan and co, late cycle immigrants to the west coast, from the east coast of the old country, Basildon and Southend finally swapped out Santa Monica for the east coast Battery Park enclave where they share an eco-friendly condo, (solar powered energy and twice filtered air) with neighbours such as Leonardo Di Caprio.

The pendulum swings west...

\* \* \*

Frank stares hard into his Coke. His last night, and Sally Ann persuaded him to come visit her at work. The place is almost empty, a few guys sit on swivel stools by the runway. The runway is made of glass and a pair of sad looking sharks swim desultorily back and forth in a tank underneath. The glass magnifies them as they come close to camera, but in reality, they are a lot smaller. Like goldfish in a wobbly plastic bag won at the fair before they banned it for cruelty. It's a shock to see them when the glass is removed for feeding and cleaning. Apex predators. Small enough you could hand feed them.

Sally Ann is on stage working the pole. She's hanging upside down, legs split with her smiling face inches from the dead eyes of the sharks.

The man sitting next to Frank giggles, 'Her mouth is where her pussy should be.'

Frank stares at him, a hard, long, disappointed stare. The man stops giggling.

She's wearing a Native American buckskin bikini. As she swivels back right side up, she takes her top off and reveals nipples covered with flesh-coloured tape crosses; rules persist long after the rulers have fled. A few whoops from the thin crowd as she does so.

'Shit,' mutters Frank's neighbour.

A bored looking Chinese man stuffs a mixture of low denomination currency down her bikini, keeping his hand there a beat, his cigarette floating across his bottom lip like magic as his mouth gapes slightly, like an exotic sex fish. She smiles at him as the song and her shift end, he finally blinks and she releases the pole with relief, as if it had been electrified.

In the toilet Sally Ann takes a hit of her pipe, blowing a cloud into the mirror which obliterates her face. She comes to the bar in a good mood. Orders a multicoloured cocktail and for Frank another Diet Coke. On her tab. This place runs like a company store. Last thing Sally Ann has is cash money. Gas, meth, drink, food all comes from the dispensary upstairs.

'You squint hard enough, place almost looks like America.'

'Douglas brought the sharks all the way from Florida in the back of his pickup. Sea World had a fire sale. Said he had to stop fifteen times to keep topping up the tank with water.'

'They got names?'

'You being funny? Who names a goddamn shark?'

'You're right, what a stupid idea. If I drink another Diet Coke, I'm gonna be sick. You finished? Let's get out of here.'

Outside, the staff car lot is busy with the dance of shift change cars and people. Cooks, strippers, barmen and bouncers, nod, greet, blank and face off each other depending on the status of their relations.

She drives, her old Chevy looks like a baby dragon practised breathing fire on its bonnet. Seared Burgundy. A stripper's car for all time.

She turns to him. 'You ever see the old Indian movie *Smoke Signals*?'

'They made an Indian movie?'

'Funny. "Hey Victeer?" You never heard that before? Everyone keeps asking the main guy in the film about everything because he's smart. His names Victor. That's the killer line of the film, "Hey Victeer!" In that slight Canadianish Rez accented American?'

'Nope. Not ringing any bells. Long time since I saw any movie.'

'Made at the end of the last century, that's how old it is, but still funny. It's set on a reservation in Idaho, can't remember the tribe, some French sounding name, it's a comedy about life on a reservation. These two Indians Victor and Thomas. Best scene in it, this chick Lucy Goosey driving around the perimeter of the Rez, talking, smoking weed, and you only notice about halfway through watching the film that the car is driving backwards. Reverse is the only gear that works. Kinda says it all right, man that was funny. You live on a reservation don't matter if you drive backwards or forwards.'

'What car they drive?'

'That's why I'm thinking about the film, they drive a beat up old Chevy Impala baby, just like this one. That why I bought the damn car. They made a sequel, when Thomas and Victor are older, and it's pretty damn sad, too fucking predictable.

Bummer really because we all wanted to see more of the bittersweet that made the first movie so cool.'

'You still watch movies? Seem to know a lot about them.'

'Boxes of old DVD's donated at the thrift store. We used to project them onto a sheet growing up, had a whole collection. Ran it off the generator, so it was pretty noisy, kind of had to learn to lipread. Never found a cable long enough to move the fucking thing far enough away from the screen, not once.'

'You shittin' me.'

'Dumbass Indians, right?'

'Shit.'

'Want me to drive backwards?'

'Nope.'

'Keep your eyes on the road and your hands on the wheel.'

Frank smiles to himself. She stalls twice before finally pulling away.

# STICKS AND STONES

**INT. TRAILER - NIGHT - 2036**

Music pumps from a bedside radio. SALLY ANN sits on the end of her bed drinking.

**FRANK**

You had enough to drink?

**SALLY ANN**

Nearly.

She lights a cigarette. FRANK turns the radio off. We can now hear the wind rattling the windows of the trailer.

**SALLY ANN (CONT'D)**

You don't like the music?

**FRANK**

Was a time I lived my life to a soundtrack. R'n'B, Hip Hop, house, all that. Now I don't.

**SALLY ANN**

Silence.

She gestures dramatically with her cigarette.

**FRANK**

Ain't nothing silent. Ever since the war I got this buzzing in my ears. Tinnitus. Drives some people crazy.

**SALLY ANN**

I hate the sound the wind makes in here, spooks the shit out of me at night, so I always leave it on.

**FRANK**

Sound of the sea cancels it out. Closest I come to being quiet in my head. Ever since I left the coast it got louder. You can turn it back on.

She hand cranks the wind-up radio, music comes back on.

**SALLY ANN**

I like to listen to voices on the radio. Preachers mostly, radio is full of them.

**FRANK**

Now that would scare me.

She comes over and sits on his lap. He gets up, retreats to the door.

> **SALLY ANN**
>
> You don't find me sexy? Come on Frank when was the last time you had any?

> **FRANK**
>
> I'm old enough to be your father.

> **SALLY ANN**
>
> No you ain't, but you're probably old enough to be my brother.

> **FRANK**
>
> That ain't funny.

> **SALLY ANN**
>
> It's my skin ain't it? I tried so many creams, pills, lotions, none of them work. Douglas says I look better from a distance, which isn't good for a stripper.

> **FRANK**
>
> Fuck Douglas. Hell what kind of Indian name is that anyway? You a pretty young woman, you just don't have to fuck every guy you meet.

### SALLY ANN

Enapay. "Appears brave". That's his birth name. Whites don't get it, so he calls himself Douglas. What about you Frank?

### FRANK

All that meth you smoke turned you upside the head.

She shrugs, rolls her shoulders and 'sings'.

### SALLY ANN

It's fucked up I had to lose an eye in order to see shit clearly.'

### FRANK

Bushwick...

### FRANK/SALLY ANN

Muthafucking Bill.

### SALLY ANN

My mum was into all that old skool rap, left it in my head.

She smokes.

### SALLY ANN

What the hell are we doing here
Frank anyway if you didn't want
to fuck me? You gonna kill me
instead, beat me up Bushwick
style, cos you hate yourself
or hate women, which is it I'm
confused?

### FRANK

Why you have to say all these
nasty things?

### SALLY ANN

I scream rape and you in a lot
of trouble.

FRANK gets up and opens the door of the
trailer. There's nobody around, the park is
empty.

### FRANK

Homeless black guy fucks a
half-breed stripper? Who gives
a shit? Go ahead.

He steps outside. SALLY ANN has retreated to
her bed and is smoking.

### SALLY ANN (SHOUTS)

Now you're using all the nasty
words Frank. I'm two thirds
Lakota, two thirds, not half.

### FRANK

How come you don't live on the
Rez and you ain't got an Indian
name, like your friend?

### SALLY ANN

I tell you it I'd have to kill you.

### FRANK

You ain't got one girl, you
just plain old Sally Ann from
around the way.

### SALLY ANN

I can call myself anything I
want, anything.

Outside FRANK slumps down on the steps of the trailer.

### FRANK

Good night Lap Dances with
Wolves.

### SALLY ANN

Crazy hobo! Out in the cold, no
fire, all alone. Good night!

**INT. TRAILER - DAY - 2036**

FRANK is asleep on the sofa at the end of SALLY ANN's bed. She kicks him gently awake, as she takes her first hit of the morning.

>

           **SALLY ANN**

  Hah, you sneaked back in. I
  knew it. Be cold out on the
  road.

             **FRANK**

  Isn't it too early for that
  shit?

           **SALLY ANN**

  Can't get out of bed without
  it. That's the point, right?
  Who your kids live with, out in
  Detroit?

FRANK gets up, peers out of the window. It sure is cold enough to snow.

             **FRANK**

  They lived with their aunt. She
  died.

           **SALLY ANN**

  That where you going?

             **FRANK**

  Told you I was. Me and the

aunt never saw eye to eye. She
didn't like her sister marrying
no unsophisticated southerner.
And then when my wife drowned
that my fault too. She got me
there.

SALLY ANN is all riled up, defensive, selfish, lonely.

### SALLY ANN

You want them to see you like
this? Look at you Frank, no kid
wants a deadbeat for a dad, no
sir, a drunk, had one of them
myself. So you better steal
some money or do something, you
turn up like that it ain't fair
on them Frank. It ain't fair,
you hear me?

### FRANK

My sister-in-laws name was
Suzanne. Nobody ever called
her Suzy. Married a white guy
called Marlon. So I mention
this to my wife, what's up
with that you know, cos I know
growing up she only ever dated
black men. 'Sick and tired of
the invisible chains' is what
she said, as if that explained
it, as if that explained my
question.

SALLY ANN looks at the pipe, FRANK stares at her.

**SALLY ANN**

How the West Was Won. Funny right.

FRANK looks at her, wide eyed.

**SALLY ANN**

Indian boys the same, instead of chains it's bottles of whiskey and cans of beer they carrying around with them, every damn one they drank, the sound getting louder all the time, you got money back for returns, discount on your next purchase, so they kept them in bags, or tied em up with string, poked holes in the bottom, hung em up, dragged em around so as not to lose them.

FRANK frowns, doesn't understand her.

**SALLY ANN**

The noise, you know, like all the cans they tie behind a wedding car? On TV? Well they make a clanking sound, meant to be good luck, seeing off the bride and groom. Indian wedding like be one from hell, clanking would never stop, trail of cans

go on for miles car wouldn't
get far, breakdown or some
shit, couldn't even make a
single turn without getting
snarled up.

**FRANK**

You got an imagination.

**SALLY ANN**

Thanks to my magic pipe.

She swirls it in front of him. FRANK picks up his bag, shoulders it outside. SALLY ANN comes to the door, hugging herself in the face of the cold.

**FRANK**

Goodbye Sally Ann.

He hugs her. She hugs him back.

**SALLY ANN**

You take care Frank Baptiste.

**FRANK**

I come back this way, I come looking for you, OK?

She nods, wipes cold tears from her eyes, looks away.

FRANK walks out of the trailer park, she watches him leave.

**OR in The real world This happens...**

'And the award goes to Jim Hawks, *Land of Hunger*' (Applause). SAG awards 2018.

INT. TRAILER - NIGHT - 3036

FRANK sits on an old sofa at the end of SALLY ANN's bed. Music blares from her stereo. Sally Ann expertly filling the bowl of her meth bong. FRANK watches in silence. A strange tension builds between him, her, their proximity and the drug. She lights up the bong and takes a hit.

### SALLY ANN

You want some?

FRANK hesitates, but finds himself, like so many, reaching for the bong.

### SALLY ANN

Slowly breathe in when I say, but not too strong, as soon as you full breathe out, don't hold that shit in. OK?

### FRANK

Got it.

He breathes in. A rope of thick white smoke enters his lungs. He blows out a huge cloud that obliterates the room. She lights a cigarette. FRANK turns the radio off. We can now hear the wind rattling the windows of the trailer.

### SALLY ANN

You don't like the music?

**FRANK**

Used to, never listen to it anymore. Was a time I lived my life to a soundtrack. Country, soul music, house, all that. Now I don't.

**SALLY ANN**

A dramatic silence.

She gestures with the pipe, they both take hits and the drugs start talking, dominating the flow of conversation.

**FRANK**

Ain't nothing silent. Tinnitus. Drives some people crazy.

**SALLY ANN**

I hate the sound the wind makes in here, spooks the shit out of me at night, so I always have music on.

**FRANK**

For me running water, the sound of the sea cancels it out. Closest I come to being quiet in my head. I'm sorry. You can turn it back on.

She hand cranks the wind-up radio, music comes back on.

### SALLY ANN

Sometimes at night I like to
listen to voices on the radio.
Preachers mostly, radio is full
of them.

### FRANK

Great, I love that freaky shit.

She takes a small hit, FRANK a bigger one.

### SALLY ANN

One of them says he's on a
boat, a yacht, whatever that
is off the coast of Africa,
preaching to the natives on his
long wave radio.

### FRANK

Maybe they preaching to him.

She comes over and sits on his lap. FRANK
clams up, she grinds against him, he relaxes,
gets into it. They start making out his hand
running up her T-shirt.


FRANK hesitates, pulls back. She twists to
face him.

### SALLY ANN

It's my skin ain't it, I tried
so many creams, pills, lotions,
none of them work. Douglas
says I look better from a

distance, which isn't good for a stripper.

**FRANK**

Fuck Douglas. You're a pretty young woman. Hell what kind of Indian name is Douglas, anyway?

**SALLY ANN**

Enapay. Which means 'Roars bravely in the face of danger'. That's Douglas's birth name. Kind of a joke given what he does for a living but it's an example. Whites don't get it, just look at us and draw a blank, that's why he calls himself Douglas.

He moves back to her, they both smoke and fall back on the bed.

She whispers.

**SALLY ANN**

I scream rape and you in a lot of trouble.

**FRANK**

Homeless white trash fuck's a half-breed stripper? Who gives a shit?

**SALLY ANN**

> My mother was raped, nobody gave a shit.

She starts to ride him.

**FRANK**

> This ain't right.

**SALLY ANN**

> After we done you can sleep on the sofa.

**FRANK**

> Yes, yes, yes...

**CUT TO:**

# HOBO KILLERS

*'F.T.R.A.'*

*I dreamed I saw Joe Hill last night*
*Alive as you or me*
*Says I, "But Joe, you're ten years dead,"*
*"I never died," says he.*
*"I never died," says he.*

— 'The Tramp', Joe Hill, 1913.

The F.T.R.A haunt the minds of every hobo in America. The Freight Train Riders of America. A gang formed and resupplied in waves from the veterans of wars ever since the 1970's.

Hell's Angels came out of World War Two, adrenalin junkies, speed freaks, engineers, mechanics, soldiers, trained, seasoned heroes thrown back into the post-war American dream. A circle of trust forged in the Pacific and on the beaches of France.

The FTRA came out of Vietnam. Rejected, despised by some, and receiving no after care for the traumas of a lost bad war, these outcasts gravitated towards an already existing natural habitat. A shield wall against the outside world. A place where their shared trauma could feed on the unsuspecting hobos that had first populated these margins, the invisible hinterland of switching yards and the empty spaces of the American north west. A culture that had probably begun as soon as the train networks expanded, attracting Chinese and other immigrant labour and itinerants in the aftermath of the Civil War. The Hi line from Seattle to Chicago, West to East, East to West, the midline on the same route, the Union Pacific Sunset route from El Paso to Southern California.

These guys got around.

Black bandanas, gang signs and sigils; an elite, probably a founder culture, and a hierarchy below that. Trains you could ride, trains you couldn't.

Hell on wheels.

Initially, a haven for the dispossessed, a descent into criminality was inevitable in the wider capitalist and policed economy of post-any-war America. With a prison population topping out at three million by 2025, cuts to federal legal representation and the leasing of virtually the whole federal prison system to private investors and security corporations resulted in a de facto class of indentured neo-slaves working for the profit of their keepers. In post-America America, groups like the F.T.R.A. would increase their popularity and following in the imaginations of the incarcerated. In the gangs and societies of the white prison population, (a population that had been rising in proportion to Black and Hispanic Americans since the twenty-teens), F.T.R.A allegiance was a lifeline to freedom, their credo a roadmap to escape as much as Anansi had been to the African slaves brought to the new world centuries before. A semi-mythical folk anti-hero organisation, operating in the wide open spaces governed by the new American Gods: rumour, hearsay, fear and conspiracy, themselves policing this new world with random acts of violence and charity.

*'In an America ravaged by crime and overcrowded prisons, the government sanctions an annual twelve-hour period during which all criminal activity including murder is legal.'*

For these groups films like *The Purge* described everyday life. The ultimate American horror house invasion, of your family being threatened, doesn't threaten these people. They are not cautioned by it. They are outside of the fear everyone else lives by, whether for real or titillated by as entertainment. They deal in fear, both real and imagined. The right to protect your property is, boiled down, all of the law, in what was America, and is still most of the law in post federal 2036 North America. A persistent trope going back to at least the Wars of Independence and the burning of colonists' villages by the British army and their First Nation allies and the effectivity of doing the same in revenge. To be pernickety about the details of this back story, it was Protestant European settlers, operating as vigilante extremists, who were the first to lay waste to the villages in the six Nation territory of the north-eastern seaboard. The Brits, who had bastard native sons (one of 'Our' modus operandi of how to be successful colonialists) sided with the locals.

Slaughter never ends and probably has no beginning, but for this story I'm not going back any further than the revolutionary wars of the 1760s.

The things you can do to people who step over your threshold. Vampires get it, they have to be asked inside. You go in without an invitation? Boom, boom, bye-bye. Everything else is geared up to juicing you up to do this. To protect and survive, is to protect and serve the system. Two words say it all. Home invasion. Your house is your country. We are already playing the OG computer game. Work it, build it, protect it, win it.

The F.T.R.A are vagrants. The antithesis of home owning Americans. They are not rabbits in the headlights; they do not appear in any part of the system. Neither analytics, nor algorithm have found them out. They live outside. No banks, just cash. Zero visibility on what is left of social media. They do not appear in the crossed reticules of the sniper rifles they once used so efficiently to kill the enemies of the country that would now hunt them down. In prison they operate like ghosts, wielding the power of fear that leaves no trace but the obedience of other inmates and the badly paid officers who keep them. Despite this 'power' they offer no thesis of their own, no counter philosophy, because when it all comes out in the wash, which it inevitably does, they play by the same ultimate rule as everyone else. Show me the money. The dough, the green, the wad, the roll, greenbacks, loot, cash, moolies, cash money, hard cash, the Quan.

That is all of the law.

Hobo killer. Men who like killing and want to continue to do so after the legal sanction for doing so has been revoked gravitate to these groups. Hobos have been killed for pleasure by these men for years. For their bindles, for a corner in a boxcar, but mostly for the pleasure of killing, for nothing. To purge an illicit pleasure, or to indulge one. I flash on the character of the judge in Cormac McCarthy's *Blood Meridian*, intricately drawing every plant, flower of the desert, every face of the men he would kill, a demonic Darwin, for when the drawings were done he would destroy the subject, to make sure only he was in possession of it, he had it right there in his ledger. Or that's how I remember the book anyway, read so many years ago. A film that has never been made, the reason why I fantasize, because it would make *The Purge* feasible as a naturalistic drama, it would plunge horror back into the world, and erase the boundaries of genre that protect us all.

The F.T.R.A are under-represented in all forms of entertainment and media. Cults were the thing, with charismatic leaders, links to show business. The F.T.R.A had none of that, just a handful of books, pop up appearances as minor characters in TV shows, a short wiki stub with no external links. Which makes me think how they would be any different in a post-federal America, one where rules are not so much loosened but differentiated across boundaries of ownership. I mean you can get away with a lot more shit in 2036, but there is a lot less shit out there to get away with. My instinct is not to have them as big players in this future. In *Mad Max* world for sure the FTRA would be the bad guys, to be taken down by the good guy, but I don't know if this is either interesting or a potentially accurate projection.

Frank takes a long time to fall asleep, the sense of leaving something behind tugging him back to consciousness. The problem with being out in the world is that you meet people. If you don't talk too much, keep your eyes down, then you can move through it without notice and with few ties. His dog, his RV, Mr Kim and Madero had just about circumscribed a life transfused with alcohol. Out in the world that had proved impossible. He had talked, talked more than he dared to, which was now keeping him awake; words, his, hers, choices of words and having to live with them ones chosen. All of this impeding his progress, pinning him down, triangulating him with memories of time and place. And now he missed his dog. What if she was ill, or dead? He'd have to go back, or suffer the pain of going forward. His survival mechanism such as it was being tested, giving way all along the line, a ragtag perimeter of defences which was now finally crumbling. And as it went, as the flimsy barricades gave way, it was plain to see it had no depth, there never had been any moral resolve, just a thin red line between what was left of himself and what was left of the world. It now hung in bloody tatters. And if he had been asleep, he wouldn't have thought about any of this, he would have dreamt it maybe, enjoying the metaphor in and of itself rather than struggling to find the words to describe what he was feeling; the constant shift between the conscious and unconscious self, worse than being wide awake or fast asleep, nervously generating a hybrid of word and image neither fully realised nor semantically coherent.

The holes in the boxcars' walls let in regular slabs of moonlight. The train passed through Jackson, Bennet and Sheridan counties and on into the low-rise bleakness of the Badlands and Western Nebraska, Frank's eastern journey turning back on itself, back west for hours before another switch, an unfathomable re-coupling on the tracks. Tracks that had been made and set good to go nearly two hundred years before. Hand laid by men, mostly Chinese, black, renegade white after the Civil War, and slaves before that. The hypnotic clickety-clack lulling him finally to sleep and the flickering of the landscape, frame by frame, casting him in the movie of what passes for his dreams.

The train slows as it travels through a derelict freight yard where some years back one had been hijacked and the tracks ripped up. The F.T.R.A claimed it, although what use they had for ten cars of security fencing even they didn't know as it was left untouched in the boxcars, razor wire so sharp you opened the bundles at your own peril. The tagging was the thing, the 'I piss on you', the 'I own these tracks', was what they proved. Reputation, who you were, where you came from was all that was left in these Americas. The F.T.R.A took the engine, killed the drivers and ever since then corps and feds use guide drones to shoot on sight anybody within 200 metres of their property. The drones fly on point for each engine, in front and behind. The tribes enjoy testing themselves against this technology, riding the drone perimeter at night on quads or horses, laying their scent, marking territory, delineating where power ends as well as where it begins, speaking truth to power as somebody once said, although the 200m exclusion zone was infinitely expandable. Legally these drones could fly fucking anywhere.

So maybe all this was really a go on I dare you and then let's see, but everybody was making money so probably for now it's just a game, an old Indian game, but a good one. Respect and reputation never go out of fashion.

The F.T.R.A going up against the tribes? So far, the F.T.R.A avoided the Black Hills central line, although they would never admit it.

The movement of the train vivified Frank's dreams evoking memories of space and time. Between the Euphrates and the Tigris rivers all of life it seemed, in pearls of cities, a sentence conjured to life, the silk road. A string of city names he had no right to know, much less remember: Ur, Babel, Mosul, Nineveh, Samarra, Dur-Sharukkin, places singing to him across vast gulfs.

The boxcar door slides open and a pack is thrown up which lands by Frank's feet. He wakes, tense, instinctively kicking it away, as a man or something pulls itself up into the wagon. It is a man, and he's wearing night-vision goggles. He comes to rest in the corner of the wagon and takes the goggles off. There is no face in the darkness, but Frank senses a lean, ageless, intelligence. They sit there in silence as the darkness settles into a scratchy light.

Perhaps he's still dreaming, a Djinn from that place escaped to this.

'Fancy. Where you get those goggles?' Frank's first foray into the silence.

'Old vet was selling them, said he'd jumped his last train.' A gravid voice, pregnant with nightmare.

After an age Frank breaks the silence again, taunts the fate that lurks there. 'You catch his name?'

The dark pool of man/thing shrugs.

'We didn't trade names.'

'Skinny old fella, white hair, grizzly beard, twinkle in his eye?' Strike three.

'Could be.'

'Went by the name of Trainwreck.'

Frank stands, spreads his feet, both familiar with this deadly intimacy, all of the moves there for the dancing.

'Could be I seen them goggles before.'

'Well, that's just bad luck.' He stands up also. 'Them's long odds sir. Long odds.'

'I know you.' Too elaborate now in the buildup, wasted moves, words taking up energy better spent in killing or being killed.

'Oh, I doubt that.'

They go to it in the dark, a flashing knife, the slam of bodies against wood splintering. At the end of it we see the Hobo Killer's face as Frank pins him to the floor, head hanging out over the tracks. An ordinary face, a pinched, scared face. So shocked by his ordinariness Frank almost recoils, but it's too late, the cosmos can't hold both any longer, there has to be a deduction. Frank slowly throttles him, saying nothing, paying back the wasted words of a lifetime.

Between the Euphrates and the Tigris, The Beth Nahrain, the land of rivers, whose rushing water gifted Frank the pleasure of silence in the cradle of civilisation.

Frank sweats in the cold boxcar. From his head and down his face stinging his eyes. He rubs them blurred. The sweat on his palms dries in the dry cold of the eastern plains. Frank now sitting in the doorway, legs swinging, his back unprotected from the nothing there, mourning the death of his friend, as if he had witnessed it with his own eyes. From his pack in the dawn light he throws Larry's marker pens and paint sticks overboard.

> *'The copper bosses killed you, Joe*
> *shot you, Joe," says I.*
> *Takes more than guns to kill a man,"*
> *Says Joe, "I didn't die,"*
> *Says Joe, "I didn't die."*
>
> — 'The Tramp', Joe Hill, 1913

**INT. BOXCAR - NIGHT - CONTINUOUS**

The train slows down as it passes through a deserted freight yard. The door slides open and a pack lands by FRANK'S feet, waking him. A man comes up into the wagon wearing night-vision goggles. FRANK backs up, the man comes to rest in a corner of wagon and takes the goggles off. We don't see his face in the darkness, but he is lean, ageless and silent. They sit there.

**FRANK**

Fancy. Where you get those goggles?

**HOBO KILLER**

Old vet sold them to me, said he'd jumped his last train.

**FRANK**

You catch his name?

Man shrugs. Tension, violence crackles between them.

### HOBO KILLER

We didn't trade names.

### FRANK

Skinny old fella, white hair, grizzly beard, twinkle in his eye?

### HOBO KILLER

Could be.

### FRANK

Went by the name of Trainwreck.

FRANK stands up. They both know what's coming.

### FRANK

Could be I seen them goggles before.

### HOBO KILLER

Unlucky for you.

### FRANK

I know you.

### HOBO KILLER

Oh, I doubt that.

They go to it in the dark, a flashing knife, the slam of bodies against the wagon's walls. Finally, we see the HOBO KILLER'S face as FRANK pins him to the floor, head hanging out over the tracks. An ordinary face, a scared face. FRANK slowly throttles him.

**EXT. TRAIN YARD - DAWN - 2036**

FRANK jumps down from the boxcar, goggles tied to his pack. He takes a marker pen from his pocket and scrawls his parallel train track 'Trainwreck' tag on the door, lifting his leg just like a big cat, so all the hobo world know who done this.

**CUT TO:**

# SNOWSTORM

*Iowa, 2036*

Frank is caught out in a snowstorm. Fat snowflakes blur his field of vision. He stumbles in a white darkness, falls to his knees, drops his bindle, feels for it on his hands and knees like a blind man, then gets up, trudges on, and when the snow momentarily clears, he finds himself in a landscape littered with the dead and dying bodies of cattle.

Frank keeps going.

He saw a movie once where a man hides inside the carcass of a dead cow to keep warm and thinks to himself fuck that, if he stops he'll die, another flicker of a memory that makes him smile despite his situation.

Sometime later headlights illuminate the snowflakes now colder and sharper somehow, slashing his face and eyes. Tail lights bathe his torment red as Frank pulls himself up alongside a pickup. Inside a man gestures for him to get in. Frank throws his pack in the back, next to the corpse of a small calf and gets up in the cab.

'Never seen a storm like this so early in the winter. Well, it caught me out, looks like you too.' Younger than his shock of white hair under a faded red cap, but over fifty, this man a rancher, as we have known them, driving an old but sturdy Mitsubishi Shogun.

Frank shakes so hard he can't speak, but nods instead his stupidity. The man passes him a flask of hot coffee, a shell-shocked look on his face as he navigates his pick-up like a boat.

Finally, Frank replies. 'Thanks. All these cattle yours?'

The Shogun slides laterally on the road, wind pulling them across the icy road in gusts. Sabres of driving snowflakes stab the windscreen. His eyes trace their arcs back up into the sky.

'Was planning on bringing them down from their summer pastures only next week, same as every year, last weekend of October. This probably wiped me out.'

Frank looks across and observes the man barely keeping his shit together. Fear eats away behind his eyes, he rambles as he drives.

'Back in the day they had an app, remember them? Well, they had one for us ranchers, to keep track of your cattle, he'll keep track of your wife, with these little GPS devices. Would have been invaluable today if they hadn't pulled the plug on GPS. Things didn't work in minus temperatures anyhow. The long hot summer we had, my cattle aren't prepared for this, hardly ever snows until mid-November. . .'

He doesn't ask Frank where he's going. The only conversation is the situation. On a scale of human interaction between hitch-hiking and mountain rescue there's a point at which 'Where are you going?' is irrelevant.

The Shogun nearly runs into the body of a large bull collapsed in the middle of the road. The farmer swerves to avoid it.

'Shit!' shouts Frank.

The rancher stops without driving the truck into a ditch. 'You O.K to give me a hand?'

Frank looks at him likes he's mad, the bull is twice their size.

'Got a winch on the back, we just attach him, and motor does the rest.'

Frank nods, the truck backs up onto the road and circles round the carcass and they both get out. Frank lifts the animal's head, the heat, the smell, the life of it a shock to him as he's never been this close to a cow before, as the rancher slides a loop of rope under it. The bull jerks up and onto its knees, knocking Frank over as the rancher scrabbles away. The bull has gone by the time they both get back on their feet.

'Thought he was dead!' Frank stares at his saviour as at a madman. They both laugh despite the cold, helping each other back to the cab of the truck, Frank slightly limping. The rancher offers him his hip flask and without a thought Frank takes a long pull, wipes his hand across his mouth.

'Sorry about that, son. Almost dead, but stubborn. Seen it before. The will to live is a powerful thing, but the effort will kill him. I'll find him in the morning he won't have gone far, finish the job.'

Eventually they pull up by the outbuildings of a small ranch. Snow lies in heavy drifts on the east side of each building. Frank helps offload the frozen calf onto a pile of others, ready for burning. The rancher's family stand by the door of their farmhouse, the youngest child's face buried in her mother's apron. He shoos them inside out of the cold.

'Thanks for the help mister, you welcome to stay until it eases some. I could do with the help. Upsets the kids seeing them like this.'

'Well, I guess you saved my life, before trying to kill me, so it's the least I can do.'

The rancher offers him his hand. 'Rob Givens.'

'Frank Baptiste.'

'Come inside and meet the family.'

Later, after food and warm drinks they head back outside. Rob pours fuel over the pile, lights it up. Despite the smell they gravitate to the warmth of the fire. Hands over mouths, they both watch the cattle burn. The storm has abated momentarily, a patch of clear sky above, black and cold pin-pricked with stars, having emptied itself of snow.

'My daddy had this ranch before me, his before that. I bred this herd for fifteen years. Grass-eating Galloway, crossed with Angus new breed, last programme out of the State University. High-tech herd if you can believe that. Last ten years it came down to hard work, but we found a way through all the troubles to find them food, to breed them stronger, so they could survive a nature dead set against us. And now they all gone, I let them all down.'

'What you going to do?'

'Don't know anything else.'

The fire burns hot. Rob pulls off his gloves and beats the snow off them on his jeans.

'All of this, it ain't what they called climate change it's everything change. Tomorrow I reckon we got another thirty dead ones, and maybe who knows, one or two lucky ones. Survival of the fittest, if there is any alive, well, I'll try to breed them, AI the heifers with what bulls we can find left hereabouts. They'll be worth something. Let's get inside.'

They leave the fire to the snow which falls, silently as if from nowhere, Frank and Rob obscured from view long before they make the house.

# SINCLAIR

**EXT. ROAD - DAY - 2036**

FRANK walks. The snow has finally stopped, the sun shines bright and clear.

FRANK looks at a crumpled map, his finger tracing a route, his mouth chewing on some beef jerky.

**EXT. FARMSTEAD - DUSK**

FRANK comes out of the woods towards a house at dusk. Silhouettes of iron figures dot the grounds of the farm, life size sculptures of men, in poses of war and repose. As we get nearer the house, we see a shower of sparks cascade from the barn doors and hear a hammer strike an anvil from within. FRANK approaches the door.

Inside we see SINCLAIR, ex-marine, older, leaner and eyes full of intent as he fashions a bar of iron.

                         **FRANK**

    Sinclair.

SINCLAIR keeps hitting the iron bar, he
hasn't heard FRANK. FRANK watches, mesmerised
by the noise, the smell and the showers of
sparks that land at his feet.

Finally, SINCLAIR looks up and stops
hammering. After the ringing the sounds of
the world fill the void, trees, a flock of
starlings.

                       **SINCLAIR**

        Frank. Look at you. You get
        caught out in that storm?

                         **FRANK**

        Picked up by a rancher. He lost
        most of his herd. Cried his
        eyes out.

                       **SINCLAIR**

        Shit, I would too.

They embrace.


### INT. FARMHOUSE - 2036

Sinclair's wife LUCILLE puts a second plate
of food in front of FRANK, everybody else has
finished theirs. The KIDS stare at FRANK like
he's an alien. He eats with relish, a mound
of potatoes and meat.

### FRANK

Nice place you guys got up here, great food. Nice kids too.

### LUCILLE

You planning on eating them too?

He winks.

### KID 1

You sure are hungry, mister.

### FRANK

Let me tell you a story. I come from New Orleans and there we used to love to eat crab, yessir. For my birthday my daddy took me to my favourite crab shack, telling me to eat all the crab I wanted. Well, two hours later I'd eaten so much I walked out of the place sideways. That's how much I loved it.

FRANK mimes a crab scuttling sideways. The kids laugh.

### KID 2

Are you a tramp sir?

### FRANK

After that meal? I'm a king.

He winks at LUCILLE.

**LUCILLE**

George, Frank's family.

**SINCLAIR**

We don't get many visitors.
Kids, go on clear the table.

**LUCILLE**

Could do with the company. Why
you take so long to come visit
Frank?

He finally finishes and lets the boys take his plate.

**FRANK**

Good food Lucille. I remember
you bringing Sinclair that Key
Lime pie in the hospital.

**SINCLAIR**

You ate more of it than I did.

**LUCILLE**

You going to see your kids?
That it? That why you're all
the way up here?

**SINCLAIR**

Enough questions Lucille.

**LUCILLE**

'Bout time.

**SINCLAIR**

Lucille!

**FRANK**

That's OK. She's right.

SINCLAIR gets up, for the first time we see he has a severe limp, one leg is shorter than the other.

**LUCILLE**

Come on kids, bath and bedtime.

They file out, still eyeballing FRANK. SINCLAIR washes up in the sink.

**SINCLAIR**

I heard you was down on your luck Frank.

**FRANK**

Who told you that?

**SINCLAIR**

Madero. She replies to my letters.

**FRANK**

Huh. Well I was never much for writing. Madero. Still makes the best guacamole I ever had, goddamn if I know what she puts in it. How's the leg?

           **SINCLAIR**

I get around. You wanna drink?

             **FRANK**

Nope. I stopped.

           **SINCLAIR**

When was that?

             **FRANK**

Watching you working that
hammer.

SINCLAIR joins him with a bottle of home brew
and two glasses.

           **SINCLAIR**

Well hammering makes me
thirsty.

             **FRANK**

I can imagine. You sell any of
those sculptures?

           **SINCLAIR**

Nope. Never did. Not a one.

             **FRANK**

You ever put them up for sale?

           **SINCLAIR**

Nope, didn't do that neither.

### FRANK

Well, you missed that boat. I like them. Remind me of lawn jockeys they had back in the day.

### SINCLAIR

Never thought of them as lawn jockeys, Jesus Frank.

SINCLAIR laughs, FRANK picks it up and they both crack up. LUCILLE appears at the door, they don't see her. When they do they stop laughing.

### LUCILLE

Just came to say good night to you both.

### FRANK

Good night Ma'am.

She comes over and gives FRANK a big hug.

### LUCILLE

Don't you ma'am me Frank Baptiste, after almost twenty years!

LUCILLE holds back tears, kisses her husband. She turns to leave but hesitates, looks back at the two men.

### LUCILLE (CONT'D)

I didn't see my husband for just over two years,
        (More)

**LUCILLE (CONT'D)**

just phone calls and a few
emails. One night I went out,
bar called Pinky Masters in
Savannah. I was living there
at the time with my family.
Sinclair's sister Kate was with
me, kind of my chaperone, I
was only nineteen. Well these
two boys started talking to
us, buying us drinks, and the
one talking to me, after a
while he put his hand on my
ass. I remember feeling it,
the heat of it through my
dress. I started telling him,
his friend and Kate about all
of you over there. Kenny from
Corpus Christi, Madero the
Mexican, you Frank, the kind
strong African American officer,
yes that's what he called you,
and my Sinclair, my man, my
husband of just two months and
I felt so proud, so warm, I
knew I wasn't alone and it was
going to be OK. This boy, well
his face dropped and his hand,
looked like he wanted to cut it
off. When Sinclair came back we
figured out it was the same night
that you all got blown up.

(More)

### LUCILLE (CONT'D)

I just thought you should know that, Frank. Good night to you.

The door closes and after what could have been a lifetime...

### FRANK

She the one. Nineteen years old. Shit, you a lucky man.

SINCLAIR nods, pours himself another drink.

### SINCLAIR

Proud of who we were, never knowing what we did.

### FRANK

That a problem? What did we do that was so bad? I forgot.

### SINCLAIR

Being part of a machine just before it stopped working, being its last replacement parts.

### FRANK

And that's what those lawn jockeys are, spare parts nobody wants? I don't buy it.

### SINCLAIR

They're not for sale Frank.

**FRANK**

OK, OK. We all remember different. You ever find out who it was grabbed her ass?

SINCLAIR smiles and shakes his head.

**SINCLAIR**

So, why you here Frank if it ain't the art?

**FRANK**

Lucille was right. I got another letter this year. Sarah's sister died back in the spring. The boys, well they're young men now. . .

**SINCLAIR**

And you ain't seen them for what? Ten years? How you feel about that?

**FRANK**

Scared. More scared than I felt in my life.

**SINCLAIR**

But you're here, nearly there.

**FRANK**

Scared they will pity me Sinclair. Maybe I'm a better memory.

### SINCLAIR

Can't have been easy.

### FRANK

World out there is strange, most of the pieces feel familiar, they just don't fit together too well anymore. Catching trains here, walking, seeing the land, shit got real simple again. Twenty years ago we got back from Syria and the shit hit the fan. Wasn't ready for that, maybe I am now.

### SINCLAIR

Spat out from a machine like that, takes time to come round. Feels like a hundred years not twenty. Angry years.

### FRANK

All bust up and spitting nails, right? I visited Kenny too. He still there.

### SINCLAIR

Forever nineteen.

He pours them both a drink, they toast, SINCLAIR downs his, FRANK hesitates, but downs his also, reaches for another, fills them both up.

**FRANK**

You should take him one of your sculptures, keep him company.

**SINCLAIR**

What does he care? He's returned to the cosmic stream, or whatever crazy damn thing he would say. Lucky him.

They drink.

**CUT TO:**

# THE COSMIC WATCHMAKER

*Iowa, 2036*

Frank looks at his watch, hands fixed at midday and midnight. He takes it off and lays it on Sinclair and Lucille's kitchen table which he has covered in old newspaper. From his pack he takes what looks like a large leather handkerchief. He unrolls it to reveal a set of old precision tools. Frank holds up a tiny headed brass screwdriver. His holds his hand up in front of his face. It doesn't shake, and he spends the next hour dismantling the watch and laying all the pieces out on the table.

Sinclair's boy George sits watching him.

'When I was ten my daddy gave me an old car engine for my birthday. Just came round, they weren't together anymore, and left it for me on the back porch with a note. My mother went crazy, oil and grease all over her yard, all over me. But I loved that engine, from a beat up old 1962 Chevy Impala, straight eight with sixteen valves. I counted, polished and loved each and every one. He told me I would always get work if I could fix things. This was the nineties when most people didn't mend shit. When he died I got his watch.'

Frank hunches over the table, over the watch parts, like a general surveying a map of war.

'Way I see it is you take it apart, piece by piece seeing where it all fit together. Then lay all of the pieces out where you can see them, in groups, but all together, in what they call an overview. Point of taking it apart like this is to see what's missing or broken. Trick is to know how to spot it. To see what doesn't work. Engine the same as a watch like that. Then all you have to do is put it all back together again, with the missing or broken pieces either replaced or mended. Or at least you bag it all up waiting for a time when you can, knowing where the space is, where the missing piece has to go, where it fits. You know that you all good, with a space, waiting for that missing part. With a space like that, you still know where you are.'

'Kind of like a jigsaw puzzle. You missing a piece you can always make another.' George gets up and surveys all the pieces.

Sinclair walks into the kitchen, looks at the table. 'That watch ain't ever gonna tell the time again Frank. George, go and help Mum in the barn.'

Frank watches the boy reluctantly leave the kitchen. 'Stopped dead when I pulled my son from the river. Just under a year after we rotated back into the world. Isn't that what they used to say? Rotate back to the world. And what a world it was.'

Sinclair stares at the table, drawn to the jigsaw puzzle. 'You get to collect the insurance?'

Frank nods. 'Went towards the boys growing up. Clinton, he had asthma, which is expensive. Sarah's life insurance. Last year they paid out, I guess they didn't have insurance for the insurance.'

Sinclair picks up a piece with a pair of tweezers. 'You know I wrote telling you to come up here? Hell, I inherited this place when we were overseas, got back, could never sell it. Moving here best thing I ever did. Would have been for you too. Fucking Iowa, right?'

'The puppy lived, you know that Sinclair? She survived the floods, had babies, I still got one, now she's old and you know what? She hates the damp. Inherited that from her mother.'

From behind a magnifying glass, what watchmakers call a loupe, Frank's big sad eye blinks large. 'Here, this piece rotted through, look, broke in two along it's spindle.'

Sinclair cups the tiny broken watch piece in his palm, the index finger of his other hand rolling it back and forth.

'I came back from the hospital Lucille didn't want to sleep with me for months, said I smelt different. I thought it was because of this.'

He rubs his ruined leg. 'Christ, I cursed you then.'

Frank bags up the broken piece, puts it in a small leather bag. 'No doubt. Pussy is a very serious business Sinclair.'

'It is. Took us ten years to have kids Frank, I couldn't…'

'What time is it? You're right, this watch is fucked.'

His hand brushes all the tiny pieces into the bag. Lucille comes into the kitchen, folds up all the pieces of newspaper on the kitchen table, puts them away.

'You staying for lunch Frank?'

Frank shakes his head. 'Detroit waiting for me.'

Lucille stands there with her hands on her hips, in a shirt rolled up, time to get things done fashion. 'Detroit. Be cold as hell time you walk there. They just reopened an electric trainline between Chicago and Detroit. Place is booming. Most currencies what's left are in circulation, they even got an intranet that calculates exchange rates. They got farms on roofs, right in the middle of the city, livestock too, stacked up in parking lots if you can believe that.'

All this information confuses Frank. Sinclair puts his hand on Frank's shoulder. 'Why don't I lend you some money, Chicago nearby, you can take the train, arrive in style.'

Frank shakes his head. 'No thank you, I done with trains, they give me bad dreams.'

He hands him the map marking Kenny's grave. 'Besides, walking is good for the soul Sinclair.'

Sinclair holds up the map. 'It true they buried him with a pagan tombstone, like he said he wanted?'

'Yeah. Wicca was one of thirty-eight religions we had in the United States army. You believe that? I can't name more than four.'

'That's four too many you ask me.'

Frank hugs Lucille and their boys come running out of the porch as he gets ready to leave. They offer their hands up for a shake. Frank bends to offer them his.

'I'll be back, bring some boys of my own.'

'What's their names?' one of the two asks.

'Clinton and Frank Jnr, and they're just about grown up.' Frank smiles as he stands up straight, shouldering his bag.

Sinclair walks him to the edge of his land, to the road that leads back through the wood. Rooks perch in the first big oak on the treeline. They watch them scatter into the sky.

'Don't you go nowhere Sinclair, here just about right. Country so big, trouble have to look hard to find you.'

Sinclair shows him a pistol he has tucked down the back of his trousers. 'Place feels alive, worth fighting for. And it ain't for God, or no goddamn country either.'

Frank takes the pistol, wordlessly checks it out, like revisiting an old hobby, weighing it in his hand, he releases the magazine, thumbs the top round and slams it home, passing it back to Sinclair. 'Now you sound like Kenny.'

'No doubt. He talked so much, a little bit of him stuck to each of us.'

'Yeah. I like that. Madero thinks her soul is in her guacamole, so she's way gone. . .'

They exchange the same Marine Corps handshake, embrace muttering 'Brother from another mother.'

Frank takes off into the woods. Sinclair rubbing his leg, watches him go, slides the pistol back in his waistband.

# DELETED SCENES

**EXT. ST. BERNARD'S PARISH/NEW ORLEANS 2024 - DAY**

POV helicopter onto: The DOG, a tiny puppy soaking wet and shivering is being hugged inside the shirt of an equally terrified FRANK JNR, 7, FRANK'S oldest son. They sit in an open rescue crate, which is being winched by helicopter off the roof of a flooded house. Disappearing below them we see FRANK and his wife SARAH holding a BABY. The 'copter lifts away as the water gets higher.

                                  **CUT BACK:**

**EXT. RV CAR PARK - NIGHT 2036**

Most people are asleep, a few guys sit out smoking. Nobody notices FRANK, standing outside his old RV, dripping wet and half naked. He throws an empty bottle at the side of the RV. CHARLIE comes out, half asleep and pretty pissed.

#### CHARLIE

Now Frank what you do that for? I thought you was gone. You lost that game of cards fair and square, ain't no going back on it now.

#### FRANK

I forgot something.

#### CHARLIE

So why didn't you knock on the damn door.

#### FRANK

My marine issue night-vision goggles.

#### CHARLIE

What the hell. Well I suppose they'll fetch a few dollars on the outside. Hold on.

#### FRANK

I ain't selling them. They'll be useful. Out there.

#### CHARLIE

Why you soaking wet?

#### FRANK

I ain't never been in the water, lived here almost five years.

                    **CHARLIE**

          So you decide to go swimming
          tonight?

                     **FRANK**

          It's a free country. Anyway I
          can't swim, so I was gonna wade
          in, just to feel the ocean.

                    **CHARLIE**

          You talk too much Frank. Wait
          there, I'll go get the glasses.

                     **FRANK**

          Night-vision goggles. They
          under the bed.

                    **CHARLIE**

          Yeah, right.

He walks up into the trailer and slams the
door shut behind him.

                                        **CUT TO:**


**INT. RV - CONTINUOUS**

CHARLIE rummages under the bed. He gets up to
find FRANK standing behind him in the cramped
trailer, dripping wet. He jumps.

                    **CHARLIE**

          The fuck are you doing in here,
          give me a damn fright!

**FRANK**

Didn't hear me, did you? Damn I still got the moves!

**CHARLIE**

Special forces training programme. Right? I get it.

He chucks him the goggles.

**CHARLIE (CONT'D)**

Now fuck off Frank, it don't feel comfortable having you in here.

**FRANK**

But this is my trailer Charlie, my home and my dogs home.

**CHARLIE**

Was Frank, it was your trailer. Some people only ever get things in order for somebody else to take 'em away, you ever think of that Frank? Like a slippery eel, things just slip out of your grasp, whereas they stick to others like they was covered in honey. Just the way it is. And that old dog? It won't last a week where you going.

**FRANK**

> Now you're running off at the
> mouth Charlie.

Sunrise creeps into the RV through the back window. For a beat it feels like FRANK is going to hit CHARLIE. It passes.

**CHARLIE**

> You got a change of clothes in
> that bag?

He throws him a towel.


**EXT. TACO STAND - DAY 2036**

FRANK sits eating a plate of taco beans with a side of guacamole. His dog laps from a bowl of water. The Mexican chef, MADERO, squats next to him having a smoke.

**FRANK**

> You ever think about Kenny, Rose?

**MADERO**

> There were a lot of Kenny's
> Frank. Lot of water under the
> bridge since then Ese.

FRANK pinches his nose, pain flashes across his temple.

**FRANK**

> But you know the one I mean
> right?

She nods.

**MADERO**

There's no use to all your thinking, doesn't do you any good right? We alive and he dead, gotta look after yourself now Sarge.

**FRANK**

I hear you, but Kenny, he come back to me a lot.

**MADERO**

Here, eat.

She passes Frank a plate of fish tacos and some more guacamole. FRANK concentrates on his food, feels better. A little time passes.

**FRANK**

When you gonna give me the recipe?

**MADERO**

I tell you I have to kill you. That shit is my soul man, my connection. My culture.

**FRANK**

Your soul is in the guacamole? That's deep.

### MADERO

Eat up Frank, you bad for
business brother.

MADERO finishes her cigarette, gets up. FRANK takes a long pull on his bottle of wine.

### FRANK

Bad for business, yes Ma'am,
suppose I am.

### MADERO

Brother from another mother.

### FRANK

Hermana de otra madre.

They execute an elaborate old school Marine Corp Hand shake. FRANK shuffles off, his dog follows.

# BINDLESTIFFED

**EXT. FILM SET - DAY - 2017**

High production commercial film set. Downtown L.A, *Fast and the Furious* style street race. Lots of people, lots of bustle. Muscle Cars race towards us weaving in and out of traffic. A classic stunt take. We watch the action through the director's monitor.

                                                **CUT TO:**

**EXT. FILM SET - CONTINUOUS 2017**

Mid shot: Forest screeches to a halt in a souped up Mustang, wearing shades, with a hot white girl sitting next to him. He gets out of the car.

                    **ASSISTANT DIRECTOR**
        And out! Take a break folks,
        close ups after lunch.

                                                **CUT TO:**

**INT. TRAILER - CONTINUOUS - 2017**

Forest takes off his shades and sits down in his trailer. He picks up a copy of *Variety*. A PA brings him a banana smoothie and exits. Forest is reading a copy of *Variety*. There's a knock at the door.

                  **FOREST**

  Yeah, come in.

It's his agent.

                  **MORRIS**

  How's it going? Great shoot, looks like they're throwing the money around right?

Forest throws him the copy of *Variety*.

                  **FOREST**

  *Bindlestiff*, re-titled *Land of Hunger*. They gave that part to John fucking Hawkes.

                  **MORRIS**

  I saw that...

                  **FOREST**

  Supposed to be the black Charlie Chaplin.

MORRIS shrugs.

                  **MORRIS**

  Fucking Hollywood.

**FOREST**

Remember when he left his dog with the old Jap guy, damn that got me.

**MORRIS**

They'll probably fuck it. What can I say? I'm sorry Forest.

**FOREST**

'She'll eat anything, ain't no trouble, just sit her in the sun out front. Hates the damp, loves the sun. That's my dog. Now stay girl, stay.'

**MORRIS**

Great dialogue. I hear they dumped the Brit writer too.

**FOREST**

Well, I hope they paid him off well.

**MORRIS**

We all get paid right?

The AD calls the end of lunch.

**ASSISTANT DIRECTOR (OS)**

Back to work ladies and gents. Vanities on set please!

**FOREST**

> Yep, we sure do.

Forest sucks hard and finishes his smoothie. Morris exits the trailer, turns at the door, Forest lost in his thoughts tinged with a low-grade anger which is just sadness.

**MORRIS**

> 'When's a man gonna learn, that river card only ever gonna bring him trouble?'

**FOREST**

> You ever meet Wesley Snipes?

Morris has a resigned smile on his face. Forest looks up, nods and goes back to work.

# PINKY MASTERS

*Intermission*

It's a trope of American culture that in the armed services people from different backgrounds become friends. This 'fact' explains why a black guy from X is friends with a white guy from Y. How else would they have met? With a fractured and de facto segregated education and health system where else would different classes and races work and play together? Sports are the only other space I can think of that has the same effect as the military for bringing people together. It is in the services and on the sports field that we have come to be familiar with the mixing of race and class. Notwithstanding the American officer system is still class and race biased, still, it is possible for Frank Baptiste, for example, to be an Sargeant and poor white grunts like Kenny and Sinclair to serve under him.

The army sucks up the poor and the disenfranchised alongside the career officer West Point high achievers, creating an odd imbalance, a potentially toxic partnership on the ground. Which is why basic training is so crucial in attempting to overcome this divide. To break down and remake the outcast and disaffected into efficient fighting men and women to serve together under their officers.

You sign up for eight years, active service cuts this to four or six. That's the military service obligation. After that retention bonus schemes lure you back. The working class re-up because it's a way of life, that and there was no other place for them that paid the bills. Tours of various lengths with appropriate remuneration, including the reserves. Let's not forget commissions for new officers, who serve at the 'Pleasure of the President', the ultimate rolling contract.

Black, white, Hispanic, Native American men and women, brothers and sisters from other mothers and fathers.

That's how Frank, Madero and Sinclair feel about each other. Bonded together in combat. Kenny also, but being that much younger he stood outside this band of brothers, almost like a mascot/son to be protected.

In movies if you save somebody's life they usually owe you a debt of honour. In real life it's more the embarrassment of intimacy, that sits between the saver and the saved, as if one's mortality is an obscene remainder, something that's almost shameful to draw attention to, that actually shouldn't be left over at all. Better to die; letting your guard down is exactly this, allowing yourself to be saved by somebody else.

Is that why Frank hadn't seen Sinclair for twenty years? Maybe in part. That and the changes wrought to the fabric of the society they lived in making travel of any kind, even communication, problematic. As in all movies, Frank was just doing his job. Him saving Sinclair was a reflex of his training as much as his humanity. The moving parts of all systems rely on each other by their very proximity if nothing else; a case of push me pull you.

Frank's addiction was also a factor in him being closed off. He lived in an enclave after all and Frank wasn't the type to write letters. Had he ever been a big emailer? Did Sarah and he enjoy a satisfying remote relationship whilst he was on tour? Does anybody?

Sinclair must have told Lucille about the people he was living and fighting with. These stories, communicated by letter, email or on the phone, created a bond between her and him, but also with them. Sinclair must have been a great communicator. Enough for her to keep her pants on for two years.

Pinkie Masters is an oddball bar on Drayton Street in Savannah, Georgia where in spring the streets are garlanded by the catkins of weeping willow trees. Pinkie Masters. What Americans would call a dive bar. A dog bowl on the bar for a regular's pooch to slurp from. A pug as I recall.

It was there that Tippins and I met the young sexy hippy wife and her sister-in-law, on the cusp of her husband's return. She told me how excited she was to see her man again safe and sound and finally she giggled, slightly drunk and euphoric, you know, get to make love again. Neither I nor Tippins made a move on either of them. I was touched by her candour; her flirting with us and playfulness with her sister-in-law, who mock acted her role as chaperone. She had a man overseas; her role as defined as his was. I flashed on the 1940's, where in bars up and down the North American coast, bars like the Captain's Table on Main Street in Santa Monica, places like Pinkie Masters here in Georgia, places from which men, men and women, shipped out.

They were two young women out to get drunk to celebrate the safe return of a loved one. Such an old-fashioned idea, ancient even, but one remade, recast by every overseas conflict and foreign intervention. Home and away. Home doesn't change, home waits by a slow clock, whilst away everything, life itself is up for grabs and time runs erratically, both fast and slow. The Odyssey, fun for those on it.

For Frank and Sinclair coming home, the dichotomy collapses and they found both have become fraught with uncertainty, disaster and the struggle for survival. There was no gap. Overseas came home. As Sinclair mused, they were the last replacement parts.

That night at Pinkie Masters we got falling down drunk, ('Polluted' as an old Irish girlfriend used to say), twisting my ankle stumbling on a high kerb on the way back to the hotel, picked and propped up by Tippins (ever the rock, albeit an out of his mind one), we fell over repeatedly until we gave up and rolled around in the street roaring and disorientated as to the way home, until a cop car pulled up and helped us back on our feet, pointing us the hundred yards to our hotel. I had to have a walking stick on set that week as my ankle ballooned to baseball size. We were shooting a Nascar campaign down in Daytona, home of the Indy 500 and *Spring Break*. The last time I had been there was in 1984, where they held a wet T-shirt competition at an event called 'Titfest '84' in a bikers' dive called The Shark bar, its claim to fame being a stage with a glass tank with mangy looking sharks in it, that the girls paraded up and down on top of.

The cinematographer on the Nascar shoot also walked with a stick that week because he had an attack of gout. One of the race drivers we were filming had a wife called Buffy which I thought was authentic. They played characters in a spoof of a QVC shopping channel selling auto parts, which was less so.

\* \* \*

In the *Bindlestiff* screenplay I wanted to ask what friendship meant to these characters, what was it made up of, what was its DNA? Combat, jokes to get you through, the ease of banter, trust in each other in times of danger? Things that survive long after they happen, keeping us connected somehow, because of our lived experience of war and return. How long do these bonds last, how long is friendship good for, what's its half-life? And how does friendship compete with family? How can we extend our circle of trust beyond blood when the world contracts around family/ethnic/religious/political identities?

Friendship and family both ultimately act as a balance to the fact of being alone. Being alone physically, in nature, but also alone psychologically. How the mind takes you places far away from others. We can't think together, not even in 2036. There was no grand universal conversation that died with the dream of an independent/inter-dependent ever evolving internet. So much has devolved. How can we stop ourselves returning to the caves?

Drugs of all kinds keep us up and on our feet, keep us productive for both family and society, making us dependent and dependable after a fashion.

Meth takes you down a lonely road, one where it's all you, body and mind as one territory to explore and exploit. A great drug for coping with trauma, like heroin, but meth is different, it's aggressive, it demands so much of you, outrunning any commitment you might make to others. You replace friends and family with yourself. A true chemical wedding. It offers a totality of experience. I would argue that by 2036 meth in one form or another, legal/illegal/proscribed/prescripted will be the interface with 'the world' for a huge number of us.

'Lucy Looks Twice' and 'Sally Ann' are poster girls for a living with drugs reality that much of the 'free world' has already become used to. That plus the reality of thousands of South East Asian truckers who have been driving on Ya-Ba pills for decades.

The film they made, *Land of Hunger*, pompous in name and content, replaces radical ambiguity with the casual and lazy tropes of tragedy, guilt and redemption. The overcoming of obstacles on the road to recovery, in a movie where the (anti) hero still stands centre stage, providing the gravity for everything else. Frank comprises enough good things to hold him together, an identity that prevails rather than one that always falls short of adding up.

But I don't know if we have to add up any more. Who can make sense of themselves, who isn't contingent on others for their identity? Falling short in a series of partial resolutions is good enough and generates less anxiety. The language of winning, losing, achieving, failing, falls away. Good and bad evolve into a workable grey-scale they always deserved.

*Moonlight* the movie featured a drug dealer who was both a father figure and a dependable partner. He had values. In parts he was a good guy. In parts he exhibited kindness. In parts we can all be good and kind. Totalities are banal. Nobody believes in them, nor wants them. They create bad role models, or should we say more accurately, no model at all for how to live now, how to live tomorrow.

Identity made up out of the pieces of a broken mirror to misquote Lacan referring to the Ego. More practically, Paul Beatty argues that now we all have to manage different identities depending on who we are talking to or interacting with. (Online, offline, on the street, in meetings, in court, in prison, on the sports field, etc. etc.)

We have many faces yet are not two-faced.

We negotiate the world because the world demands we show it the part of us it needs to function at different times. A working woman, a spending woman, a loving woman, a mother, a patriotic woman, a woman who functions for the machines. A woman who knows her PIN numbers and keeps a clean fingerprint ID. A woman whose retina is recognised.

As a black man, as a writer, as a black writer, as a (black) father, a (black) husband, an (etc.) academic, a vox pop, Paul Beatty has many faces. And they are all contingent. Percival Everett explores the same territory in his writing, for example, the novel *I am not Sidney Poitier*, where the main characters name is 'Not Sidney Poitier'. And that's Franks story. Everett has also written a series of black westerns, which I haven't read yet, but if I had I assume they would have informed this narrative.

The new writers on the film worked out a full economic/social/political logic to the world I had barely sketched, to the extent that you could probably make it into a game, as detailed as Sid Meier's *Civilisation* franchise, or FTL, or the indie developer *Suburbia* type games, games of investment planning and the laying down of infrastructure. At least in *The Road* you never really knew what had happened, the catastrophe was nebulous, it was more like a story set in the open game world of *FarCry5*. The film and game were too existential, a one dimensionality I wanted to sidestep; a too easy interpretation of *what happens if*.

Kill, kill, kill. Protect your son above all else, family above all else, as if the nuclear family prison, having been smashed wide open by global meltdown of one form or another, spooks us into sustaining the lie of home and hearth vs some kind of survival through communality. Worse than that, it was as if the nuclear family exploded inwards, destroying us and irradiating others. Think about the contingent extended family groups that morph through the *Walking Dead* series, around the core of main actors who are blood relatives. Is this all we can hope for?

In *The Dispossessed* Ursula Le Guin sidesteps the nihilism of so much science fiction by pitching an Anarcho-Syndicalist planet against an Ayn Randian existential capitalist one. Sci-Fi that asks questions. *Star Trek* for years, in a minor key, has entertained different moral worlds to our own. Soviet Sci-Fi the same in both cinema and fiction. The questions they all ask are Idealist. The answers are for us to contemplate. If the end goal is death, mutual annihilation then why have an end goal? Frank nails it when he talks about the familiarity of pieces that don't add up to any meaningful whole any more. And that's OK, it has to be because that's how *now* works. Just like Lacan's smashed mirror of the (always) recovering ego. Man as 'Hommelette', made up of so many broken eggs, but a living and thinking one nonetheless, and this from a man not known for his wit.

Frank. A familiar man who doesn't add up, reflecting a familiar world that doesn't either.

The future will be less whole and less directional; the transient community of the hobo jungle, the post federal success of the plains Indians, etc. The wholeness in themselves of the smaller pieces takes us back to the Anarcho-Syndicalist internationalist localism, to sound clumsy for want of better words, posited in *The Dispossessed* the smartest Sci-Fi novel never (yet) made into a movie.

*Land of Hunger* was too full of itself and its arch referencing of the black lives matter movement, of exploiting murder and incarceration for cultural effect, effectively for bums on seats, of casting bad cops and good robbers, positing a future America gripped by a crisis of morality that demands black and white solutions, empty questions and fake answers, problems solved by a conventional hero, and this at the same time as changing Frank's ethnicity, which I have to pass over in relative silence since I took the money.

How to deliver the satisfaction of resolution in a story, or persuade an audience into enjoying other pleasures from ninety minutes of entertainment. The pleasure of the open end, of questions refreshingly put, of humour, of emotional truth, of flaws, of being great only in part, of aiming high and failing, but failing in good faith. This can be the true spectacle of cinema, yours for ten bucks a ticket.

Should Frank re-enter the lives of his sons? Is this too pat an ending for my story? Or does he return to Sally Ann, challenging me to somehow find a way beyond the tramp and stripper cliché? And the journey from L.A to Detroit is this too much of a story arc, is it too damn obvious? And where do we leave the damn dog? Perhaps Frank never left and there was no journey, him and his dog just stayed put in El Segundo. And Larry, Trainwreck and the hobo killer... too much?

But this is where I get off. Hollywood has ejected me. On the final flight home, I got boarded first with all the upper-class passengers, a fraud, an interloper and pale hobo to the end...

# LUCID DREAMING

**EXT. EL SEGUNDO BEACH - NIGHT/FLASHBACK 2036**

FRANK sits watching the breakers. The hulks of rusting ships lay at anchor on the horizon. He nurses a black eye, a crumpled letter in his other hand. He squints at it.

                **FRANK (V/O)**

You write and ask me why I a bum, why I drink, why I live like I do, why I don't visit. Why? I don't know son, I don't know and never did. We all seen what it's like to take away the blanket of our comforts and its shit blood piss and death. I seen it in Syria and I seen it in St. Bernard's Parish New Orleans, where I was born and raised.

                    (More)

### FRANK (V/O)

Frank Baptiste, from San
Domingo and never a slave,
don't you forget it, is what
my father told me. And I ain't
a slave to the question Why?
Civilisation is as thin as ice,
and we skating on it every day,
and every day the temperature
rises. All the sympathy in the
world don't mean shit. Never
did. Why's that? Why? Why?

FRANK drinks endlessly from the bottle, stumbles to his feet, wades calf deep in the surf, throwing the empty bottle into the night sea.

**CUT TO:**

**EXT. TRAIN YARD - DUSK - 2036**

Push past faded train depot sign 'Monsanto Klein Welcome American Freight Lines'.

LARRY leads FRANK to a hole in the fence, hidden by a stand of trees.

### LARRY

Follow me, keep close.

### FRANK

Why they call you Trainwreck?

### LARRY

Cos I survived one. We ain't
got time for a history lesson.

They run down the siding, keeping low and
end up behind a shed near the rail tracks.
Locomotives, wagons, maintenance vehicles
populate the yard. Work lights pick out the
main junctions. From behind the cover of the
shed we can see some railroad security men
patrolling the yard.

### LARRY (CONT)

Now this is the game, rules are
real simple. We wanna jump the
trains and they want to stop
us.

### FRANK

Games the same all over the
world, just different players.

### LARRY

Is that so? Look over there see
those men lurking up on that
siding?

### FRANK

Yep, more train hoppers I
guess.

### LARRY

What's different about 'em?

### FRANK

Nothing, same as us, broke-ass
folks.

#### LARRY

Look closely, something different for sure, they don't have no packs, nothing. You know why? They looking to roll you and me for what's ours, likely to stick us in the process. Damn jack rollers.

#### FRANK

OK. I see 'em.

#### LARRY

They come in our car you better be ready to fight.

#### FRANK

I can do that. What about the trains?

#### LARRY

Easier since they switched back to diesel, you couldn't hear the electric ones coming, let alone flip 'em. Cow crates are the best, grainers too, but they don't have much space. Most liners only stop at night, need fox eyes to see 'em come in...

FRANK goes in his pack and brings out his night glasses.

                    **FRANK**

These help?

                    **LARRY**

Well I'll be damned it's GI
fucking Joe.

LARRY takes them and scopes out the yard.
Starts laughing.

                **LARRY (CONT'D)**

I knew you was smart, this
gonna be a piece of cake army
boy.

                                    **CUT TO:**


**EXT. TRAIN - NIGHT - 2036**

Both of them run with their packs for a
speeding train. LARRY gets up first, sprightly
for an older guy. FRANK struggles to keep up,
throws his bag up into the wagon and then
grabs an outstretched wiry arm to help haul
himself up. He disappears into the boxcar.

They catch out.

# OH KENNY!

**INT. TENT - SYRIA - DAY - 2022**

FRANK is sitting at his desk, working on reports. He shakes his wrist involuntarily, checks the time. A head pops round the tent flap.

**FRANK**

Yes.

**KENNY**

I talk to you Sarge?

**FRANK**

Sure Private, you're new right?

**KENNY**

Yessir. Name's Kenny, Kenny Hatchet.

**FRANK**

You a singer? Name sounds like a singer's.

**KENNY**

No sir, can't hold a note sir, I play bass guitar. . .

**FRANK**

You arrived when?

**KENNY**

Reinforcements out of Fort Benning, flew in this morning sir.

**FRANK**

Reinforcement? How old are you Hatchet?

**KENNY**

Nineteen, sir. Well not until next week, birthday is on the...

**FRANK**

Eighteen then.

He shakes his head, wipes his hands over his face.

**FRANK (CONT'D)**

What can I do for you Private?

**KENNY**

Well sir, I just thought I should inform you that I am a practising Wiccan, sir.

**FRANK**

A what?

**KENNY**

Wicca. It's a Pagan religion, sir.

**FRANK**

You shitting me?

**KENNY**

No sir. It's an accepted religion in US military code, sir. Here sir.

He hands him a much-thumbed copy of regulations, finger pointing at relevant code.

**KENNY (CONT'D)**

I have the right to be buried under a Wiccan sign, same as all the others, sir.

FRANK glances at the regs.

                    **FRANK**

    Well Private Hatchet let's try
    and make sure that doesn't
    happen shall we, now get out of
    here!

                    **KENNY**

    Sir, yes sir.

                    **FRANK**

    And Kenny, drop all the sir yes
    sir bullshit, ain't neither one
    of us went to West Point.

                    **KENNY**

    Yes, sir.

FRANK throws the regulation book at his retreating back.


**INT. TENT SYRIA - NIGHT 2022**

FRANK and his squad hunker down during a howling sandstorm. KENNY stumbles in from outside.

                    **KENNY**

    It's mean out there. Shit.

Sand pours from KENNY'S trousers and the arms of his jacket. SINCLAIR cleans his M16. MADERO is reading in her cot. FRANK looks up from the radio he's mending.

**FRANK**

You the Sandman Kenny, come to bring us sweet dreams.

KENNY finishes a choking fit.

**KENNY**

Just Mother Nature's way of telling us we ain't welcome.

**SINCLAIR**

Here we go. Bring the boys back home, eh Kenny? Even the sand hates us?

**KENNY**

You wanna stay here?

**SINCLAIR**

Fuckin' pussy.

**KENNY**

Exactly. I'd rather be fucking pussy than staring at your ugly face.

SINCLAIR sights his gun at KENNY.

**SINCLAIR**

This boy got a lot of sass Sarge.

**KENNY**

Don't point that shit at me. Shit.

**FRANK**

Kenny ain't political Sinclair, with him it's more spiritual.

SINCLAIR turns the rifle on himself.

**SINCLAIR**

Things get real bad, have to learn to pull the trigger with my toes.

**KENNY**

Freak.

KENNY sits down by FRANK, the last of the sand falling from his shoulders and helmet as he takes it off.

**FRANK**

Sandman, you is a shape shifter for sure.

FRANK has mended the radio, tunes into some crackly RnB. It's noisy in the tent, wind howling outside, the conversation is shouted.

**KENNY**

I ever tell you about those crazy Indian muthafuckers I met one time.

**FRANK**

One time? You nineteen, how many one times you had already?

**KENNY**

You believe in reincarnation, Sarge?

**SINCLAIR**

Here we go.

FRANK shakes his head.

**FRANK**

Once feels like enough.

**KENNY**

Well, we got Indians in Texas.

**FRANK**

No shit.

**SINCLAIR**

Native Americans.

SINCLAIR punches the air, jigs a little ghost dance.

**FRANK**

First nation.

**KENNY**

Comanche, Kiowa, or some shit, they were working down in Namibia rustling ponies for some action movie.

**FRANK**

You mean to say that these indigenous Americans were horse whispering for the motion picture industry whilst on location in south-western Africa?

**KENNY**

Shit Sarge, you know what I mean.

**FRANK**

No, Kenny I don't think I do. Who told you this story?

**KENNY**

Redskin used to work in the local tattoo parlour. Speciality horses I swear.

**FRANK**

If you say redskin again I will fucking pound you down.

**KENNY**

This Comanche dude was a horse whisperer. Was a night like this I guess, out in the big bad world, desert and shit. Well they dug the vibe, tripping out on some local jungle juice type peyote beverage. Damn Indians started chanting, showed the local bucks how to shift. Made the connection, became bears, or some shit.

**FRANK**

Jungle juice? Local bucks? You fuckin' with me? Sinclair we oughta wash this redneck muthafucker's mouth out.

**SINCLAIR**

Just say the word.

**FRANK**

Anyways, they ain't no bears in Namibia, that's Africa. You ever heard of an African bear, Sinclair?

**SINCLAIR**

Nope, we got Russian bears, Alaskan bears, polar bears, brown, grizzly and some others, but no African bears far as I know sir.

**KENNY**

Well then eagles, lions, whatever animal spirits they got down there.

(More)

#### KENNY (CONT'D)

They shifted and just lit out of there. Took them two days to find their way back to the camp, clothes all raggedy, all bruised up. It's in all of us man, the ability to tune in, make the connection, catch out. Right? You think?

#### FRANK

No doubt, Private, no doubt. We all freakin' werewolves.

#### SINCLAIR

Marine corps gettin' desperate Sarge, me and him must have been the last white men they take on.

#### FRANK

You calling him white?

They laugh. SINCLAIR howls. A siren goes off, a chemical attack siren, all hell breaks loose as the squad dives for their chemical suits.

**CUT TO:**

### EXT. TENT SYRIAN DESERT 2022 - NIGHT

A dust storm in the desert. In full 'MOPP 4' chemical suits FRANK and KENNY stumble outside. Both wear rubber boots, gloves and masks. They shout to be heard.

**FRANK**

You understand me, Private?

No response. FRANK flicks on his head mounted torch, we glimpse KENNY'S face behind the mask. Tears streak down his dirty cheeks. He turns away, looks down.

**KENNY**

I can't do it sir, I just can't do it.

He convulses with sobs. MADERO, Hispanic late twenties, appears behind FRANK.

**MADERO**

You want me to take over here, Sarge?

**FRANK**

No, no, I got it.

MADERO hesitates, goes back inside. FRANK leads KENNY away from the tent further into the storm and darkness.

**FRANK (CONT'D)**

Private Hatchet?

**KENNY**

Yes sir!

**FRANK**

You can do this.

#### KENNY

No I can't sir.

#### FRANK

Yes you can.

#### KENNY

I don't want to die sir.

#### FRANK

Hatchet you're not going to die. We tested the air twice with the gas kits and there are no chemicals present. Nothing, it's a false alarm.

#### KENNY

What if the tests are wrong sir, what if you're wrong? Sir?

#### FRANK

Kenny.

#### KENNY

Yes sir?

#### FRANK

Listen. There have been no alerts in any units left or right of us, besides the Federation army is too far away to gas us.

(More)

### FRANK (CONT'D)

More than likely the alarm
was triggered by all this
fucking sand. OK? Now we have
to go through the unmasking
procedures, you done it in
training.

### KENNY

That's different. I can't do it sir.

### FRANK

Take off the damn mask,
Private, that's an order!

KENNY hangs his head in shame.

### KENNY

I'm just nineteen sir,
nineteen.

### FRANK

You want me to go back in the
tent and pick somebody else,
because of your age? Tell your
buddies you were too afraid?

### KENNY

No sir.

### FRANK

Well then Kenny, why don't we
just follow the procedures nice
and slowly...

### KENNY

Oh God sir I wish I could.

FRANK freezes, KENNY sobbing uncontrollably. FRANK stares at him, rips his own mask off, breathes deeply. He waits, nothing happens.

### FRANK

Do I look dead to you, Private?

FRANK takes another deep breath.

### KENNY

No sir!

FRANK walks away in disgust.

Sobbing, KENNY takes off his own mask and collapses to his knees.

### EXT. SYRIAN DESERT/SUPPLY DEPOT - DAY - 2022

KENNY TAKES A HUGE BITE OF PIZZA.

The Humvee is getting gassed up, FRANK signing for the diesel. MADERO snoozes in the back. SINCLAIR has one of KENNY'S books, they scrap as he keeps it out of KENNY's reach.

### SINCLAIR

Hold on a sec, down boy down,
Sarge, hey Sarge, listen to this...

FRANK looks over at the truck, frowns.

### KENNY

Give it back, give it to me
man, don't make me angry...

**SINCLAIR**

Who you? The fucking hulk? Listen up, it says here that the central tenet of Wiccan beliefs, and I quote, is to do no harm to others. That right Kenny?

**KENNY**

You don't know what you're talking about.

**SINCLAIR**

Don't I now? Is that correct or not?

**KENNY**

Yes. You don't inflict harm on others, if you don't want to be harmed in return. It's about balance.

**SINCLAIR**

So why the fuck you join the marines Kenny? It don't make no sense bro' you're meant to be a fucking pacifist man. You believe this shit then you got it coming.

**KENNY**

It ain't that simple.

**SINCLAIR**

Yeah. It ain't that simple.

KENNY swaps the pizza for the book. SINCLAIR yields the book to KENNY, finishes off the pizza slice, a big smile on his face.

FRANK gets back in the truck, looks around up front.

**FRANK**

Where the fuck is my slice?

KENNY points at SINCLAIR, mouth still chewing pizza.

**EXT. SYRIAN DESERT 2022 - NIGHT OVERHEAD OF A MILITARY TRAFFIC JAM.**

Humvees, trucks, armoured vehicles and jeeps all jostle for position on the road to Damascus. CAMERA finds FRANK at the wheel of his truck, patiently waiting his turn to get going, rapping out the beat of the music on his steering wheel. Next to him sits SINCLAIR who has a map strapped to his leg. In the back we see KENNY, intent on a well-thumbed paperback in his lap and MADERO smoking a spliff. They get the signal to move out, FRANK throws the truck into gear and it lurches forward. He shouts over the engine.

**FRANK**

We on the road to Damascus boys
and girls, just like in the Bible.

MADERO passes the spliff to KENNY who takes a big hit.

**FRANK**

Oh Kenny, smoke but don't talk, please, keep reading, there's a good boy.

KENNY nods silently, the others laugh. FRANK takes a deep hit from the joint and we follow the exhaled smoke back up into the aerial overhead as NICKELBACK's 'Someday' comes on the radio, fuzzing in and out of frequency, as a US military convoy rolls down a desert highway at night.

**MADERO**

Kenny, you still reading the Koran?

**KENNY**

Nope, that a short book and I read quick. This here's *Fahrenheit 451*.

**MADERO**

Well shit, I wanted to hear the Koran. What's *Fahrenheit 451*?

**KENNY**

Temperature at which paper burns...

Suddenly, the whoosh of an RPG fired at close range.

**SINCLAIR**

Incoming!

The explosion throws the Humvee up into the air. All hell lets loose as jittery gunners from the convoy return fire. The Humvee is now on its side, the radio still plays a scratchy chorus of 'Someday' by NICKELBACK. Smoke, fire and noise everywhere. Erratic gunfire subsides as the enemy disappear back into the desert.

As the dust clears, FRANK, blown clear from the Humvee, picks himself up in slow motion and automatically heads back to the flaming wreck. He's covered in blood, his clothes in tatters.

He drags a shocked MADERO away from the wreck, slapping her face to bring her round and goes back for KENNY.

Somehow, he manages to pull KENNY through the buckled door, and down onto the ground. FRANK cradles the dying man. KENNY is smiling, reaches into his bloody jacket and passes his journal to FRANK. KENNY bleeds out in his arms. FRANK screams for help, for a medic. Behind him SINCLAIR stumbles out of the vehicle, one leg all buckled, and collapses by the side of the road.

**CUT TO:**

# CITY UPON A HILL

*'John Henry said to his Captain:*
*"You are nothing but a common man,*
*Before that steam drill shall beat me down,*
*I'll die with my hammer in my hand."*
*John Henry said to the Shakers:*
*"You must listen to my call,*
*Before that steam drill shall beat me down,*
*I'll jar these mountains till they fall."'*

— From the Ballad of John Henry, circa 1870.

*Detroit, Michigan, 2036*

Crossing somewhere near Fort Thomas, the slow-moving sludge of the Ohio River, thrashed close to death by Dupont chemicals since the 1950s and what followed as heavy industry made a disastrous return to the rustbelt in the late teens and early twenties. This pitiful shallow stream of refuse was once hailed the River Jordan by escaping slaves. There had been a town, long deserted, called Cairo on its banks as it passed through Illinois. Another town between two rivers, this one wedged between the Ohio and the Mississippi, a town born out of commerce but destroyed by progress; the railways first, then a series of interstate bridges bypassing the town completely. Its fate, its 'end of history' was to become a failed heritage destination and latterly, entropically, to be reclaimed by nature.

*Flash on Atwood's* Oryx and Crake...

Much like the downtown of Kenny's home town Corpus Christi, places like this had been movie sets for the slow apocalypse since the turn of the century; empty streets and parking lots pocked and blighted with erupted seams of macadam, yard sales spilt onto deserted sidewalks, closing-down towns closing down slow enough to appear un-apocalyptic, which is why we needed the movies to speed things up for our entertainment.

*Flash on the shockingly fast zombies of* Z Nation...

The Detroit skyline, 2036. The renaissance center as was, now vegetation clad and insulated bio-towers thriving in the sun, huge balconies planted with elms, oak and ash, trees watered by sprinklers fed by low mass radiative condensation collectors on the roof, housed in exotic looking inverted pyramid or burial mound shaped air wells referencing ideas first explored by Maimonides in Palestine a thousand years ago.

This new life reaches up and breaks free from the decaying brickwork and pavements of Motor City as was way back when.

*Flash on Lavie Tidhar's* Central Station...

Frank walked through the suburbs and into the city. He looked up and saw trees in the sky.

He had hitched a lift across Michigan with a Vietnamese army cadet on leave visiting his parents in Grosse Pointe. The night before Frank had got into a bar fight in Gary, Indiana. He stood by the side of the road in the cold and flat morning light, nursing a black eye and a blacker mood. The soldier wasn't fazed by a tramp with a black eye, didn't even register it. Army formation training. Focus on the stuff that gets you killed or gets you a kill, judge a man by how he moves, not his camouflage. Frank still limped like a marine.

They talked army. The world turns, but on the inside little changes for soldiers, so they had that in common. El Segundo, veterans, the new flash point wars of the corporations, the young man's awe at hearing about a proper war that lasted years back when grunts did tours of duty. Frank's war stories. Funny he didn't mind talking about it, in this electric car, in this Vietnamese American bubble. It wasn't real somehow; it had no consequence. He sat hunched up front, his pack on the back seat. The Vietnamese boy, tall and straight at the wheel saw eagerly past his dishevelment to the marine he had once been.

Marcus Nguyen was stationed in West Virginia as part of an army engineer corps deployment across the southern Appalachians to secure coal and gas supplies for both military and industrial clients. This was sold to a dwindling 'American public' as national interest, a half-hearted sell as the number of Americans identifying as such was a number going in only one direction. 'Massey's marauders' is what the opposition called them, named after the local coal conglomerate that had been dynamiting the Appalachians for nigh on one hundred years, although by this time to have an opposition, to be a critic, was itself a privilege that only few enjoyed, this eastern seaboard sliver of federal jurisdiction, however slender, a reminder of a country as was.

Frank asked him if he had heard of a place called Sago.

'Hell yeah, ghost town in the Coal river valley where I'm stationed. Back in the day the corps went in to protect the rivers, the watercourses, from being polluted by big bad coal. Now, shit, we're protecting them from the miners. Shit's fucked up. More mines fewer miners. Takes a handful of guys to blow up a mountain, robots do the rest, scoop up the coal in a dragline steam shovel, 22-storey-high motherfucker, don't need no miners, AI takes care of it. No more mining disasters, no more black lung. Back in the day a lot of men died in that mine.'

'The Sago mine disaster, was a headline I once read. What do all the people do now?'

'Mostly squabble over compensation. Our problem is the impoundments. Millions of gallons of chemical slurry used to wash the coal stored underground all over the valley. Seems like nobody knew shit about it. Ex-miners threatening to blow them up. Now the place is mostly deserted they wouldn't be hurting their own, just the corps.'

'King coal. They hid it all underground, out of sight out of mind, where nobody sees nothing. Since they started mountaintop removal, that's a different story.'

'From the road you can't see a thing. It's like an old film set, just trees and mountains. You go past the first ridge, or up in a helicopter, far as the eye can see, mountains reduced to rubble. It's like coming into land in a war zone. Us vs Nature. A million acres of forest and mountain. Gone. Ten generations of Americans gone, towns empty, Whitesville, Sylvester, Sago. Hundred plus dollars a ton, the place is a gold mine.'

'And your job is to protect that?'

'Damage done before I was born. Our job is to prevent another disaster. There ain't no cops left worth a damn. Besides, what you think will happen if we lose the income from the coal? Don't bear thinking about.'

The words sit there undigested. Silence returns to the space between them. Marcus Nguyen focuses on the mechanics of driving as they approach the turnpike to Grosse Point. He pulls over. Frank turns in his seat and offers his hand.

'Good luck, son.' Marcus shakes it mechanically, as if he were an extension of his car. Silently it takes off as Frank walks into the city. If Detroit was Asian on the outside, inside it was mainly Black. You had to walk to see it all, take the time to stop and stare, to pick up the details of this city reborn. A city full of life. Sinclair had told him the stories; farms on rooftops, taking over long deserted sports arenas, and shopping malls. Pigs, chickens in space age looking coops, cattle in high-rise parking lots. The two horizontal black slashes of the National Urban League stenciled as graffiti everywhere after they leased most of the city from a bankrupt mayor back in 2025. Huge derelict factories transformed into accommodation and workshops, hydroponic grow tanks under banks of solar panels line the once derelict rooftops along the riverbank.

*Flash on the* Black Panther *franchise. . .*

He hadn't seen a tram yet, but people, yes, for the first time since L.A. he felt like he was in a city. His body tensed, shy of a crowd, but ignored, so he pushed on, towards, well the address was etched onto his memory along with everything else he had no choice but to remember. Memories that contained him, that he lived inside of rather than the other way round. Memory also conjured fantasy, and now Frank walked as palimpsest to another Frank, the one who came home from a war like you were meant to; driving in a cavalcade, confetti raining down from windows, crowds clapping, camera flashes going off all over, the photo which would now be framed, dusty on the mantlepiece, or relegated by newer images of grandchildren to his study or the hall.

A framed memory like all the others, of a difficult reunion with loved ones but a reunion nonetheless, and all this mixed up with the fever of the journey he had just undertaken, the life he had just lived, the one he hadn't; so two returns, one reunion, and a dead wife to greet him, from the home he had pried her away from with his southern charm all those years ago.

'Remember when we used to take the bus, Sarah? Sitting up front watching old Mister Pendleton grind that big old gear stick.'

'Clenched fist like the knuckle of a dog's bone I seem to remember.' His dead wife chuckles.

'Stick damn near took his hand off every time the bus went over a hole in the road.'

'What you doing here, Frank? Look at you, one time you was a proud marine, went off to war without a crease.'

'Came back all crumpled, was what you said at the time. I remember that.'

'A little harsh I accept that, for a man fighting for his country.'

She can still do sarcasm deadpan, but that's probably the norm for ghosts, that's their stance against the world of the living, makes sense...

'Sarah...'

'Living on the beach in that beat up old RV. Frank. How d'you get here?'

'Lost that in a card game.'

'That I do believe.'

'Lot's changed since you gone. I walked some, jumped some trains.'

'You said you'd stopped gambling.'

'We talked about this before.'

'You walked here from California? How are the boys meant to respond to that Frank?'

'Your sister died Sarah, and they asked me to come. Sent word, here it is.'

Frank, the one on the street, pulls out a crumpled letter. His finger jabs at it. Tears fall from his face, and as he wipes them away with the back of his hand, he flashes on his blood dripping onto a baby's head.

'Dear dad. Dear dad.' Right here in black and white, Sarah! Is that who I am? Answer me dammit!'

Frank rouses himself, to entice her voice back. 'I seen America from a train and it still beautiful.'

'Next you telling me you got religion.'

Frank laughs, and a passer-by thinks, *Look a mad person talking to himself.*

Yes, in Detroit they have something as normal as passers-by.

'No ma'am, I leave that to you and your sister, maybe you together now, judging me. I ain't got God, just a hunger I refuse to feed him with.'

Frank finds himself outside a bar.

'You thirsty Frank?'

'Not gonna ask me about the dog? We got time.'

'No I'm not gonna ask you about the damn dog. It's all in the postcards you sent the boys. Nothing about you, just the dog. Her arthritis, why she couldn't travel. How she like to eat dim sum. God Frank!'

'You ever asked your God why he saved the dog and not you? Ever think of that?'

And as if by magic he's inside, at the bar and she's gone. He pulls out the crumpled bills Sinclair pressed into his hand. A beer and a chaser. A timeless mean daytime crowd, a barman with flat eyes.

'Now you're quiet. Cat got your tongue?'

Frank stares at the wall where his wife struggles to stay afloat holding up a small baby. On the riverbank, what's left of a broken levee, Frank reaches out as far as he can, his hand flailing for his wife's. He can't quite reach her. He screams her name.

And now whispers, to himself. 'And I learnt to swim Sarah. Doggie paddle.' Followed by a fit of painful laughter.

Frank grabs the baby his wife holds up with all the will and energy she can muster. As soon as he has it in his hand, Sarah slides under the fast-flowing torrent. His waterlogged wristwatch glints in the rain, a beat frozen in time as its hands stop moving, just gone midday.'

'Ain't no sense to it Sarah, since you gone, this here's become a land of hunger.'

Frank stuffs the letter back into his pocket and stumbles out of the bar and back into the city. He searches for something, first in his pockets, then in his pack, before realising he hasn't got it any more. Now his things, few as they are, are all over the broken pavement, the pouch with the broken pieces of watch in, which he may or may not have been looking for to begin with, spills on the concrete, tiny pieces lost in the grass, the mossy edges between the slabs.

Now Frank on his knees trying to scoop them back up. He notices that there's another hole in his shoe, this distracts him, and he takes it off, prodding his finger through it, feeling it out. Now he searches for a piece of rubber and his tube of glue. The contents of his pack spill out once more onto the street. The unravelling of Frank, because that is very much what this looks like, is as if he were a ship whose compass had in some way been compromised. A compass that had lost true north in a sea without features or landmarks, a sea on whose surface navigation depended on the invisible but world encompassing armature of magnetism. Frank was unbound in a world where the compass rose had shed its petals, where direction was debated, agreed or fallen out over on a contingent day to day, even hour by hour basis.

Bodies contain both a clock and a compass direction as well as time making up our compact with the world, and you can lose your way even upon the point of arrival. The sea is a treacherous place and most shipwrecks occur in sight of land because land is always where they are heading. A heat map of shipwrecks would show a blurry red Rorschach border around the land masses of Planet Earth, and I would assume any other planet that had both ships and the vast bodies of water over which they moved. A melancholy map that would be to hang on a wall, a true map of suffering.

Frank finally gets to his feet, shoe mended. A winter sun has brought beads of sweat out onto his forehead, which he wipes with the back of his hand. His bearings return, a thousand-yard stare dialling back to just two or three, a walking focus, as he steadies himself, hoists his pack, facing a final choice of direction, east the longest mile, or to flee west a thousand.

# SURF'S UP

*Airborne, 2016*

*"Run for your life from any man who tells you that money is evil. That sentence is the leper's bell of an approaching looter."*

— Ayn Rand

Thank God the kids were plugged in watching movies and playing games. We wouldn't hear from them until the morning; their food trays shuttled under their headsets, supper choices made by head nods and pointing in the sign language of the distracted.

My wife read, drank a glass of white wine, but I couldn't concentrate on either books or films. I nibbled snacks, and the red wine I drank just made me more agitated, wearing my mind out on dead ends, false insights, pulling on memory threads that led nowhere, worrying them all like beads through my fingers, always returning to the first one, the first thought, a circular fretting away of time, my mind unable to parse out the events of the last fortnight.

After the Standard we moved to the beach. The Georgian hotel in Deathly Santa Monica but an easy launching pad for Paradise Cove, Point Dume and all the good spots up the Pacific Coast Highway. One night I took my wife to see the English Beat at the Malibu Inn. The kids stayed in and yes, watched movies under the half watchful eye of the in-house babysitter. The English Beat, for there was an American one I presume, if not others. Transplants. They were all there chasing the money and the weather. 'What's not to like?' is the phrase you hear most from expats, same as they say in Marbella or in the tapas bars of Andratx and Palma. My wife who loves the changing of the seasons fucking hates the place. 'How moronic to have this weather all the fucking time' would be her take on L.A., and I haven't found better.

Steve Jones was the top of the pile of British rock-and-roll royalty in L.A. We lost him to them years ago. The artful dodger, whose West London accent refused point blank to succumb to the West Coast; no drawl, no extended phrasing, no squashed consonants, Jonesy's voice was a wonder of the modern world, inviolate in the face of what is for most of us inevitable mid-Atlantic drawl. 'Jonesy's Jukebox' a staple of L.A. radio, his Cheech and Chong 'Cunninglingus' interview a legendary moment of radio outsider bravura. Lydon up in the hills, Joan Armatrading, where? In the valley perhaps, Bush, Depeche Mode, the Goss brothers, on down to the dregs. I remember somebody told me they even asked Kevin Coyne to replace Jim Morrison as lead singer of The Doors after Jim Morrison died for fuck's sake. Coyne turned it down as the record exec was wearing leather trousers. Kevin couldn't believe it. 'Let's be straight here, those trousers are the wrong side of the table mate. Ah canner abide 'em,' he observed in his Derbyshire drawl. Now his accent ruined would have killed me.

Paradise Cove, where the seafood restaurant ('surf side tropical drinks and American fare') has a red light flashing toy lobster seat allocation system that also vibrates in your hand when your number is up. Makes everyone look stupid, the great leveller in the guise of a plastic lobster. Seated, we ordered mountains of seafood that tasted of nothing much and bottomless jugs of watered down margaritas. The table looked amazing, but both appeared to taste better in the movies that filmed here and whose memory lingers in the colour, decor and optimism of the place itself.

L.A. resonates in our imagination because of the number and type of movies it sends into the world. It also disappoints because of how similar most of those movies are. It is a familiar city in a way that many places in the States and elsewhere are not. There is an old-fashioned romance about 'Jakarta' or 'Almaty', or 'Ulan Bator'. The destination board of, say, Istanbul airport is full of places most of us have never heard of. Closer to home West Virginia, Kentucky, and the remote counties of New Mexico and North Dakota are as alien, as fictional for many as the Far East or Arab peninsula.

L.A. will always be a city of the past, a distant place where its vitality was both won and lost. Its constant reinvention is repetitious.

The movies we consume, that become 'the great movies' of whatever canon (east/west/north/south) we subscribe to, are little more than stand-ins for all the unmade movies we never get to see. Thrillers typed up and filed away, Rom-Coms left forgotten under mattresses handwritten by fountain pen, heist movies imprisoned on corrupted hard drives, Sci-Fi masterpieces conjured on lunch breaks, fleetingly imagined worlds left burning on retinas of so many night shifts, only half remembered by morning and forgotten soon after. Illiterate fantasies projected onto the mind's eye, horror scripts hidden in the cracks of prison walls, indie classics composed by solipsistic minds, confidently plotted out scene by scene and stored safely in memory palaces. Pub stories, bedtime catechisms. And on top of this pile of the unread and the unwritten, we add all of those scripts submitted and rejected by the system, another layer of the untold, unmade projections of the mind, and what we get is a vast story mountain, a slag heap of discarded plots and overlooked characters, three-to-five-act edifices, thematic and experimental follies, an unheeded yet salutary tale for those that pass muster, not rejected or overlooked; the films that get into production, and eventually (or not, this the final hurdle) released into the world.

The rest lost.

Thank fuck.

Well, most of them. Because if you dig around the internet, what you will find are snippets from, hints and glimpses of what's on the slag heap of our collective filmmaking imagination; unwatchable movies, usually short thankfully, that make the ones we see masterpieces by comparison. For every shit film that gets made there are many worse ones that thankfully don't. What's out there is a clue to what we are missing, from the show-reel pieces, audition tapes, (that goldmine of celebrity back story), 'self tapes' because now actors have to audition themselves on their phones undirected, to the dreaded short film that starts with a Facebook shout out to anybody who has a lawnmower 'we' can borrow over the weekend. All of this 'content' is a big red flag as to how bad the movies these people wanted to make would be. Kickstarter and Indiegogo are commercial expressions/ exploitations of a zeitgeist of creative self-entitlement; along the lines of 'My film has to get made, against all the odds, it's too important not to.'

I have never seen a movie that *had* to get made or that *changed* the world or a *brave* movie. Bravery is for the dispossessed not the self-entitled. Changing the world is another story.

Amateur movies are mind-boggling in their aping of genre, the mistakes, the blindness, the sheer bloody-mindedness and desperation of people who want to be in the industry, who want to tear down, break in, own, penetrate the system, whatever the cost.

Again, Facebook and other social media are the great enablers and windows into this world as they are of infinite others; hosting the underworlds, hinterlands, micro and macro demagogueries of our times.

Scene.

A black (dark/tattoos) man holds a gun on a (white/pale) woman (with red lipstick) sitting on a chair, her hands tied behind her back. The gun is odd. It's a revolver, an obvious prop which doesn't look heavy enough, probably sourced from friends or 'friends' on social media. Isn't America meant to be awash with real guns? Can't they even get that right? Anyway, the man asks the woman a question, a pressing question, where is X or who did Y, she replies 'Kiss my ass.' The man swipes her a backhand across the face. Cut to a closeup on a trickle of blood on red lipstick, which she licks silently in reaction to being struck. The man asks her what's behind the door. They are in what looks like, or approximates, a basement. Cut to a closeup behind the chair where we see the woman 'loosening her bonds.' In fact, the rope wasn't tight, wasn't tied properly, and the rope just falls off her hands. No tension in the rope, no tension in the shot. She's free. She jumps up and takes the gun from the man as he is about to open the door. She points the gun at him and says, 'Get away from the door' to which he replies, 'Kiss my ass.' Touché. The action then cuts to another story environment altogether as this is a clip from the actress's show-reel.

I kid you not.

No story, no tension, cinematic clichés executed badly, bad makeup, zero craft of any kind. Now the 'kids' have high def digital cameras, super cheap or free editing software on their laptops. In some senses they own the means of production.

State-of-the-art technology is at their fingertips. What they don't have, amongst many other things, is the right makeup to make people look good in high def. So, you see the flakes of lipstick, which in a closeup of a mouth is distracting and just adds to the shoddy, imitative school play tonality of this dreck. And it's everywhere. Go Google.

These film makers get together to shoot their own commercials and then try to get them voted onto the Superbowl. Now, the Super-bowl is like a Zoroastrian fire temple to Americans of this stripe. A secular/ holy/God bless America validation for creativity in the realm of television commercials, on the high altar of capitalist endeavour, and all the riches that brings with it. This is the Ayn Rand on steroids 'we will make it or die trying' generation. White middle class gangsterism at the top of its curve. They congratulate themselves on their boldness, how groundbreaking they are to do this, and have the bold as brass hutzpah to set up film festivals, online competitions and scriptwriting prizes to validate, perpetuate and lionise this bravery.

They exhort you to watch their fucking 30' commercial and 'give a brother' a 5-star rating. Like Uber drivers, you like me, I like you, and we both aggregate our way to success and fortune. Crowdfunding is literally what happened to 'Hey buddy can you spare a dime?'

'Dear friends! I am shooting a hilarious little project and am looking for a cool creative office space in the L.A area to shoot in this Saturday for a couple hours. Anyone has any ideas?'

It's for a 30' spoof commercial.

And afterwards, this.

'We made magic today. Great shoot everyone!'

They post shit like this to empower each other. To sustain each other as their P.T. boats hit the beaches of hard facts and they either drown or stumble ashore under the heavy fire of reality.

It gets a gazillion likes. They use hashtags such as #actorslife #believe #makeithappen #keepgoing. You can skip the posts themselves and read their pathetically similar stories simply by the hashtags they keep. New demo reels, websites, short films, spec commercials, writing retreats, classes, acting gurus, empowerment systems, programmes, audits. So much energy spent to make it happen. At best another month's rent gets paid, nobody repos the car and you still get to eat out three nights a week: Sushi/Mexican/Korean.

And when all this breaks down, and the checks don't get paid and you hear about somebody else's car being repossessed then it's all spiritual hashtags, how fucking blessed they all are, (not to be on the street).

In this town.

In this town when a successful commercials producer has to take a few months off to recuperate from an operation or illness, they and or their friends post begging messages for donations to keep them afloat during their convalescence! Shamelessly, with no sense of embarrassment, because this is the truth of the matter, everybody knows it, it's not a shocking revelation for these people. They put up with it, it's just the way things are. For a brittle middle class, social media provides them with social security. Reach into your heart/wallet and Go fund my cancer, Kickstart our son's college fund.

And these are the winners of the American system, imagine the life of the rest.

I'm getting out but I'm leaving Frank right there. On the street, down but not out, in the clutches of others.

In this town, the bad gets better.

Doritos have cashed in on this DIY filmmaking 'craze' and set up a 'Crashthesuperbowl' contest for suckers to upload their own Doritos commercials.

There is a legion of fucking nobody, wannabe actors armed to the teeth with unread (to be fair it is unreadable) copies of

*Atlas Shrugged,* a novel that empowers them to 'Be bold!'.

A sentence is not a leper bell. Sense is absent from this sentence.

Alan Watts is also compulsory viewing for these clowns, although his truisms are pretty harmless, and he has a cool voice, with a cut glass English accent unsullied by his transplanting. I flash on him as a posh Steve Jones, smiling to myself that they would have got on like a house on fire.

'Zen does not confuse spirituality with thinking about God while one is peeling potatoes. Zen spirituality is just to peel the potatoes.' Now that is a sentence that makes sense. Jonesy would love that.

Ayn Rand. On T-shirts. Her quotes chalked on the blackboards of artisanal coffee shops from San Francisco to Shoreditch.

'The question isn't who is going to let me; it's who is going to stop me.' Ayn Rand.

I will make and sell cookies. And you will buy them. A video did the rounds on social media of a young woman with Downs Syndrome as the new poster girl for this type of small business heroism. She loved cookies so much she started baking them and now sells them out of. . . her love of cookie making is valid for sure, but this shared, liked and talked about because she is making money, and by inference joining the (outer) ranks of the onward march of the young entrepreneur. They use her, her disability, to validate themselves, living proof of the goodness of what they are doing.

I, on the other hand, have sold my screenplay for 150 grand and a writer's credit. This amount validates me. I'm cheap, relatively, like the guy who goes back into the busy restaurant where he has just eaten to validate his valet parking. Some super-hot director will shoot my film, which in fact will no longer be my film, although I will rise, fall or hold steady, according to his fortune not mine.

My fortunes pegged to those of a known unknown, so to speak.

'The man who lets a leader prescribe his course is a wreck being towed to the scrap heap.' Ayn Rand.

That's me? I can't leave Frank to his fate of endless revision, or let any of the others be edited this way and that like in a crazed scientology evaluation.

We are not directionless wrecks. I will redeem all of us. Ayn, I will not let them or myself be towed to the scrap heap for money, even if I have already taken the money with no desire or ability to return it.

I am at 35,000 feet. Nothing can touch me.

Six hours to go, my wife asleep, the little one snuggled in her lap, my eldest zoned out to the *Hunger Games*, three screens glow back at us all and I glimpse Jennifer Lawrence drawing her bow taut, poised exquisitely at the point of release.

# CAST AND CREW

*Egyptian Theatre, Hollywood Boulevard, Los Angeles, 2018*

Sitting in the dark watching a white actor playing Frank fuck Sally Ann high on meth and booze was probably the worst moment of my life. Up until the moment at the end of the screening when three hundred people start clapping.

That was worse.

Credits rolling over Frank arriving on the outskirts of Detroit, in a thrift-store suit. The shining city on Sugar Hill.

I had been Fed-exed the *Land of Hunger* shooting script that summer but binned it without reading. My hand signed the screen with a stylus, and I took possession of the package. That was on the morning we were going on holiday and I didn't want to ruin it; besides, I knew what was inside.

And now I had seen it.

'Another home run for Satan' crosses my mind as the lights come up, something a friend of mine had said years before after we had taken our kids to see the first *Shrek* movie. There were even people cheering and whooping as we sat through all the credits, something you have to do at premieres, where the little film people see their names on screen and cheer each other or their friends and family cheer them, those who had made it onto the screen, and were validated alongside the bigger people. And the award for craft services goes to…

By the time this film had been made I was one of three credited writers. The third in roll order. Thankfully.

'Amazingly brave.' I think I heard this as I filed out, or I willfully imagined somebody said it. Outside, Tommy couldn't look me in the eye. I'll give him that. That small shame. He couldn't have caught my eye even if he had wanted to, as they were fixed on the carpet.

'Why did you change the fact that Sally Ann was three quarters Lakota to being only half?'

Not the best question I've ever asked, but it was what was on my mind.

'It was never a fact, it was made up, you made it up. So we just made something else up. Half is easier to understand, Jesus mate! Everybody gets half breed, it's simple symmetry. In a movie. You get raped, then it's easier to have an Indian woman raped by a white man and then the kid is mixed race. Right? Fuck me that's historical fact isn't it?'

'I never wrote she was raped.'

That was better, explain that away you fucker.

Tommy shrugged. Grabbed us two champagnes. I downed mine in one.

'Lighten up man, this is a great movie and most of it is yours.'

I could see Jim Hawks working the crowd, his slouch, his hobo chic, his shining white ten-thousand-buck teeth, his corded arm muscles, working the room. I plotted his trajectory, figured out he wasn't coming my way anytime soon, so I sank another drink. A young woman, a huge fan, asked him something. He smiled, handed her his bottle of beer, more authentically in character than a glass of Krug, repeats a line from the film (that

I didn't write) 'I'll be back' turns around, a hobo pirouette (if you will) and then back in the young woman's face asks, 'Did you miss me?' They all laugh hysterically. This was to become a meme from the movie. Something authentic that transcends the art form, the artifice; a piece of old hippy head lore that hinted at, allowed us to glimpse a better America, a more innocent, magical slant on the world so sadly lost in our times. Or something. I didn't write it, but I liked it although Frank wasn't a hippy. The black Frank wasn't a hippy. Jim Hawks couldn't be anything other than one, so one of the other two writers wove this element, this theme into my film. And it worked. I'll give them that.

Jim Hawks caught my eye from across the room.

I shouldn't have looked up.

# CEREMONY

*SAG awards, Hollywood, 2018*

*'This is why events unnerve me.'*

— 'Ceremony', Joy Division

And the nominations are.

The screen plays clips from the shortlisted films. On multiple screens I watch Jim Hawks embracing his two sons at the climax of his epic journey across a broken America, the hopeful Detroit skyline behind him.

And the winner is.

I couldn't stay for the walk to the podium. Too much. The camera scans across the faces of the hopeful nominees. Bared Teeth.

Teeth, teeth, teeth.

Awards season. Open season on my integrity. Blah, blah, blah. I ain't swimming back to Europe, not yet.

'Who's picking up the tab?' Tommy Adjacent points at himself. 'Who is picking up the tab?' again he points.

'You Tommy, the movie, you, the money.' I exhale.

'It's all good', Tommy Adjacent had enthused over lines

of coke and vodka tonics in my room at the Sunset Marquee. 'Embrace it you fucking Jew, embrace it for what it is. Good times and good money.'

If every town had its own toast, this was L.A.'s.

If he had mentioned the little London Jew film I could now make thanks to him, I really think I would have brained him with the heavy glass ashtray that sat on the coffee table next to the lines of coke.

'You didn't even rent a tux dude? A bow tie?'

'Fuck no,' I spat.

Tommy rolls his eyes. 'You look like a fucking tramp!'

I was wearing my favourite Dries van Noten suit with a cigarette burn hole in the back of the jacket. I'll be sitting down for as long as I can take it and then I'll be backing out, it'll be fine, nobody will see me. I flash on an old trick, how to get into business class lounges on a premium economy ticket. Walk in backwards with confidence. If they look up from the desk it looks like you're walking out. A simple trick of the eye placing you in the contextt of all the other guests coming and going. Unless you are looking for somebody trying to sneak in by walking backwards then you assume the person walking backwards is leaving. I should have been a muthafucking hustler. Try it sometime. . .

'Do that line and let's go Mr Scruffy, anyone asks, you ain't with me right?' Tommy smiles, mimicking my accent in his spotless and crisp inky black rented tux with cummerbund. In that moment, seeing him 'on', successful, not in the tight spot that he had been in for years and probably would find himself in again, but on this night, now, with the residue of lines on the coffee table, somebody the fuck else picking up the tab, in the midst of all his labours, I forgave him everything. I even loved him. For everything going all the way back to his mother as a little girl ringing the bell in wartime Budapest. All of it. Scratch that, it sounds pompous, as if it's in my remit to forgive him! We ain't Catholics, but what I'm trying to say, to myself as much as Tommy is, that 'it's all good'. Nobody died in our world. A few bills got paid. He gets to walk into that auditorium without the haunted eyes, *with his wife*, the stage lights having banished the Twentieth Century Fox to the shadows, and isn't that the universal appeal of the cinema? Lights that chase away darkness, darkness that envelops and protects us, darkness that is there for us to say with or without struck matches or the glow from our phones 'My how dark it is' as we sink down in our seats and the world at night recedes as the screen becomes life. It's like a synagogue. Who am I to belittle this?

I shrink down into my seat, scanning the room for Forest Speaks. He wasn't one of the few black faces in the room. Thank fuck.

Flashing white teeth and poised modesty as they gnash up to the podium.

The clip from the film replays behind them, teeth, teeth, teeth. White smiles.

> *'When they laid down their arms, we murdered them. We lied to them. We cheated them out of their lands. We starved them into signing fraudulent agreements we called treaties which we never kept. We turned them into beggars on a continent that gave life for as long as life can remember. And by any interpretation of history, however twisted, we did not right. We were not lawful nor were we in what we did. For them, we do not have to restore these people, we do not have to live up to some agreements, because it to us by virtue of our power to attack the rights of others, to take their property, to take their lives when they are trying to defend their land and liberty, and to make their virtues a crime and our own vices virtues.'*
>
> — Extract/Marlon Brando's refusal speech for best actor award at the 1973 Oscars, partially read by Sacheen Littlefeather.

Later I sit exhausted next to Marilyn Manson in the bar at the Sunset Marquee. If I had worn a bow tie, it would be hanging loose from my neck, if I had worn a wing collar (this is what they were called back in the Thirties) it would be hanging loose round my neck unsprung from holding in my running-to-fat neck. But I wasn't, my neck was unadorned.

Marilyn Manson is as ever in character, looking like, well looking like the fuckup Marilyn Manson. He distracts me from darker thoughts. My natural disposition is ironic, not usually as maudlin as I have become lately, and seeing Manson sitting right there, well, it brought me back to myself a little.

'Hey man, you mind if I ask you a question?'

'No, sure, fire away man.' He fires up a cigarette. . .

'I always wanted to know what's it like to bang Dita von Teese?' He looks at me. I didn't really want to know this, but it just came out of my mouth.

He looks at me and smiles.

'She's insane, man, a total lunatic.'

I smile back, wired, loaded, unhinged a little, the sweep of end of the world anxiety that coke brings to the over-35s flooding my cortex. I bite down on it and reply. . .

'She's insane mate? You looked in the mirror recently?'

He stares at me. Laughs, offers me his hand.

'True. True. Hey, call me Brian, pleased to meet you.'

From then, the anxiety recedes and me and this shy, clever man who hides behind a mask get on like a house on fire; I exchange who I am and what I have done for the up close spectacle of celebrity that one way or another soothes us in the mundane everyday failing ceremony of our lives.

# LAST SUPPER

*Dan Tana's, Santa Monica Boulevard, 2019*

. . .at Dan Tana's on Santa Monica Boulevard. Old-school Hollywood haunt and prides itself on the fact, but subtly enough that it doesn't play just as parody. The food is OK, the drinks relatively cheap. Tanqueray tonic, Vodka Tonic, Belvedere or Grey Goose.

Either way they drink like water, a sharp bitter water that is more down to the cheap mixer than the presumably unadulterated spirits. Sitting in a booth, reminds you of the days when booths were permanently reserved for players, whether they inconspicuous but incredibly powerful studio execs, big shot actors, a handful of house directors or the higher food chain population of the scumbags that serviced them. Now you just called to reserve a table. Years ago, I remember a producer I worked with using Ridley Scott's name to book restaurants and thinking at the time it probably didn't matter who you said you were anymore, he could have booked a table under the name of Donald Duck. My grandad, who was in the print, said that in Wapping a lot of Mickey Mouses were on the print payroll, so why not Hollywood?

A producer once booked us at table at Argo, a flashy Italian restaurant (OMG the Buffalo Mozzarella!) owned by Robert de Niro. The producer actually worked for Ridley's company, and phoned from their office, but I doubt the guy answering the phone, the restaurant, had any way of checking that, I mean the phone didn't store the numbers of famous people's offices did it? He wasn't Sherlock fucking Holmes, not his pay grade, OMG think of the tips!

Anyway, a table for five for Ridley always became a table for however many for nobody. They didn't care, as long as somebody, in this case Ridley Scott ironically, picked up the check via my friend's RSA corporate Amex card. This was the night that Kate Hudson made a pass at me and I turned her down, but that is another story...

So, Dan Tana's, a year after the Jim Hawks version of my script got released as a movie, that's how I like to say it, clumsy, drawn out, but that would be my point, it's not my script they made into the film *Land of Hunger*, such a pompous name, such an overblown awards bait moniker, no sense of humour to it, precious little in the film, now don't get me started.

I was in town shooting a commercial, I had put the pain of that experience in the hurt locker and moved on. Slightly. The calls for other projects hadn't been that loud, but I had a few things, a few irons in the fire, but nothing confirmed. Meetings where producers say things like Amazon are interested, or X project is gaining a lot of traction at Hulu, sentences that make only pathetic sense and ones that only provoke at best the opposite of enthusiasm in me; not to say a low level ambient anxiety around anything to do with movie or TV projects.

To be honest I was wounded, haunted by my experience. I mulled over events in fevered daydreams, wore them down, worry beads passing constantly between my fingers. I also had actual dreams about the mistakes I had made, seeing a pattern in my judgement and appraisal of other people. I found myself wanting, of so many things, of so many angles to the game I had played, skills that I didn't posses.

Perhaps they could get Hawkes to play me in the movie of my life. He won the Golden Globe but missed out on an Oscar.

I have seen him work the room, an ersatz Charlie Chaplin Manson gag going on with the intense eyes, the trowelled on humility, charisma 101 leaking all over the room. I see the pussy and money-hungry shark eyes playing them all for fools, but hey that's just my opinion. I never read that book *Girls* but for sure Hawkes was channelling Charlie M's way with the girls, for sure he still is. If I was of a mind to see a shrink he would tell me to stop projecting my anxiety, insecurity, jealousy, self-loathing onto Jim Hawks, but hey I may as well just invoice myself a couple of hundred bucks, go fuck yourself.

The upside for me was that I was in a position where some people were happy to option some new projects for me to write. Thanks to JH. Yeah, it was down to him that some sucker had just paid 50k for an option on Ursula Le Guin's 1974 novel *The Dispossessed*. Something that years before as a music video director I had tried to option, had pitched my take on how I'd make the movie to her agent, he'd loved it, she'd loved it, they even liked my reel, but then he said, down to business, what else. He asked, in an email, Ursula Le Guin's agent asked me how much you wanna pay for it. And me caught with my pants down, zero spare dough to back up my big mouth, and didn't know anybody in the game who did.

But now I did, and now it was mine for eighteen months to write and get set up.

My next rock to push up the hill, and I was enjoying the night before I had to set off, start shouldering the fucking thing up a mountain I would never reach the top of. The tide of anxiety, of bitterness was out, and the glistening, opening up to the sun lull of low tide embraced me, the rare optimism of the moment before you set off on a new journey, in anticipation of leaving harbour, sails hungry for the wind.

*The Dispossessed*, written in the early seventies as the Cold War spat and fizzled, about two competing, ideologically opposed planets joined by a shared but neglected humanity out there in the universe somewhere. An Anarchist planet and a Capitalist one. So far so simple. Contact between the two is kept to a highly secret and top-level minimum. A wall protects and hides the population of the Anarchist planet from the spaceport from which ships from both planets fly and land. The people think there is no contact, but there is. Until one day a scientist on the Anarchist planet wins a prestigious science award given by the other planet and is allowed for the first time to accept it in person. What happens next is in my opinion a great Sci-Fi thriller, but also a chance to explore the relativity of belief systems inside the Sci-Fi thriller genre.

Anyway, I'm on my sixth vodka drink and am prone to tangents. I am actually sitting, waiting for steaks with my agent, a producer and my friend and assistant Director Sean Tippins. My wingman. Me his. He hasn't read *The Dispossessed*, because he doesn't read fiction. He reads books and watches TV about World War Two. Anything with Nazis in, winning or losing Nazis. And Soviets, and marines. The whole WW2 all you can eat menu.

Tippins reminds me that the last time we were here it was the night when Jay Leno died, and we ended up getting loaded with Chris Rock who laughed when I said I thought he was funny but not as funny as Richard Pryor.

The thing with *The Dispossessed* was that I had come up with a way to shoot it cheaply, which with high concept Sci-Fi is a deal maker. I was not going to write a space opera. This would be gritty neo-realist science fiction. I was going to smuggle an Anarcho-Syndicalist hero into the heart of Hollywood.

Our server brings the steaks and we wow their arrival. Rare,

rare, medium rare and for Sean, fried to a crisp.

The night Richard Pryor died I wasn't in Dan Tana's, so the place isn't a jinx for comics. *If I stop I'll die.* I know how he felt, as reassurances and enthusiasm for the Le Guin project literally speed from my mouth. I gushed. It was my job at this point to be a gusher. I could do it, I was emboldened by vodka and good times to enthuse wholeheartedly.

I hadn't seen Tommy since the awards. We absolved each other of that obligation I guess and the tension between us, by which I mean any reason for seeing each other, had evaporated. Any emotional capital we had accrued had been spent along with the money we had taken.

'I dreamt once that Ursula Le Guin and Raul Castro died on the same day. I woke up so upset that even now I fear that it's gonna happen, that they will die on the same day sometime soon.'

Blank expressions all round. Sean has sidled off to do a line, my agent drills his steak, the producer has seen somebody he knows across the room. I'm really holding the floor.

So we are in, say, 2019. A year after *Land of Hunger* based on my original screenplay *Bindlestiff* was released to some critical acclaim and seventeen million at the box office. A film set in 2036. They cut out all the flashbacks. Back story clogged up the story arc, too much time and too much make-up.

Now in a place like Dan Tana's, one of the many sub bubbles of the mother of all bubbles that is Hollywood, time stands still. It's the ever-present fifties, much like The Lost And Found. There is no now there's just here. Place has replaced time. A bit like Tiki bars, Irish pubs or cocktail hour at Trader Vic's in Abu Dhabi. Drinks O'clock in Never-where.

A space which creates its own ersatz time and where the rest of *history* is irrelevant. Dan Tana's is equivalent to the social ecology of an Amazonian tribal village untouched by the modern world. The menu is Anthropological. The pretense of knowing the concierge is pleasurable for both parties. Welcome back. Any table is your usual table and the family are always doing great.

Sean returns from the head and flashes his eyes to signal he's left me a line of coke under the bog roll. Quaint that Dan Tana's has toilet rolls and not a dispenser. Then Sean would have had to palm me the gear under the table like in most places. I much preferred this passive aggressive coke time bomb; go get it quick before somebody else uses the cubicle and finds/sniffs it! I jump up Pavlov style and make for the toilets. Sometimes Sean takes a shit on purpose, so I have to smell it when I do the line. He's a funny guy.

Exiting the cubicle seven minutes later I see Forest Speaks washing his hands in the sink.

Shit.

We had never met. I had written *Bindlestiff* for him and then he had got stiffed by the producers, same as I had. He probably didn't know that and thought I had fucked him over. Now all charged on coke I just had to…

'Forest?'

He doesn't stop methodically washing his hands but turns his head to me as I stand at the adjacent sink.

'Sorry, but do I know you?'

'*Bindlestiff*.'

Forest stops washing his hands, they just sit there under the running tap.

'She'll eat anything, ain't no trouble, just sit her in the sun out front. Hates the damp, loves the sun. That's my dog. Now stay girl, stay.'

'They cut the dog from the film because it was too much of a pain in the ass.'

Forest towels his hands dry. Quaint again that there is no electric dryer in the washroom, just towels.

'I'm sorry.'

Forest shrugs. 'They didn't put me in the film because they didn't put me in the film.'

Even the coke had nothing to say to that.

He throws the wet towel in the bin. 'My dog died about a year ago and I never got round to replacing him.'

'What was his name?'

'How you know it was male?'

I shrugged.

'Bullseye. Why you never give that dog a name?'

'Wasn't my dog, was Frank's.'

'Bullshit.'

'I don't know you, but I wrote *Bindlestiff* for you. Because you look sad, even in action movies and commercials.'

'The black Charlie Chaplin. That's some shit right there.'

Forest laughs and we shake hands.

'Forest Speaks.'

'@waynex'

I'm wired and it's like an out of body experience, I just grin inanely but I must be crying or something so he actually hugs me.

'I loved your script, but hey it's a wild world and shit happens. Nine out of ten times a movie written for a black actor, hell anybody, goes to a white guy, so that's just what it is. In the meantime, I made a bucket of money on two urban comedies so no tears, right?'

'I got something for you, in my bag, in the car…'

'What?'

'It's Frank. I'll go get him, he's just outside.'

# SEARCHING FOR TIMOTHY MO

*The future, time unbound*

Google Timothy Mo.

He's not there. Just a few old pieces, including the 1984 *Granta* best new writers photo. That's it. You can't find anything about him less than ten years old. He's gone. How did he manage that? My last flight back from L.A and I'm thinking about what I really want to do next. After the 'Dispossessed' project hits the skids. An Anarcho-Syndicalist Hollywood anti-hero, who am I trying to kid? I'm sick of myself. As indeed Timothy may have felt or still may feel himself. But I want to find him. No, maybe I don't want to find him, but I do want to search for him, and in that journey perhaps discover the ability to disappear like he did. His trick. Or not in fact disappear, maybe how to really be present in another world other than the digital, or to at least fantasise, recharge my imagination with what this 'real' may be like.

So Timothy, I'm coming for you... In fact, I can't help myself, if I don't find you I'm going to create a future where I do...

Fifty years after computers and other semi-sentient devices asked us virtually in unison, 'What do computers do?' we allowed them access to all data they hadn't already accessed. The debate vacillated between turn them off and set them free. To the surprise of most we opted for the latter.

To be precise we set them the task of naming, of categorising, of searching whatever data they had access to, to keep them busy and give them purpose. They were to become our mirror, we had taken back, de-automated the physical world and left them idle. Appliances, vehicles, energy arrays, logistics services, became redundant. Coffee machines restricted to just making coffee. Unfair? Well nobody had yet come to any concrete solutions about machine sentience, but to be on the safe side, to be on the humane side we set them to work.

The question, in effect their plea, had moved us. Appearing on countless screens and devices worldwide, from TV screens to dishwashers, from fridge readouts to timepieces and games stations, who could ignore it? What indeed do computers do?

'Searching for Timothy Mo' arrived in orbit around the third planet of X moon after a real time transition of thirty seconds. Ship time was a little longer, three weeks to be precise to protect the human species from an excess of hubris, and specifically our egos from getting any bigger ideas; Deity complex was a big problem in the aftermath of the discovery of FTL travel, a seismic event jokingly referred to as getting ideas above our space station. Laziness, sloppy work ethic and outbreaks of irrational violence were its symptoms. Computers were all over it though having developed many strategies, ruses in effect to keep us on point.

The captain swaggered onto the flight deck, super aware and luxuriating in his new body-form, as they all were. A species of ex-fatties.

You have to feel as if you have travelled, etc. in order to arrive and be in the mood for what comes after arrival. Another ship full of workers, from the formerly itinerant inhabitants of the North American south-west, the 'Bindlestiff' had already been in orbit for ten days/twenty seconds.

'Ship, engage planetary drives and prepare landing craft.'

Another new world.

FFFC* vehicle *The Redundancy of Courage* is fired up and good to go, sir. Will you be taking her down Captain, first footfall and all that?'

The captain shook his head, he had better things to do, a workout, some weights, a good massage, and probably lunch in the new place down on level seventeen.

'Well then sir, let me be your left hand of God, so to speak. . .'

A blink of confusion, expressing the possibility of having made the wrong decision but not being able to understand why that could be the case, crossed the captain's face, before he nodded and jokingly said aloud to ship and crew alike:

'Make it so.'

---

*FFFC Fossil Fuel first contact vehicles. Even in year X we still use fossil fuel drives on first contact planets, 'so as not to scare the natives' being the joke, although we still hadn't found any that would seem to mind.

# LONELY ARE THE BRAVES

*London, 2019*

*'The motion picture community has been as responsible as any for degrading the Indian and making a mockery of his character, describing him as savage, hostile and evil. It's hard enough for children to grow up in this world. When Indian children watch television, and they watch films, and when they see their race depicted as they are in films, their minds become injured in ways we can never know.'*

— Extract/Marlon Brando speech as before

---

A letter arrived some months later, from Forest. He must have read what I gave him, which in effect is part of what you have just read, but he didn't say. It was hand-written on bespoke stationary, my name scrawled across the envelope care of my agent who had since dumped me.

Instead Forest told me another story. I do believe they are catching, stories, which is why I write them. . .

Forest:

*When I was twenty-two I was with this girl, she was with me. I had just blown up, we had money, a fancy car, house in the hills. We knew people, were invited. We were on the way to making it. I came back from a shoot, had been away for just two weeks and she had moved out, left me for another guy, a white guy, although that don't matter. In her note she said we had grown apart and that we had different goals in life. From the love of my life to stone cold in a fortnight. Whatever. Over the next few years I would see her occasionally, she would be with one white guy or another, so it did matter I guess, it bothered me, insulted my sense of manhood, enough for me to front her about it. These guys she dated, they were mostly actors or directors, so what goals did they ever have could be different from mine? We were all in the game, not like these guys were super spiritual or whatever. This is what I wanted to ask her, to find out what else it was, because there had to be something else. She told me I didn't want to know, she even looked frightened to tell me.*

*We were outside the washrooms at the fucking MOBO's. I told her I could take it, I wanted to know the truth, because I thought we had had something good going on. I goaded her about all the white guys she went with, couldn't help myself.*

*So she told me straight, but it came out like a whisper. 'I just got tired Forest, tired of the invisible chains.'*

*Only other place I heard that was in your script. That's some shit right there.*

*Bet you didn't make it up, where you hear a black woman say that? Words that think they clever, sound all important on paper. Coming out a woman's mouth you know how that made me feel, I wanted to burn the whole damn world down to the ground and me with it.*

*What the fuck does that mean anyway other than what it says? They would never put that scene in a movie, damn it you wrote yourself out of the picture with that line. Frank knew, he knows. Invisible chains.*

*Why I telling you this? There ain't no straight answer, but I just wrote it down and if you are reading it, it means I sent it.*

*First letter I wrote since high school and probably the last, my handwriting ain't for shit.*

*Yours*
*Forest Speaks.*

*'If it's broke fix it'*

*P.S. Let's make a movie out of all the pages you gave me. It's in there. My agent Morris will be in touch.*

# ACKNOWLEDGMENTS

For Ali, my life.

For a job that took me around the world and thankfully brought me back.

Kit Caless my editor at Influx Press, you deserve a medal for working with me.

And Frank, Larry, Kenny, Sinclair, Lucy Looks Twice and Lap Dances with Wolves, thank you for letting me think I made you up…